THE *Matchmaker's* MATCH

OTHER BOOKS AND AUDIOBOOKS

BY BRITTANY LARSEN:

Pride and Politics

Sense and Second Chances

a novel

THE *Matchmaker's* MATCH

BRITTANY LARSEN

Covenant Communications, Inc.

Cover image: *Bunch of Peonies* © AnnaPustynnikova, istockphoto.com
Cover design by Christina Marcano.

Published by Covenant Communications, Inc.
American Fork, Utah

Printed in the United States of America
First Printing: July 2018

24 23 22 21 20 19 18   10 9 8 7 6 5 4 3 2 1

ISBN-13: 978-1-52440-676-9

To Shawn, my own Knightley/Darcy/Edward

Acknowledgments

As always, I owe a large measure of my success to the people who provide me with love, support, advice, and chocolate.

Thank you to Covenant Communications, for continuing to publish my books, and to Kami, for your editorial support.

Every writer should have a critique group, but no writer has a group as great as mine. Thank you, Tiffany, Aubrey, Melanie, Teri, and Jen for your input on this book and so, so much more.

Every writer should also have a Josi Kilpack, but sorry, you can't have mine. Thanks for making this story so much better and for making my life a little brighter.

Tatum Frampton is my new best friend for agreeing to read this manuscript and make it florally accurate after only knowing me for roughly five minutes.

Melanie Christofferson loaned me her tattoo, for which I am forever grateful. Also, she's a pretty awesome sister-in-law.

And thank you to my own Liza Belle for being the name inspiration for this story. My fictional Liza Belle is almost as smart and sassy as you are!

I always save the best for last, so here it is: Thank you, Shawn, Emma, Tess, and Jane, for being you, for loving me, and for all the things. There are too many to name.

Chapter 1

The louder-than-usual clanging of the wind chimes at my shop door should have warned me change was coming, but I was too engrossed in my flowers to notice. I had light-pink peonies and seeded eucalyptus laced through my fingers, and with a few twists of my wrist and a quick wrap of tape, the separate stems of flora and fauna would be transformed into one beautiful bouquet of living art.

Is that overly dramatic?

Probably. I don't care. That's how I feel when an arrangement I'm creating comes together. Total zen. I capture the flowers at the peak of their beauty, and then I get to share that moment with someone else. In this case, that someone else was my sister, and the arrangement would be her bridal bouquet.

But in the seconds before the flowers became the work of art I intended, Parker Knightley's voice caused me to lose my concentration.

"Little Liza Belle has her own business?" he called out just loud enough to make me jump. His teasing had been a part of my life for as long as I could remember, but I hadn't seen him in three years. In my surprise, the peonies slipped through my fingers, hit the table, and showered the floor with delicate pink petals. I would have cried if it had been anyone besides Parker standing in the entrance of my flower shop.

"Parker!" I squealed and ran the twenty feet from my workspace to the front of the store and had my arms wrapped around his neck before he had the door shut behind him.

He circled his arms around my waist, squeezing tight. "It's good to see you."

"You too," I said, and he squeezed tighter. "Except I can't breathe."

I tried to break away, but before I could I felt his fingers creeping toward a certain spot under my rib cage.

"Don't do it!" I ordered, but it was too late. He'd found my most ticklish spot and had already started his torture tactics. I broke away, but he grabbed my wrist before I could escape and dug his fingers into my side, pulling me close again.

"What do you say?" His grin spread wide, and the light reflecting off his glasses couldn't hide the blue of his eyes or the way I knew they were dancing with laughter at me.

"Please!" I pushed against his chest, but there was no getting away, especially once he started wiggling his fingers up my spine and then toward my armpit.

"I'm waaaaaaiting." He drew the word out, proof he could outlast me.

"Okay!" Tears streamed down my face. I gasped for air, unable to stop laughing but also painfully aware of how close his hands were to places we'd both be embarrassed by if he accidentally touched them. "PARKER IS THE KING!"

He let me go but kept his hands on my waist, staring down at me with a smile playing on his lips that shouldn't have made me notice them in a way I never had before. The gold undertone of his glasses complemented the shades of blond in his short-cropped, wavy hair. Hair so close in color to mine that people sometimes thought we were brother and sister.

"That wasn't so hard, was it, Miss Liza Belle?"

"You are as bad as ever." I pushed his hands away and smacked his chest, unintentionally taking note of its firmness. The seven-year gap between us wasn't as notable in our sizes anymore—he only had four inches on me now instead of a whole foot—but he was obviously still strong enough to tickle torture me the way he had when I was six and he was thirteen.

"And no one calls me Liza Belle anymore. It's just Eliza."

Parker stepped back and pointed his gaze and his finger upward in the general direction of the sign that hung outside my shop. "But that's the name right up there. *Liza Belle*. In a swirly font and everything."

He glanced down at me, his smile no longer playful. In fact, it was full on making me think things about him that, as his "faux baby sister," were totally inappropriate. Especially now that Preston—Parker's younger brother—was marrying my sister Caroline. In two days Parker and I would be more sister and brother than ever before.

"Well, it's a good name for a shop, but not for a grown-up." I smoothed my skirt and readjusted my T-shirt. I'd spent most of my childhood trying to catch up to my sister and the Knightley brothers, aka the Three Musketeers. But I wasn't six years old anymore.

Parker picked up a soy candle and smelled it before turning it over to look at the price. His eyebrows went up and his gaze bounced from me back to the candle. "You sell many of these?"

I took it out of his hands and set it back where it belonged, making sure he knew I was running a legit business, not playing pretend. "I grossed ten thousand dollars last month, if that's what you're getting at." Technically that total included payment for an event Caroline and I had planned, and my net pay was lower. Much lower. Possibly in the negative range.

He let out a low whistle. "Selling candles at that price, I'm not surprised."

I rolled my eyes and put my hand on top of a larger candle as he reached to pick it up. "When did you get back in town?"

"A few hours ago. Caroline said I should come see your place." He walked to the brick wall lined with cards, pulled one out, put it back, and then reached for another. I itched to ask him what he thought about my shop but wouldn't give him the satisfaction of thinking his opinion still mattered to me. I wished he'd stop touching things.

"Did she tell you I'm doing all the flowers?" I walked toward the back of the store, and he followed. "That's mostly what I do . . . weddings. I've done some pretty big ones." I inspected the peony I'd dropped while trying not to look at his reaction. Like any little sister, I'd always had this insane need to impress big-brother Parker, even if he wasn't really my big brother. His parents were Daddy's closest friends and had always lived next door until five years ago when they'd decided to cash out and move to a retirement community in Arizona.

I couldn't remember a holiday or vacation we hadn't spent together—at least until he'd left for college, followed by law school and an internship in Hong Kong that had led to a job there. The last time I'd seen him was three years before, when he'd been in town for a night. Even with his years of absence, he was still the closest thing I'd ever have to a big brother.

He leaned his elbow on the other side of my high worktable, resting his chin in his hand. "I honestly never thought you'd do anything besides surf and party."

"Party?" I pushed his elbow off the table, and he lurched forward before catching himself. "I don't party."

"I didn't mean it like *that*." The corner of his lip twitched, wanting to grin. I squeezed my lips tight to keep them from following his lead. "But you do like parties." His face broke into a smile. Mine didn't.

"Laugh all you want." I brushed the peonies onto the floor already littered with pink petals, dead flowers, and cut stems. The peonies would have been okay for a different wedding, but not my sister's. "Parties are what bankrolled this place." That and Daddy. But Parker didn't need to know that part.

"How do you feel about being out of the party business now?" He pulled up a stool and sat down.

I shrugged and swallowed the lump rising in my throat. "It wouldn't be the same without Caroline. She's the one who's really good at it. I prefer the flowers."

"Really?" His voice held just enough of an I-don't-believe-you to remind me how much older and wiser he thought he was.

"Caroline's the event planner, not me." I grabbed three new peonies and some eucalyptus from the full bucket in front of me, regretting that I'd ruined my first bouquet just to hug Parker, who was determined to ask questions I didn't want to answer. "It made sense to shut the business down once we knew she'd be moving."

"You're not going to miss it?" His eyes bored into me.

I shrugged again. "I'll still do little things here and there."

Of course I would miss planning events with my sister. It had been our dream since I was in high school, and we'd not only made it happen but we'd been pretty successful at it. Then she'd gotten engaged and Preston had matched to a residency in San Francisco. She'd always wanted to live there, so they decided not to wait until he was done with med school before getting married. I was happy for her. It was no use crying over what might have been, especially since I'd been the one to get her and Preston together in the first place.

"Well, if I ever throw a party, I'll be sure to hire you."

"Thanks."

Maybe my face gave away what my heart was feeling, or maybe he regretted his moment of sympathy, but either way Parker changed the subject and went back to joking with me.

"I'm impressed you actually have a job," he jabbed. Didn't matter. Teasing was better than needling. "I expected to find you on the waves."

"*Rude.* What made you think I wouldn't be working?"

"Um, you." He took a rose from the bucket and smelled it. "If I remember right, and I do,"—insert smug grin—"your exact words when I asked you what you planned to do with a degree in fine arts were, 'I don't have to work. I'll take care of Daddy and surf.'"

I remembered saying something like that—maybe even exactly that—but not in the snooty voice he'd used. "Whatever," I mumbled and rolled my eyes again.

"Don't be mad." He laughed and handed me the rose I reached for. "I'm proud of you, Liza Belle. Looks like you've got a good thing going here."

"Thanks. Now tell me about Hong Kong," I ordered. After law school and his internship, he'd ended up starting a nonprofit law firm to advocate for domestic workers' rights.

"There's too much to tell. You should have visited me. Tell me about Caroline and Preston." He unwound some floral tape and rolled it into a ball.

"Stop playing with that, and wrap it around these stems." I held the flowers and indicated where to wrap the tape around the stems. He didn't know anything about flowers, but my bestie, Taylor, still hadn't shown up to help, so Parker was my only option. "Daddy won't travel anymore, otherwise I would have visited—"

"Not at all?"

I shook my head. "What do you want to know about Caroline and Preston? How I got them together?" I'd much rather talk about them than how much worse Daddy's quirks had become in the last three years.

I called them "little quirks"—we all did—because it kept us from having to use the words "mental illness." Someone with a little quirk checked the clock three times before leaving the house, but he still left the house. Someone with mental illness needed medication and therapy, maybe even hospitalization. Daddy didn't believe in any of that. He believed he was sick all the time, but he wouldn't set foot in a hospital, let alone a psychiatrist's office.

I handed Parker the bouquet, placing his hands above the green floral tape but not so close to the peony heads that he might accidentally touch them and risk their turning brown before they reached full bloom. Peonies were particular.

"You got them together?" he asked, looking around the bouquet at me. "That's interesting, considering they've known each other since they were four."

"Knowing someone is not the same as dating someone. It would have taken your brother another twenty-five years of 'knowing' Caroline before he asked her out if I hadn't stepped in." I bent under the table and pulled a vase from the boxes stacked there and then exchanged it for a different one, taking my time more to irritate him than out of necessity.

"So, you bailing on your sister and convincing Preston to take her to the charity thing—"

"Christmas for Kids in Foster Care. It's a really great event. One we helped plan."

"And that you bailed on—"

"I was sick." I stood up and set the vase on the table.

"That's my point. There wasn't any matchmaking involved—just bad luck on your part." Parker rocked his head side to side, stretching his neck.

"Hold still." I wound floral tape around the stems then put my hands over his and moved them and the flowers close to my face until his fingertips grazed my cheeks. I put the tape between my teeth and tore it off. I could have taken the flowers from him and done it. I don't know why I didn't.

"How much longer do I have to do this?" he asked as I let go of his hands. The tips of his ears were red. "My fingers are starting to cramp."

"Just until you admit that without my matchmaking skills your brother would not be marrying my sister the day after tomorrow." I blew one of my curls out of my eye, but it fell right back where it had been. I'd given up long ago trying to get my curly hair to do anything it didn't want to do.

"Fine. Whatever. Can we please be done now?"

I stuck the arrangement into the vase, and he breathed a sigh of relief. A sigh of relief cut short when I held his hand up, spread his fingers wide and reached for more flowers.

"How do you do this when you're here alone?" His eyes narrowed with suspicion. He was on to me, but I was saved by the bell. Literally. My wind bells at the door jingled, carrying my BFF's voice with them, before I could answer Parker.

"Eliza? Are you in back?" Taylor called.

"Yep, and I've got a surprise," I said over my shoulder before I stuck a rose between Parker's fingers.

"Parker!" Taylor said seconds later when she walked into the back room.

"Don't touch him until we're done," I ordered, stopping her and her hug in their tracks.

"When did you get here?" she asked him, her arms dropping. Normally she would have been all over him. We'd been best friends since the sixth grade, and she'd had a crush on Parker for just as long. If she hadn't been in a serious relationship—with a guy I set her up with, thank you very much—nothing could have kept her from Parker.

"This morning."

"And she's already suckered you into this? Dude." Taylor shook her head. "Has she given you the speech yet?"

Parker looked from Taylor to me and back again before slowly shaking his head.

"'Flowers are a metaphor for life. You have to be present to see them in full bloom, or you'll miss it.'" Taylor waved her hands and swayed like a drunk yogi, imitating my words in a soft, husky voice that sounded nothing like me. At least, I hoped not.

Parker laughed. "It sounds like what she used to say about surfing."

I glared at him. "Shut up." I examined the peonies stacked in the bucket in front of me. "You're just jealous that I'm younger and wiser than you both." I found my perfect peony, pulled it from the bucket, and gently slid it between Parker's pinkie and ring fingers. "Tomorrow, when these flowers are in full bloom, we'll all be there together to experience a moment in time when nature and humanity are brought together. But it takes the wiser ones among us"—I swept my hands to my chest so they'd know exactly who I meant—"to bring others—"

"Into awareness," Taylor finished with me as her phone dinged. She pulled it out of her pocket. "I know, I know," she said while reading her text. "Ride the wave, enjoy the journey, yada, yada, yada. You need to give all the zen yoga, om-lightenment crap a rest."

"Om-powerment. Which has nothing to do with flower arranging—that's ikebana." I grabbed Taylor's cellphone-free hand and held it up. She spread her fingers wide, knowing they were about to be filled with flowers. She'd been to my shop enough to know what to expect.

"Om whatever." Her phone dinged again, and she voice texted a message back. "Come by tomorrow."

"What are you talking about?" Parker asked Taylor as he took the flowers out of his hand and passed them to her. "You're not entrapping the human rights crusader into any more slave labor," he said to me and stuck his hands in his pockets. He was catching on quickly to my employee recruitment tactics.

"It's this yoga class she's been going to that promises enlightenment for the low, low cost of two hundred and fifty dollars a month," Taylor answered Parker in a perfect infomercial voice.

"Sounds like there's some definite enlightening of your wallet going on." Parker smirked and looked to Taylor for backup, which she readily gave by putting out her fist for him to pound. Which he readily did.

"You two are hilarious." I rearranged Parker's flowers between Taylor's fingers. "We planned an event for the owner—Elton—so he gave me a few months free. The name may be hokey, but he does have some good meditation techniques if you can get around the other stuff he's trying to sell. Mostly I go to the other instructor's class—Mary. She's great."

"Yeah, but how much of the stuff have you bought?" Taylor asked and arched her eyebrow.

"I think what you meant to ask," Parker said to Taylor with a playful grin before he turned to me, "is 'how financially *enlightened* have you become?'"

Taylor burst out laughing, and I told them both to shut up.

"Don't be mad. We're only teasing." Parker wrapped his arm around my shoulder. "I've gotta run."

"Are you going to come over for dinner tonight?" I leaned into the semi-hug he offered. He smelled nice, like sage with a touch of cedar—probably from the candle he'd picked up and not because he usually smelled that good. It had to be the candle. "I want to see as much of you as possible before you head back to the other side of the world."

"You'll probably be seeing more of me than you want for a while. I'm not going back to Hong Kong." He pecked the top of my head like he hadn't just dropped a bombshell.

"You're not?" I tried squirming out of his arm before he could do what he always did next, but I wasn't fast enough.

"Nope. In fact . . ." He dug his knuckles into the top of my head and rubbed before I could get away. "We're going to be neighbors. Your dad's letting me crash out back."

"I haven't missed *that.*" I pushed his hand away and glared at him. "You're staying in the garage apartment? Why didn't he tell me?" The detached garage out back had a nice apartment above it that Daddy usually rented out, but over the past few years, he'd refused to rent to anyone he didn't know.

"Because he offered it to me right before I came here," he said and hugged Taylor goodbye. "What time is dinner?"

"Whenever you get there. I've got food I'll pop into the oven. Caroline and Preston are going out with some friends." I kept the smile off my face until he walked out the door. We hadn't talked much over the past three years, so I couldn't explain the drumming in my chest that had started when Parker said that not only was he not going back to Hong Kong but also that he'd be living in the apartment above our garage. It would be nice to have him back, and in close proximity. Even with the inevitable teasing I knew it meant.

Chapter 2

"Eliza?" Taylor's voice reminded me where I was and what I was supposed to be doing.

"Yeah, sorry." I closed my hand around the flower stems so she could pull hers out.

"I guess you're happy Parker's back," she said with a sly smile while she wound tape around the bouquet.

"Of course. Why wouldn't I be?" Heat crept into my cheeks. Had she read my mind? Had she sensed all the un-sisterly thoughts I was having about him? And was she as creeped out by them as I was?

"No reason." Her shrug said almost as much as her grin. "You didn't hear a word I said after he walked out the door."

"Yes, I did." I pointed to the vase I needed and let her do the work of getting it out of the box. I'd make her pay for her teasing in hard labor.

In all honesty, though, if I could have hired Taylor, I would have done it in half a second. I could have paid her almost as much as her job as a social worker did, but she wouldn't do it. She loved her job too much.

"What did I say about Hailey?" she asked.

"Hailey who?"

"You just proved my point." She held up a bow for my approval. "Hailey who you were supposed to meet nine months ago at the Christmas for Kids in Foster Care event. Hailey who had a baby right after aging out of the system. Hailey who I've been telling you about for months."

"Okay! I remember!" I held out the bouquet, and she attached the bow to it. "I didn't forget. I just wasn't thinking."

"You were thinking about *someone*," she muttered under her breath.

"Shut up." I stepped back, eyeing my creation.

"She's coming tomorrow to help you," Taylor said and then, as if she'd read my mind, handed me a branch of eucalyptus.

"Good. I can use it." I stripped the leaves from the bottom half of the branch and then prodded between the flowers to find a spot for it. "Does she have experience?"

"No. She has nothing."

"Except a baby?" I eyed Taylor as critically as I had my arrangement. Part of her job was helping kids transition out of foster care when they turned eighteen. Ideally, she'd be able to find relatives the girls could rely on for a support system. When that didn't happen, she brought the girls she thought had the most potential to me. I provided part-time jobs that allowed them to go to school while also gaining work experience.

Taylor nodded. "She's not going to college, and she needs more than any girl I've ever sent you. With some encouragement she'd go to school, I just know it. With one good chance to prove herself, her whole life would change. Not just hers. Her baby's too. Plus . . ." She handed me the ribbon I needed before I asked. "She surfs."

I took the ribbon and returned her stare. "How good is she?"

"Like, really good."

That was the nail in the coffin. "Okay, I'll see what I can do," I answered slowly. It wouldn't be easy, but surfer girls stick together.

Along with the rotating cast of girls Taylor sent my way, Caroline had been my steady part-time assistant as we'd shut down our event-planning business and opened my shop. But in the last few weeks, not only had Taylor not had anyone to send me but Caroline had also quit in order to get everything ready for her wedding, pack for her move to San Francisco, and look for a job there. What I really needed was someone full-time, with experience. Hailey didn't sound like she'd fit that bill.

I thought about Hailey and her baby after work as I left downtown San Clemente and drove home, passing housing developments that had once been the rolling green hills my family had ranched for generations before my grandpa started selling off parcels to developers. By the time Daddy had inherited the family business, there weren't any cattle left, just land leases, a healthy bank account, and trust funds for his father's grandchildren to inherit when they turned twenty-five. I had six more months before I had access to mine.

Until then, Daddy was my financial backer. Which worked to my benefit in some ways because he refused to let me pay back the money he'd loaned me to open my shop. The trade-off, however, was his unsolicited input into how I ran my store and what I did with the profits, if I ever had any. Luckily, he didn't ask often.

I'd grown up rich, and I would die rich without ever having to do anything to earn a penny of my own. It wasn't fair, so I tried to balance the scales by doing charitable things with the money I had. One thing I'd learned from seeing Parker fight for human rights was to use the advantages I'd been given to do good. Not that I'd ever let him know he'd inspired me.

My "inspiration" was already at my house when I got there. As I walked through the living room, his voice floated through the open back door from where he and Daddy sat outside. The curtain covering the opening blew in billowing waves that kept Daddy and Parker from seeing me but didn't keep me from hearing them.

"The shop is nice," he said to Daddy. "Liza has done well."

"She's not making any money," Daddy replied, and I stopped in my path.

"Does she need to?" Parker asked.

"A business has to make money, even if it's just a hobby," Daddy answered. "If she's not making money, she should settle down and get married." It wasn't the first time I'd heard him say that, but it still made my eyes roll so far back in my head I could almost see behind me. Their conversation had gone on long enough.

I pushed the curtain away and walked outside. "Hi!"

"Hi again," Parker answered. He and Daddy sat across from each other on couches surrounding a gas fire pit. The flames from the fire lit their faces, giving them the same orange glow as the sun hovering on the horizon. Seeing them together gave me a warm feeling I would have liked to blame on the fire, but I think had more to do with having Parker back with us. It felt like wrapping up in the fuzzy blanket I'd slept with every night until I was twelve . . . okay, *fifteen*.

I walked behind Daddy, wrapped my arm around him, and kissed the spot where his gray hair was thinnest. "Sorry I'm late. Are you starved?"

"Not at all." He patted my arm and leaned into my hug. "How's my girl?"

"Perfect." I let go and walked around the couch to sit next to him. "Are you warm enough? Do you want me to get you a sweater?" He already had a blanket draped around his shoulders, but once the sun set, the ocean breeze would turn from refreshing to chilly.

He pointed to the sweater folded on his lap. "I'll put it on in a minute. After the sunset." Every night he sat on the patio until the rays of orange and pink dipped into the Pacific Ocean then disappeared, leaving behind a gray twilight and the sound of waves lapping against the sand. It was his favorite time of day, and he swore it looked different every time. He was right.

I nestled into the crook of his arm, breathing in the smell of honeysuckle and the sea. The scattered clouds in the sky promised a spectacular show as the sun dipped below them, taking its time to change their color from white to a million different shades of pink. Patches of dusty-blue sky broke between the banks of clouds. The sun rested momentarily, a bright-orange spot perched on the shoulder of the darkened cliffs jutting into the ocean. It teased us into believing it would stay there but within moments had quietly slipped away.

I let out a sigh of contentment. Daddy patted my arm in solidarity.

And Parker?

Even in the dim light I could tell he was itching to do something besides stare at the sky. He never could sit still long enough to enjoy the sunset, so he should have known better than to come before it was over. It's not like he hadn't ever met my dad before.

"Will dinner be ready soon?" he asked after glancing at his phone. "I can help if you want," he offered quickly, realizing he'd ruined the moment.

"Give me a minute, and I'll put it in," I answered. Daddy wouldn't eat take-out—too many germs—and I didn't cook, so we had someone who prepared most of our meals for the week. All I had to do was pop them into the oven. "Do you have somewhere else you need to be?"

"No."

He lifted his glasses to rub the bridge of his nose. "Just hungry and jetlagged."

"Right. I'll get it started." I should have known Parker would be hungry and tired. It was after eight o'clock, and he'd flown across the world that morning. I hurried into the kitchen, turned on the oven, and pulled out some brie and crackers to put together an appetizer plate.

After putting dinner into the oven, I carried the appetizers out to the deck and walked into the conversation Daddy and Parker had been having when I'd first arrived home.

"She needs someone to look at her books," Daddy said to Parker then glanced at me as I set the cheese plate in front of them. "She won't listen to me."

"I'm right here. You can include me in this conversation." I kept my voice light, even cheerful, but I hated when Daddy treated me like I was still a little girl instead of a businesswoman with a college degree.

"I'm sorry, sweetheart," he said as I sat down next to him. Then he turned back to Parker, who cast me an apologetic half-smile. "You could show her where to make some changes."

I returned Parker's look with an exaggerated eye roll. I couldn't imagine loving anyone as much as I loved Daddy, but he was old when I was born, and losing Mom had only aged him more. And somehow he'd missed the whole women's-movement thing.

"You don't need to worry about it, Daddy. I promise." I spread some cheese onto a cracker and handed it to him.

I'd never told him—and never would—that he'd spoiled me too much for any other man to want to take me off his hands. Like Daddy would let him anyway. He said he wanted me to get married, but really he didn't. I had no intention of finding a husband and no intention of giving up my shop even if I did. Not to mention the fact that the only reason I was okay with Daddy sometimes treating me like a child was so he could feel like he was taking care of me. In reality, he was the one who needed to be taken care of. He couldn't live on his own.

"What makes you think she'd listen to me?" Parker took a cracker and tossed it into his mouth. "I'm not really qualified to tell anyone how to run a business even if she would listen."

"You know enough to help her," Daddy said. "She needs someone she trusts to show her how to make money instead of lose it. She won't talk to my accountant, and I don't want her throwing good money after bad once she has access to her trust."

"I don't care about the money, Daddy." I jabbed a cracker into the cheese, breaking it into pieces. "I don't need it. I just enjoy what I'm doing." Even as the words came out of my mouth, I knew I was reinforcing Daddy's unstated belief that women were more suited for marriage, motherhood, and hobbies than for careers. "Plus, why would Parker know more about business than I do?" I waved a new cracker in Parker's direction before popping it into my mouth.

"I do have an undergrad degree in business," Parker said, forcing a glare from me. He wasn't helping my case. "And, in case you've forgotten, one of the goals of my charity is to provide financial advice to our clients, and, until recently, I was the provider of that advice," he added with a confident shrug. As though helping domestic workers avoid predatory lenders qualified him to advise me on how to run my flower business.

"That settles it, then." Daddy slapped his hands on his knees and rubbed them back and forth. "Parker will help you out."

It wouldn't do any good to protest. Daddy wouldn't rest until Parker had taken a good look at every penny coming in or out of my business. Daddy may have believed my shop was a hobby, but he was financing it, so he'd make sure it was turning a hefty profit whether I cared or not.

"Whatever you say, but I really don't need him." I jutted out my chin and held Daddy's sweater open for him.

He laughed as he stuck his hand through the arm. "She's still as stubborn as ever," he said to Parker in a voice tinged with pride.

"I noticed," Parker responded, his eyes dancing with the laugh I knew he wanted to let out. "She's still got that stubborn chin."

"What are you talking about?" I asked at the same time I tucked my chin into my neck.

"You stick your chin out when you don't want to do something," Parker answered, still trying not to laugh.

"It's true," Daddy chimed in. "I think the first time you did it was hours after you were born. The nurse tried to take you from your mother. You stuck your chin in the air and then wailed louder than anything I'd ever heard."

"You've never told me that story before." I fastened the top few buttons of his cardigan and then covered his lap with the blanket that had been on his shoulders. He hardly ever talked about Mom, but I'd put up with an eternity of Parker's teasing if it meant I got to hear stories about her. "I'm going to get dinner. Should we eat out here, Daddy?"

"You'll catch cold in that thin dress. Better eat inside. The fire in there will be warmer than this little thing." He waved his hand at the flames in the fire pit.

"June is a little late in the year for a fire," I said to him while trading a conspiratorial look with Parker, who took a sip of water to hide his smile.

"I'll come get you once dinner's on the table." I patted Daddy on the shoulder then walked to the door.

"I'll help you," Parker said, following me through the door and sliding it shut behind us.

"You really don't need to—with the dinner or my finances." I shot him a quick smile to let him know I was joking, even though I wasn't. "Your name doesn't have to be an adverb. It can just be a name."

His forehead wrinkled with confusion.

"You don't have to act all *knightly*," I explained. "Rushing in to rescue anyone you think needs help."

He let out a laugh, but he didn't listen. Instead he pulled plates out of the cupboard behind me. "I don't think there's any way I can get around doing what your dad asked me to do," he said lightly, as though he were telling me he'd promised my dad not to let me stay up past my bedtime.

"You could try saying no." I pulled the pork out of the oven and hip-bumped the door shut.

"What's the big deal?" He set each plate in its spot, making noise loud enough to compete with the loud clang I'd forced out of the oven door.

"It's not any of your business." I jutted my chin toward a trivet on the counter. "Put that on the table," I ordered and then elbowed him out of the way once he'd done it so I could set down the pork.

"Hal asked me to make it my business." He leaned against the counter and crossed his arms, his blue eyes taking on the gray of hardened steel.

"And I'm asking you not to." I glared at him, trying to get my eyes to take on the same look as his.

He stared back and then blinked. "Your dad asked first," he said, cocking his head to the side to meet the shoulder he shrugged.

I sucked in my lip and took a breath. "I'm not a little girl anymore, Parker."

"You're acting like one," he said sternly enough I felt stinging behind my eyes. "Your dad asked me to look at your books. He's not charging me anything to live here right now, so I need to do something in return." He let out a deep sigh, and his eyes softened. "I know you love what you're doing. I can help you figure out how to make money doing it."

"I'm making money!" I snapped, still smarting from his accusation.

Parker looked as surprised by my words as I was that I'd said them. I didn't mean to. I had no idea if I was making money or not. I entered numbers into my computer program. Sometimes the figures it returned were black, and sometimes they were red.

"What are you doing with it, then?"

"Nothing." I turned around and walked outside to get Daddy. I told myself I wanted to get away from Parker's questions, but really, I needed to get away from him before I did something stupid. Like punch him. Or kiss him. I had the overwhelming urge to do both.

Chapter 3

Taylor brought Hailey by the shop the next day, and I couldn't help but fall in love with her and Xander. Hailey because of her willingness—if not her actual ability—to help and Xander because I could not resist his big brown eyes.

"Can I hold him?" I asked after he'd given me a toothless grin.

Hailey hesitated, looked at Taylor who bobbed her head, and then took him out of his carrier. "He likes to be on your shoulder," she said as she handed him to me. Before I could get him to my shoulder, Xander had one of my curls in a vice grip and was sucking on it. I didn't know two-month-old babies had that kind of strength.

I gently bounced him up and down while Hailey pried his fingers loose. Once she had him detangled, she took him back from me. A long strand of drool followed from my shoulder to his fist. Hailey grabbed a cloth from the bag slung over her shoulder and wiped up the wet spot Xander had left behind.

"Sorry." Her nervous giggle left me less irritated about what the baby had done to my shirt. "I guess he likes blondes," she said and giggled again while fingering her thin, shoulder-length brown hair.

"No problem. He's adorable." I took an elastic off my wrist and pulled my mess of blonde curls into a ponytail in case I wanted to hold him again.

"We're here to help," Taylor said and then nudged Hailey.

"Oh. Yeah. Taylor said you're doing all the flowers for your sister's wedding tomorrow and you might want to hire me." Hailey clutched Xander and kept her eyes on the floor.

I gave Taylor a look I meant for Hailey to miss, but she caught it.

"I mean, not to work here all the time—just for today," she sputtered before her eyes darted to Taylor. "You don't even have to pay me. I'm happy to help. Whatever you need."

She blinked quickly then squeezed her eyes shut. I could have pinched Taylor for mentioning the job before I'd even had a chance to meet Hailey. As much as I wanted to help her, I really needed someone who already knew flowers and could work full-time. Especially given all the pressure Daddy was putting on me to make money.

I looked at Hailey again in her ratty jeans and stretched-out tank top that did little to cover her black bra. The skin around her nose ring was red with infection, and she touched it gingerly. Her Vans had seen better days too. If I had to guess, I'd say they were probably worn-out before she'd inherited them.

Who was I kidding? Taylor knew the minute she brought Hailey in I'd be giving her a job. Dad was right that a business wasn't a hobby, but helping people could be. I could teach anyone to work with flowers, so why not a girl who needed a break?

"You know what?" I bent my knees and tipped my head low enough to meet her eyes. "I do need help. How about I hire you on a trial basis, and we'll see how it works out?"

"Really?" Her eyes opened wide, and she almost smiled before taking a deep breath. "Sick. Thanks."

"Do you have a sitter you can leave the baby with?" I asked and picked up my clippers. I had a bucket of roses to de-thorn.

Hailey bit her lip and looked at Taylor, her eyebrows knit together.

"He's still so little," Taylor said, taking a step toward Hailey. "He'd probably be okay in his carrier for most of the day. Don't you think?" She wrapped her arm around Hailey's shoulders, and I didn't know if the question was for me or for Hailey. Either way, I felt cornered. I couldn't run my shop and be a babysitter.

"You don't have anyone you could leave him with?" I asked. Hailey shook her head slowly.

"I could even get one of those"—Taylor pantomimed a square—"Playpen things."

"I don't know. What about daycare—"

"I swear he'll be fine," Hailey blurted. As if to prove her point, she laid the baby in his seat and stuck a binkie in his mouth when he let out a cry of protest. He quieted right down, which soothed my concerns.

If it hadn't, I couldn't have said no anyway. While Hailey was bent over Xander, Taylor mouthed, *She has no money*, and then made a big zero with her hand to emphasize her point.

I nodded, embarrassed I'd been so clueless. Hailey had been in and out of foster care most of her life, so of course she didn't have anyone to leave her baby with, even if she'd wanted to. And there was no way I could pay her enough to make daycare an option.

"We can give it a try. Sure," I said as Hailey stood up and bounced the seat to keep Xander quiet.

"Oh, thank you!" She let out a deep breath. "It's been so hard to find a job where I don't have to leave Xander."

She was near tears, and the relief on her face assured me I'd made the right decision. I'd make the situation work somehow, because that's the kind of person I was. Maybe other employers couldn't find it in their budgets to hire a young mother who needed a break, but most other employers didn't have my resources or—if I was being honest—my heart.

Although, I nearly lost heart when the first thing she did was pick up a rose by the head.

"What should I do first?" she asked, handing me the flower. "I'm a quick learner."

"The first thing you should do is never touch a flower's petals, especially if it's white." I took the rose by its stem and set it aside, knowing it probably wasn't usable anymore. "Flowers bruise easily and turn brown if you touch them."

"Oh. Sorry."

I thought I'd said it pretty gently, but she looked terrified. I'd have to be more careful about how I talked to her.

"It's not a big deal. Here." I handed Taylor the stem scissors. "How about we start with the basics? You can be the stem cutter today. Taylor will show you how." Hailey would require a lot more training than I'd planned on if she didn't even know how to properly pick up a flower. I'd have to start small.

Her head bobbed up and down with nervous gratitude as Taylor showed her how to snip the thorns off the stems without cutting the stems themselves. A pretty easy task, but Hailey was so shaky she cut the head off a rose.

"Tell me what your biggest dream is, Hailey," I asked to calm her nerves.

"Hailey wants to do nails. She's really talented," Taylor answered. "Show her," she directed Hailey and took the clippers from her.

Hailey held up her nails for me to inspect at the same time Taylor's phone dinged. As Taylor pulled the phone out of her pocket and read the message, her face broke into a grin. "I've gotta go," she announced. "I'm meeting Weston."

She set the clippers down, and with a wave goodbye, she was out the door before I could protest. She'd told me weeks ago she could help me get the arrangements done for Caroline's wedding, but she'd been ditching me more and more for Weston. It was my own fault for setting them up, but without Taylor things would take twice as long.

I sighed, shifting my attention back to Hailey's fingertips. "You did these yourself?" I asked as I inspected her pink nails with tiny designs. "Are those apples? They're so cute!"

She nodded.

"Did you paint them yourself, or are they decal things?" I let go of her hand and motioned for her to sit.

"I did them myself." Color rose in her cheeks, along with a shy grin.

"Why did you choose apples? I've never seen anything like that." A little too busy for my taste, but the girl had skills.

She didn't answer right away, but when she did she kept her eyes on her nails, and the color in her cheeks went from a pleased pink to a dark red. "I was having a rough day and started thinking about this time my mom took me apple-picking, and I kind of just painted them on there. It's one of the only good memories I've got of her, so I want to hold on to it."

Her rushed words and all the unspoken ones attached to them hung heavily in the air like the marine layer that had kept the sun from shining on us that morning. But I was glad she shared them with me. Everyone needs a break from the sun sometimes. How else would we learn to appreciate it?

"I don't have any memories of my mom," I said. "Sometimes I think that's better than if I had a lot of super bad ones. I think it's cool you're focusing on the good ones." The little Taylor had told me about how Hailey had ended up in foster care wasn't good. She had to have a lifetime's worth of experiences with her mom she'd like to forget. I knew she had the physical scars that wouldn't let her.

"Thanks," she answered softly.

"Your nails are really good," I said brightly. It's not good for the sun to stay hidden for too long.

"Thanks," she said again, with more confidence. She took the rose I handed her and clipped the thorns. "I tried to get a job at a nail salon, but I don't have a license."

"It would be a tough gig making any money doing nails." I showed her a thorn she missed. "But it's a great hobby."

There's no way it could be more than that. She'd have to go to cosmetology school and then try to find a job in a salon or a spa if she wanted to support herself and Xander. Those spots had to be hard to get. Hailey deserved more. If she could see her full potential, she could rise to it. That's where I came in. I had the money to help her realize dreams she probably never thought were possible.

"Have you ever thought about going to college?" I asked her. "You could take some classes to see if there's something else you might love as much as nails. You could even take some business classes to see what it would take to start your own nail salon."

That suggestion was a stroke of genius. I mentally high-fived myself. Without even meaning to, I imagined Parker getting in on the high-fiving too since I'd kept Hailey from pursuing a job with employers who would likely exploit her.

Feeling very satisfied with myself, I handed Hailey a bunch of flowers and showed her where to cut the stems.

"Is that what you did to open this place? You took business courses?" she asked as she cut each stem with careful precision. A little too careful. It took her so long I didn't think I'd ever get started on my next bunch.

"No, not exactly." Majoring in fine arts had allowed me to stay as far away as possible from anything that had to do with math. "But my dad and my sister know all about that stuff, so they help me out."

"I never really thought about going to college. I don't have enough money." She shrugged, as though the idea had never been real enough to believe in. Maybe it hadn't. Maybe no one had ever encouraged her to get an education. Maybe no one had ever told her she could be so much more than she imagined. Maybe that's why she'd been placed in my path. I could be the person who helped her reach higher than she ever thought possible . . .

"Eliza?"

I shook myself out of the vision of glory I had for Hailey. "Sorry, what was that?"

"Did I cut those okay?" She pointed the clippers at the stems.

"Perfect." They weren't, but fate had put her in my path for a bigger reason than to help me with my flower arrangements.

I pictured a brighter future for her and Xander than I'd seen that morning. And a brighter future for myself now that I had not just one person but two who could fill the giant hole Caroline would leave in my life within twenty-four hours.

Chapter 4

Those twenty-four hours were gone in seconds. Suddenly I was watching Caroline walk down the aisle of our tiny church on my father's arm in her simple but elegant sheath dress. Daddy's eyes were on her, shining with pride, joy, and tears. Her eyes brimmed with similar emotions, but they were on Preston.

For the first time in my life, I actually had pangs of jealousy for a bride. A picture popped into my head of what I'd want for my own wedding. Every detail was startlingly real, right down to my bouquet—peonies and roses, of course. But the moment Parker's face appeared on the groom side at the end of my aisle, I put a stop to the craziness going on in my head. I refocused my attention on my sister and was very careful not to look at Preston's best man, who just happened to be his brother.

It wasn't until the reception that I allowed the reality of my sister's marriage to set in. Until then, I'd put all my focus on helping her prepare for the wedding, ignoring the aching that had crept into my heart every time she chose to spend time with Preston instead of me. Ever since she'd announced her engagement, I'd been as thrilled about it as she was. I even faked excitement when she announced they'd be moving to San Francisco after the wedding. But now I couldn't ignore the fact she wouldn't be living at home with Daddy and me anymore. She wouldn't even be living in the same city.

It hit me hard, as I stood in front of the dessert table, that we'd never live together again, sharing midnight snacks and trading dating disaster stories while Netflix-binging on *Gilmore Girls*. My vision blurred, and all I could do was stare at the desserts in front of me. Why the tiered trays of petit fours would trigger the tears that followed, I don't know, but suddenly they were there, and so was Parker.

"Are you having a hard time choosing, or is it something else?" he asked and handed me a napkin. "Because you can take one of each, you know. That's what I'm doing." He loaded his plate with three different desserts and then filled the empty plate I was holding.

I tried to laugh, but it came out in more tears. "It's not the dessert." I set my plate down on the table so I could wipe my nose. "I'm losing my sister."

Parker set his plate down next to mine as if in solidarity to my pain, but a smile tugged at his lips. "Did you think Caroline and Preston were just going to have a wedding and not do the marriage part?"

"You're laughing at me." I blew my nose to cover my own laugh, because he was right. I hadn't thought past the party part of my sister's wedding.

He quit fighting his grin, but it was just serious enough to be sympathetic. "Come on," he said and grabbed my hand, leading me to the dance floor. I didn't resist. When we stepped onto the parquet floor, he took my left hand in his right and wrapped his other arm around my waist, moving me in time to the slow drum beat of "At Last."

"I wasn't laughing at you," he said, holding my hand against his chest and gazing down at me in a way that made me feel more grown-up than I'd felt since he walked through my shop door. His heart pulsed as steadily as the beat in the song.

"You still are," I answered, but my tears were gone. "I can see it in your eyes."

His smile grew. "What happened to the happy matchmaker?"

"I'm still happy I got them together." Daddy was much better than Parker in the sympathy department. He never had a problem letting me feel sorry for myself. "I'm just going to miss her when they move."

"San Francisco is a short flight away. You'll have somewhere to visit." He moved his hand to the middle of my back then back down again, sending a sensation down my spine that made me want to bury my head in his shoulder and stay there forever. Instead, I put a few inches of distance between us.

"Daddy won't go, and I can't leave him." That's all I had to say for Parker to understand. Caroline was the only other person who knew how little Daddy left the house anymore, but being in Parker's arms felt safe.

"He's that bad?" Parker's smile faded.

I nodded, and he pulled me close enough for me to lay my head on his chest. Parker had known Daddy before I was born, and he had more memories of my mother than I had. He'd seen what the car accident that killed her had done to Daddy. In a way, he knew my father better than I did.

"I can help," he said into my hair. "I'll stay with him whenever you want to visit Caroline."

"Really?" I pulled back to look at him.

"Of course. And she'll visit too."

I closed my eyes and rested my cheek on the space between his shoulder and heart, feeling its steady rhythm. Parker was home. Things would be okay.

"I feel better already," I whispered, and he patted my back like any big brother would. He'd never be able to replace my sister, but he was the one other person who understood me the way Caroline and Daddy did.

That fact, however, didn't keep me from avoiding him for the next month after we'd said goodbye to Caroline and Preston. Most of my reasons for dodging him stemmed from Daddy's insistence that I needed Parker's "business expertise." I thought Daddy would forget about it—or that, at least, I could put him off until I quit thinking about Parker holding me while we danced.

I should have known better. Daddy kept asking if Parker had been by the shop yet, and I kept finding myself humming "At Last." Even when I directed all my energy into training Hailey and going to my Om-powerment yoga classes, I couldn't get that song out of my head. On top of that, I really missed my sister. So when he texted on a day I was especially homesick for her and asked if I wanted to go to lunch, I didn't hesitate to say yes. I needed a hug as much as I needed food.

Parker hadn't bought a car since moving back to the U.S., so I picked him up. We drove to our favorite taco place, and as soon as we got out of the car, I told him, "I need a hug."

He pulled me into his arms right there in the middle of the parking lot and asked, "Missing Caroline?" before laying his cheek on top of my head.

I nodded, noticing—despite my misery—the firmness of the pectoral muscle under my cheek. Somehow it comforted me.

"Tacos will help," he said and pulled away.

"They always do," I answered and followed him into the restaurant.

He took my mind off things with stories of Hong Kong and the domestic workers he'd helped there. Most of them were Filipino women who had left their families in order to earn money working as nannies or maids. They earned a lot more in Hong Kong than they could in the Philippines and sent everything back to their families. However, they had few rights, and when they were mistreated by their employers they didn't have anywhere to go for help. Many had also gone into debt to illegal "brokers" who found them jobs but then charged the women such high interest on their brokers' fees that the debt couldn't be paid off.

The nonprofit Parker started helped women not only find jobs without paying exorbitant fees, but also gave them resources if they needed help getting out of an abusive situation.

"I can tell you love it," I said as I double-dipped a chip into our shared salsa.

"It's intense and hard, but yeah, I love it." His eyes shone in the same way they had when he used to talk about volunteering at the homeless shelter in high school. Social justice had always been his thing.

"Why'd you come back here?" I'd been wondering about that since he came home but had never asked for fear he might decide to go back.

"My partner can manage things on his own, and we need more money." He pursed his lips. "We're going to expand our outreach to include workers in the U.S., which will hopefully make fundraising easier. That's my job now."

"What do you mean workers in the U.S.? We don't have the same problems as they do in Hong Kong, do we?" I hoped not, but if we did, maybe he'd have a reason to stay.

His laugh made my cheeks burn even after he noticed and got serious again. "A lot of people think we don't have slave labor here, but there are plenty of sweatshops in L.A."

"Oh." I sat up straighter. I *did* know what he was talking about. "I don't buy cheap clothes because I know how underpaid the piece workers are who put them together."

"That's a good start." A smile tugged at Parker's lip. The same smile I'd seen every time I said something he found funny when I didn't mean it to be.

Before I could protest, the cashier called our order number, and he got up to get it. I didn't know why what I said had made him come close to laughing, but I didn't like it. I may not have been on the front lines fighting for social justice, but at least I was doing something.

That's when I decided Parker needed to meet Hailey. I could prove to him I wasn't just some spoiled trust-fund baby. I was doing my part to help people who didn't have the same advantages as me.

I jumped out of my seat and met Parker on his way back from the counter with our tray of food. "Let's get it to go. There's someone I want you to meet."

I took the tray from him and carried it back to the counter to have it bagged. I had over-ordered—as usual—so I knew there'd be enough for Hailey. Once I'd decided to tell Parker what I was doing for her, I could hardly wait for him to meet her.

I only wished I'd done it a month earlier, before I'd taken her shopping for more professional clothes to wear to work. She didn't have to get super dressed up, but now instead of see-through tank tops and booty shorts, she wore nice jeans and cute tops. I'd even taken her to get her hair cut and styled so it was more Emma Stone than '80s stoner. Her transformation would have been more impressive if he'd seen her when she first walked in the shop. It also would have been more impressive if the clothes and haircut had made an impact on her job skills. Those still needed work.

Back in my car, I started to tell him about her, but he had other concerns.

"How long has that engine light been on?" he asked, looking at my dash.

"I don't know." I'd noticed it a while ago and meant to ask Daddy about it but kept forgetting.

"You need to get it checked. When was the last time you had the oil changed?" He grabbed the emergency handle and pointed. "That's a red light!"

I slammed on the brake then calmly said, "I know what a red light is." There were still inches between me and the car in front of us, but Parker gave me the same disparaging look I'd seen a thousand times on my first driver's ed instructor's face.

"Where's the sticker that says when your last oil change was?" he asked when he was done lecturing me on how and when to brake.

"I took it off. It was ugly." The light turned green, and I pressed lightly on the gas, keeping my speed well below the limit, as per my self-appointed instructor's advice.

"How do you know when to get your oil changed?"

"Daddy takes care of it." I shrugged. "He's got a guy who picks up my car every few months . . . except I think he might have retired, and Daddy hasn't found anyone he trusts yet."

Parker let out a deep sigh. "That engine light means something's wrong. You need to get it looked at today." He took out his phone and googled *car repair*.

While he had decided he needed to manage one more part of my life, I'd decided I wasn't all that excited to introduce him to Hailey anymore or tell him how I'd figured out a way to pay for her classes at community college without her ever knowing.

To be honest, I should have been grateful he wanted to take care of my car, but he'd been so rude about it. I couldn't muster up any gratitude for him or his bossy attitude. And I certainly didn't need him to tell me how to manage my employee.

Unfortunately by this point we were back at the shop, and I didn't have another choice but to bring him inside so we could eat our lunch. And it didn't take him long to meet Hailey. Almost as soon as we opened the door, we were met with the sound of shattering glass, followed by a wail that sounded like a cross between an air-raid siren and a fire alarm.

"Is that a baby?" Parker asked before stepping around me and heading toward the back where the sounds had come from.

"I'm so sorry!" Hailey yelled as I rushed ahead of Parker to see what had happened.

We stopped before we got past the counter to keep from stepping on the shards of glass spread from the table to the back wall. Hailey already had Xander in her arms and was soothing him. Even from ten feet away I could see her flushed cheeks and the tears ready to spill.

"Are you okay?" I asked. "Is Xander okay? What happened?" I stood helpless, separated from comforting her and Xander by the sea of broken glass and my thin sandals that would offer little protection.

"I dropped a vase." Hailey's chin quivered. "I finished my first arrangement, and I think it was okay. I wanted to show you, but it slipped out of my hands."

She choked back her tears, and all our eyes were drawn to the floor where a dozen roses and their petals were lying. They'd have to be thrown away along with the vase, but I reminded myself it was more important that she not beat herself up over things that were easily replaced.

"I am so, so sorry," she said quietly. "I'm so dumb." I couldn't hear her over Xander's crying, but I saw the words.

"You're not dumb. I've done the same thing a hundred times." I smiled and got a half-smile and a sigh of relief in return.

"Parker, get the broom." I pointed at the closet then turned back to Hailey. "We'll clean this up. You take Xander to the back and get him calmed down."

They both followed my directions. Hailey fled to the couch, and Parker brought me the broom, handing it to me as he whispered, "Who is that?"

"Her name is Hailey." I handed the broom back to him and pointed at my practically bare feet. "I hired her to help me. You get the glass, and I'll clean up the rest."

"You're making enough to hire someone?" he whispered.

"That's none of your business. Remember?" I replied and pointed him in the direction of his task.

"Your dad's asked me to make it my business. Remember?"

"That doesn't mean I've asked you to." I stuck out my chin and stared him down.

"Your chin's out," he said and then turned around to sweep, ignoring my glare.

Despite my "stubborn chin," there was a ninety percent chance I would lose the battle to be the master—er, mistress—of my own finances. Daddy may not have had the willpower to leave the house, but he had the stubbornness to get what he wanted. Right now he wanted Parker looking at my balance sheet. And I was one hundred percent sure I wasn't going to like him poking around my business.

"Hailey!" I called as soon as I could be heard over Xander and before Parker could bring up my finances again. She emerged from the back with the baby cradled in her arms and a bottle in his mouth. "This is my faux brother, Parker," I said, pointing at him.

She scrunched up her nose and eyes like a puppy who doesn't know where his ball went. "What's a 'foe brother'? A brother you fight?"

I laughed until I realized she was serious then stopped abruptly. "No, Parker is like a fake brother. I've known him my whole life, and he bosses me around like I'm his little sister."

"Someone needs to." He walked to Hailey and stroked Xander's head full of hair. "And who's this little guy?"

"Xander," Hailey answered in a squeak.

"How old?" Parker stepped back but kept smiling at the baby.

"Three months." She kept her eyes on Xander, rocking him with so much nervous energy he let out a whimper that threatened to turn into more.

"I don't know a lot about babies, but that is a cute one." Parker glanced at the floor and gripped his broom tighter. "Careful of the glass right here." He swept near Hailey's feet then went back to sweeping the rest of the room. "And before you get smart about me playing big brother to you, Liza Belle, I'd like to point out that I *am* your big brother now, since your sister is married to my younger brother."

"That's a pretty big stretch, but if it makes you feel good, I'll allow it." I picked up the flowers one by one to see if any had survived.

"You'll allow it. That's cute." He bent down and swept his pile of glass into the dustpan. "Speaking of big-brother responsibilities, I found a place you can take your car."

"You need your car fixed?" Hailey piped in. "I know a really great place. A friend of mine works there. Tony's Auto Repair."

"That's the place I found too. They have great reviews." Parker smiled at Hailey like he'd found an accomplice. Which he had.

"I can call him if you want," Hailey offered, pulling her phone out of her pocket and deftly scrolled through her contacts with one hand while holding Xander's bottle in place with her chin.

"See if he can get her in today," Parker answered.

"Oh, was that question for you?" I chirped. "I thought maybe it was for me since it's my car we're talking about."

He held his hands up and took a step back. "Sorry. You're right."

Hailey's eyes darted between us. "It's ringing. Should I hang up?"

I shook my head and walked past them both to get the mop. "It's fine."

I knew they were just trying to help, but it was more annoying than anything. The last thing I wanted to do was spend the day at a car-repair place. I could only imagine how gross that would be. I mean, I'd never actually been to one, so I really did have to use my imagination, but it was conjuring up some pretty yucky images. If Hailey hadn't been so intent on making up for the vase disaster, I would have called Daddy and asked him to take care of it.

Hailey got ahold of her friend, and by the time I had the water on the floor mopped up, she'd set up an appointment for me.

"He says to bring it right over." She beamed with pride.

"Great. Thanks," I said through gritted teeth. "Do I just stay there until it's done, or how does this work?"

"I could follow you over in the delivery van if you don't mind Xander riding with you, and if Parker doesn't mind staying here," Hailey offered, oh-so-helpfully. "Then you can leave your car and come back here until it's done."

"That sounds like a fantastic idea." Now Parker beamed as brightly as Hailey had a few minutes before. But it was a different kind of beaming. A gloating kind of beam, pointed directly at me. "It'll give me a chance to go over your finances."

"Let me put Xander in his seat, and we can go!" Hailey grabbed the keys to the van and hustled to gather up her stuff with an energy I'd rarely seen from her before.

I turned my gaze to Parker and glared. "Nicely played, Big Brother. Nicely. Played."

He shrugged and then smiled.

"Do you know what to do if a customer comes in?" I asked, hoping to wipe the smug look off his face. He might know finances, but he didn't know a thing about flowers.

"How hard can it be?" He shrugged again, so smug in his confidence I had to believe he was purposely trying to make me lose my mind.

"I'm ready to go!" Hailey shouted from the back before I had a comeback for Parker.

"Don't worry." He rubbed my shoulder. "I won't do anything you wouldn't do."

I pushed his hand away. He hadn't earned my forgiveness yet, and he wouldn't until he quit acting like I couldn't run my own business.

"Just to be sure you don't mess something up, I'll go ahead and put up the closed sign," I said before turning my back on him and adding, "Don't touch anything."

Chapter 5

By the time I got to Tony's Repair Shop, Hailey was already inside. I would have begged her to come in with me even if she hadn't wanted to. To my surprise, it wasn't nearly the dungeon of filth I had imagined. In fact, it was pretty nice. For a car place, anyway. With a quick scan I saw clean linoleum floors and barely worn leather couches. They even had good magazines, not just *Fish and Stream* or whatever it was old men read in car shops. If it hadn't been for the smell of hot pavement and disinfecting wipes, I wouldn't have minded being there at all.

"Hey, Hailey!" A young guy with short dark hair shaved on the sides and slicked back on top yelled when we walked in, practically running to meet us at the door. He wiped his hands on his coveralls and then stuck one out for me to shake. "I'm Ashton Martin."

I looked at the grease-stained hand then back at him, smiling politely. Luckily he shoved the hand back in his pocket before I had to actually shake it.

"Sorry." He shook his head. "I'm usually not this dirty. Been doing brakes on a car I'm fixing up."

"Is it the El Camino?" Hailey asked.

"Yeah." He looked her up and down with the same admiration I imagined he used for his El Camawhatever. If his eyes had landed anywhere besides on Xander, I would have dragged Hailey out of there faster than a coyote with a captured house cat.

"How's this little guy?" he asked as he reached out to stroke Xander's black hair then glanced at his own dirty hands and dropped them to his side. "Xander, right?"

"Yeah." Hailey's face lit up. "He's good. A little fussy. I think he's teething."

"Oh man, that bites." He laughed at his own joke. "I didn't even mean to do that. What's that called when you, like, say something that sort of relates to something else for a joke?"

"A pun?" I offered.

"Yeah, that's it!" He snapped his fingers and pointed at me. "No pun intended!"

"I love puns," Hailey said. Her eyes radiated with the same El Camamawhat'sit glow Ashton's had. I didn't share their love for puns, and I wasn't interested in spending the day in Tony's Repair Shop, no matter how good the magazines were.

Hailey, on the other hand, looked *very* interested in spending the day there. She didn't seem to mind Ashton's wrist-to-shoulder tatts, the ring in his lip, or the gauges in his ears. They could have gone on talking puns and cars all afternoon if I hadn't cleared my throat to remind them why we were there.

"Sorry!" he said and then glanced apologetically at Hailey. "Tell me what's going on with your car."

"It's been making some weird noises for a few days," I answered then gave Hailey my own glance. She was flushed and smiling more than I'd ever seen her smile. She was obviously into Ashton, who seemed like a nice guy . . . just not a college girl's kind of a guy.

"Her radiator light's on." Hailey interrupted my thoughts.

"It is?" I asked. "Parker said it was the engine light."

She shook her head. "I'm pretty sure it's the radiator. I noticed it yesterday when we drove to lunch," she said to me. Then she turned back to Ashton. "I'm probably wrong, but it sounds like it might be the water pump."

"Could be. I'll have to drive it around, but I wouldn't be surprised if you're right."

"So, should I leave it here?" I broke in before they started whispering sweet nothings about radiators while gazing deeply into each other's eyes. "Or are you going to test drive it now?"

"I'll take it for a quick drive and give it a listen before I put her up on the lift. You can leave it here or wait, but it may take a while. We can call a car to take you home." His return to professionalism didn't change my mind about him. He might be the right guy to fix my car, but he wasn't the right guy for Hailey.

"I'll leave it. Just call me when you have a diagnosis. We'll take the van back." I handed him the keys and turned to Hailey. "Should we go?"

"Yeah," she answered without taking her eyes off Ashton but then turned to me in a panic. "Oh no! We can't take Xander in the van!"

It took me half a second to realize what she meant, and then embarrassment crept over me. The van only had two front seats. That's why Xander had ridden with me in the first place. We hadn't thought about how we'd get him back to the shop after we dropped off my car.

"I'll take the van and have Parker come get you and Xander." I reached for my phone, already hearing Parker laughing at me before I'd even dialed.

"Or you and Xander could ride with me," Ashton offered, his words spilling out faster than Superman rushing in to save the day. "We'll take Eliza's car around the block once, and then I'll drop you where you need to be. We can see if your diagnosis is right."

Hailey looked at me for an okay. I didn't want to give it, but I wanted to call Parker even less, so I nodded yes.

"I swear I won't keep her long," Ashton added. "I'll have her back to work in half an hour, tops."

He seemed like a decent guy, but I had a hard time trusting anyone who thought giant discs in his ears looked good. I didn't know a lot about Hailey's past, but I did know she had a lot of reasons not to trust men.

"Could you come out to the van really fast?" I asked, sounding more awkward than when Daddy tried to use surf lingo.

Her brows knit together. "Sure," she answered slowly. "I'll be right back, Ashton."

She buckled Xander in his carrier then followed me outside.

"Are you sure you'll be okay?" I asked her as I opened the van door. "How well do you know him?"

"Pretty good," she said. "I mean, I haven't known him that long, but we text and stuff." Her confidence waned with each word, but mine increased. I was positive he wasn't the right guy for her.

"You've known him long enough to trust him?" I asked carefully.

"Yeah," she said slowly. "I mean, I think so. He seems nice. And he's cute. Don't you think?"

"He's not really my type." I picked a piece of hair off my shirt and tossed it to the ground. "I've always liked more of the nerdy college type." She might like driving around with Ashton-types now, but I could plant the seeds of something better.

"Oh, like that Parker guy!" She smiled broadly and moved Xander to her other arm.

"What?" My eyes shot to her face. "No!"

"Really? It seemed like you were totally into him."

"Parker?" I forced a laugh at the ridiculousness of that idea. "No! He's practically my brother."

"Hmm. My bad." She didn't seem convinced.

"Listen, I know I'm being overprotective, but if you're not back in twenty minutes, I'm going to start worrying." I looked her straight in the eye and didn't blink so she'd know how serious I was.

She nodded and twisted her nose ring.

"Thirty minutes and I call the police." My eyes burned they wanted to blink so badly.

"I think I'll be okay, but thanks for looking out for me." She almost smiled before walking back to my car, where Ashton was waiting for her with the door open.

With that, I had no other choice but to drive back to the shop thinking about what I'd done that would give Hailey the idea I thought of Parker as anything more than a friend. A really good friend, but still, just a friend.

A friend, I was reminded as soon as I walked in the door, who needed to mind his own business when it came to mine.

"I'm going to have to take a closer look at your books when I have more time," he said before I even had a chance to say hello. "I can show you how to document your expenses better. It looks like you could cut some of them so you could actually turn a profit."

"Thanks, but no." I crossed in front of him and shut down my computer.

He let out a low laugh. "I'll take that as a sign you've had enough interference for the day."

"You could say that, yes." I turned to face him, relieved he got the message without my being any blunter about it.

"I'm sorry." He pulled me into a side hug. "You're doing a good job with this place. Better than I expected—"

"You know how condescending that sounds, right?" I tried to squirm out of his hug.

"Yes, but it's the truth, and I mean it as a compliment." He squeezed my shoulder and then let me go. "I didn't think it was possible to make money on flowers and candles."

"I did. That's why I opened this place."

"You could be doing a lot better though. I can show you how to make a sustainable profit." Of course he had to follow his almost-compliment with some unsolicited advice. There wasn't any point in arguing with him. I didn't want to tell him where the money was going, so my only real option was to distract him.

"You want to come over for dinner tonight?" I asked as I walked past him to my worktable. A change of subject seemed like the best way to divert his attention. "I've already invited the Bateses. I'm sure they'd love to see you."

"Martha and Nancy?" His eyebrows shot up over his glasses. My distraction had worked. "I haven't seen them in years. How are they?"

"The same," I sighed, and he laughed.

"So, you're not so much interested in feeding me as you are in having me there to provide a different kind of interference, right?"

"If that means I want you there so someone else has to listen to Nancy talk about nothing for three hours straight, then yes, that's why I want you there. But I'll reward you with filet mignon and crème brûlée." I put on my most convincing smile and batted my eyelashes. I really needed someone for backup when it came to conversation with Nancy. But I also wanted Parker there. With Caroline gone and Taylor spending most of her time with her boyfriend, I was short on people to hang out with. And, despite his teasing and bossing, Parker made a pretty good friend.

"Are you cooking?" he asked tentatively.

I wanted to be able to say yes and then prove to him I could cook delicious food, but I couldn't do either. "No. Daddy's chef is coming."

"Then I'm in. I love steak." He pulled his keys out of his pocket and kissed the top of my head. "I'll see you tonight."

"I'm putting you next to Nancy, you know," I called to him before he walked out the door. The spot on my scalp where his lips had been still tingled. He'd never done that before.

"Looking forward to it!" Without turning around, he held his keys in the air and waved goodbye.

Chapter 6

Parker's good-friend attributes came on full display that night the moment the doorbell rang and he jumped up from the couch to let in Martha and Nancy Bates. Since Daddy hated to leave the house but still liked people, I invited dinner guests over at least once a week. It gave him something to look forward to, and usually those were his best days.

Martha had been married to Daddy's friend, Jack Bates. Nancy was Martha's forty-year-old daughter who had also been Daddy's secretary. He'd hired her after Jack died—which was right around the time everyone realized Jack had squandered every dime he'd made by investing in a real estate scheme that went bust, leaving Martha penniless. The fact that Nancy talked nonstop and had never had a job that didn't involve rescuing animals didn't matter to Daddy. She worked for him until he retired, but since then she hadn't kept a job for more than a couple of weeks at a time. I suspect she didn't actually do much for Daddy either, but he'd kept her on the payroll to help where he could.

Parker let them both in and led them down the hall, with Nancy jabbering the whole way about the sweater she wore despite the summer heat.

"Dad bought it for me on my twenty-fifth birthday. He knew I'd like it because of the Scottie dog button." She pointed it out to Parker, who showed the proper amount of admiration for it before leading her to the table.

"You look so pretty," Nancy said to me when she saw me in the kitchen. "Of course, you always look pretty. I didn't mean to imply you don't look pretty every time I see you. You're such a pretty girl it would be hard for you to not look pretty, but that dress makes you look especially pretty. Don't you think so, Parker?" She turned to him, blinking rapidly while her shoulder twitched.

"I completely agree, Nancy. Eliza is a very pretty girl, especially in that dress." He lowered his head in a slow nod that made his words seem less like a compliment than another teasing jab. Plus, he'd called me a girl. I was twenty-four, not twelve.

"Thank you both," I said politely and brushed past them to set plates on the table.

"You see, Eliza?" Daddy said, hugging Martha and then Nancy. "I'm not the only one who thinks you're beautiful, so you can stop accusing me of being biased." He took his seat at the head of the table, and the rest of us sat down. I'd suffer through a thousand dinners with Martha and Nancy if it meant seeing Daddy so much more like himself.

Nancy prattled on through dinner, cutting her mother's meat while telling us about each and every dog in the shelter where she'd recently found a job. I forced myself not to look at Parker, who, while he would never say anything mean, did give me one or two looks that nearly made me burst out laughing.

"And Jami emailed me just last night to say she's coming for a visit. I'll read you the whole thing." Nancy looked around for her phone, and I prayed she'd never find it. The last thing I wanted was an email-by-email account of Jami Fairfax's life.

"Oh, it's in my purse. Parker, do you remember where I put my purse? Could you get my phone for me? And my glasses? I can't see anything without my glasses anymore; my eyes are so bad . . ."

Nancy kept talking while Parker found her purse, phone, and glasses in the entryway closet. By the time he got back with them, she'd told Daddy and me everything Jami had said in her email. That didn't stop her from reading it to us anyway.

"She says, *Hi, Grandma and Aunt Nanc . . .*" She paused to put on her reading glasses. "She always calls me Nanc; she has ever since she was a little girl. *I'm taking some time off before going to grad school and would love to come visit you . . .*"

I noticed a spot on the table runner and made a mental note to include it in the load scheduled for the dry cleaners on Tuesday. Then I got distracted by how pretty the little pots of succulents looked as centerpieces. Then I started thinking about the wedding I'd been hired to do and how I could incorporate succulents in the bride's bouquet and the groomsmen's boutonnieres.

By the time Nancy stopped talking, I'd planned out every flower arrangement for my client.

"I'm sure Eliza would love to show Jami around while she's here, won't you, sweetie?" Daddy asked, and I nodded before realizing what I'd agreed to do.

I hadn't seen Jami in almost fifteen years. Her parents divorced when she was four, and she'd spent a lot of time at her Grandma Martha's house when she visited her dad for the next several years. Since we were the same age, Daddy and Martha had thrown us together a lot.

Then Jami's dad—who'd always been out of control—was killed driving drunk. Jami's stepdad had adopted her, and her mom, who'd never liked Martha, made sure Jami didn't visit anymore. A few years ago, Jami had reconnected with her grandma and aunt through Facebook but hadn't been to visit them. Now, every dinner with Martha and Nancy meant more news about Jami than any one person could ever want.

"When does she get here?" I asked Nancy, sure I would have known if I hadn't spaced off ten minutes before.

"She'll be here for Thanksgiving, and if she gets a job, she'll stay for Christmas," Nancy answered. "She could be here until she goes to grad school!" Nancy's shoulder twitched as though to add special emphasis to her excitement.

"When is she going to grad school?" I asked, cutting my meat and trying out the European way of eating by not switching my fork to my right hand. I'd learned that once in an etiquette class.

"Well, um . . ." Nancy clutched her silverware and then glanced at Parker.

"She has to work for a few years to earn the money for it," he answered for her. "Maybe you missed it when Nancy said it. Twice."

"Oh! Of course, I heard you," I lied. "I don't know where my head is." I knew exactly where it was. Back in etiquette class. Because even that was more exciting than talking about Jami Fairfax.

"There's a coffee shop right next door to my store." I smiled and forced myself to reengage in the conversation. "Maybe she can apply there. I'd be happy to put in a good word for her." I put on my brightest smile for Nancy, and when she looked down to smooth her napkin, I shot a withering look at Parker.

"I don't think she drinks coffee," Nancy said slowly.

"Maybe you also missed the part where Nancy said Jami is at a Mormon university where they can't drink anything with caffeine in it," Parker answered again. Parker liked to be helpful. Sometimes too helpful.

"I think it's just coffee and tea they can't have," Nancy piped in, going into a lot more detail than I cared to know about the Mormon health code before switching gears back to Jami. "I wish we could do more for her so she didn't have to work. I doubt her mother would be happy about it. She's not happy at all that Jami's coming here, but Jami thinks she'll be able to earn more money here than she did while she was in school in Idaho. And she wants to get out of the cold." Nancy looked at me, expectation written on her face more clearly than a dry-clean label on silk. "So, if nothing else, maybe a few months on the beach will cheer her up."

"I'm sure it will. A good day on the waves cures anything," I said brightly.

"Does she surf?" Parker asked. "There probably weren't a lot of opportunities to learn, growing up in Utah."

I sent Parker another look. I knew Jami had moved to Utah after her dad died. I'd just forgotten for a minute.

"Hanging out on the sand is a legit remedy too." I took a bite of my steak so I wouldn't have to say anything else. By a massive stroke of good luck, a knock at the door saved me.

I could tell by its *knock, knock, knock-knock-knock* rhythm it was Taylor.

"I'll get it!" I yelled and jumped up before anyone else had time to move. I had no idea why Taylor would be at my house when she was supposed to be out with Weston, but I didn't care. Listening to her cry hysterically if they'd broken up would be a hundred times better than Parker outing me one more time for ignoring Nancy's boring email from Jami.

The front door flew open before I reached it, and Taylor barged in.

"I'm engaged!" she squealed as soon as she saw me.

"What?"

"I'm engaged!" she squealed again before throwing her arms around me. She squeezed me tight while Weston stood behind her, grinning ear to ear.

She let me go and stuck out her hand to show me the ring. I grabbed her fingers, and we jumped up and down, yelling, "You're engaged" and "I'm engaged" until Parker came down the hall.

"What is going on?" he asked as he turned the corner. "Your dad's worried there's a mob out here ready to storm the house. He's ten seconds away from calling 911."

"Taylor is engaged." I hugged her and then turned to Parker. "Another successful match to add to my list." I curtsied then pulled back my shoulders and dared him to make fun of me.

"You have a matchmaking list?" he asked as he passed me and pulled Taylor into a congratulatory hug.

"Preston and Caroline and now Taylor and Weston." I did a showcase model hand motion to introduce Weston. "I met Weston when he came in to buy his mom a flower arrangement for Mother's Day and knew he'd be perfect for Taylor, so I set them up."

"It's true. I owe all my happiness to her." Taylor beamed at Parker then wrapped her arms around Weston's waist.

"Humph," Parker scoffed. "Well, congratulations to both of you, no matter who the credit for your approaching nuptials goes to."

"You know it's me." I twisted back and forth in front of him, making my dress twirl like a six-year-old. "Do you know how one percent you sound when you say, 'approaching nuptials'?" I added because he deserved to be roasted.

"Says the girl with a trust fund." He raised his eyebrows, challenging me to try again.

"Fine. Then you sound like a Harvard professor wannabe." I turned my back to him and faced Taylor. "Daddy will want to congratulate you."

I grabbed her hand—the one with the giant ring on it—and ignored the panic dueling with my excitement. This was the outcome I'd wanted from the moment I introduced her to Weston. Now that it was here, though, all the implications I'd been pushing aside for months took center stage. Taylor would always be my best friend, but I wouldn't be hers anymore. She'd have someone else to talk to and lean on and spend time with. Weston would be her right-hand man.

I pulled Taylor into the dining room, parked her in front of Daddy, and said, "Guess who's engaged."

He frowned and focused on me. "You haven't been dating someone I'm not aware of, have you?"

"Daddy! No, of course not." I wagged my head toward Taylor. "It's Taylor."

She held her ring hand up as proof, and Weston took his place beside her.

"Oh yes, that does make more sense." Daddy stood up, his joints working at the speed of a sloth, while Nancy clapped with excitement and Martha continued to say nothing.

"That is such happy news! I'm so glad Mother and I could be here to hear it." Nancy stood and rushed to Taylor, beating Daddy there. "I love weddings! There's nothing more fun than dancing and eating cake. What kind of cake will you have? I hope it's chocolate. I've had lemon before at weddings, but it's never very good. Except at one wedding I had a piece of white cake with raspberry in the middle. I liked that kind. The cakes I like best are the ones with all the layers, and each layer is a different flavor. I always do a taste test with a piece from each one . . ."

Taylor and I had been inseparable since we were ten, so of course she knew the Bateses. They'd been a part of our lives even longer than she had. She didn't, however, really know them well enough that they would have made the wedding guest list, but obviously they would have to now. She shot me a plea for help as Nancy rambled on and squeezed Taylor's hand, fingering the ring on it.

"Do you remember whose weddings those were?" I gently guided Nancy away so Daddy could hug Taylor. "I'd love to ask them who did their cakes."

“Yes!” Nancy looked so excited, I wished I’d found another diversionary tactic. “You can give them to Taylor. Of course, it’s been a long time; before Dad died, I think.” I sat her down in her seat, and she kept right on talking. “I’m sure I can find the names. I’ve saved the invitations somewhere. Maybe Jami can help me find them while she’s here . . .”

I loaded her plate with more food, despite her protests. Back in the day, she’d been a debutante. She’d never talk with her mouth full or leave a plate with more than a bite of food on it. I added another spoonful of roasted potatoes to make sure she’d be occupied at least long enough for Taylor to get through her story of how Weston proposed.

Weston watched Taylor as she spoke, his eyes swimming with love. The more animated she got, the more he lit up, until finally when she finished he wrapped his arms around her and kissed her like they were the only two people in the room.

My eyes accidentally met Parker’s, but we both pretended they hadn’t. After that, I kept them glued to Taylor and Weston. They were so cute and happy together, it almost made me want to get married.

Almost, but not quite.

Chapter 7

I'm convinced yoga is the answer to most problems. I bet if Putin and that crazy guy in North Korea spent some time in a yoga class, they wouldn't be nearly so mean and world domination-y. Whenever my world gets out of whack, I go straight to my mat to get centered again.

That's exactly what I did Sunday morning after Taylor announced her engagement. I ignored all my icky panicky feelings until she said they wanted to get married in Hawaii. In February. And she wanted me to help plan it. Insert screaming emoji face here.

Basically I had a little more than six months to plan a destination wedding. That I could totally do. Probably. The thing I didn't know how to handle was the date looming ahead of me when Taylor would disappear into married life. As much as I wanted to believe nothing would change between us, I'd already seen what marriage had done to Caroline. We were down to talking once a day, and it was mostly about how happy she was being married and living in San Francisco. In six months, I'd be doing the same thing with Taylor.

Obviously, I couldn't talk to Taylor about why I was freaking out, so yoga was my only option for unloading all my negative energy. Unfortunately, my regular yoga instructor was out of town for a month, which meant yoga with Elton—or Roshan, as he preferred to be called.

Before he became Roshan, Elton had been a friend of Preston and Caroline's in high school. Then he got into yoga and decided a Hindu name suited him better. Roshan, as Elton frequently pointed out, was Hindi for "shining light," and as a shining light, he had determined to devote his life to using yoga to empower people. Not a bad idea. Except he wrapped up all that light and devotion into a shiny multilevel marketing package called Om-powerment.

I didn't want to get involved with that part of his program, but I did really like the meditation part. For all his cockiness, Elton said some enlightening things. I was hoping he'd say some that night because I needed them.

When I walked into the studio, Elton pressed his palms together against his heart and greeted me with a slight bow. "Welcome back, Liza," he said in a voice barely above a whisper. He'd added more meditating god statues since the last time I'd been there. I chose not to comment on that or the fact he'd called me Liza instead of Eliza. I was determined to find my zen.

"How are you?" he asked, pressing his cheek to mine. "It's been a while since we've seen you."

"Doing well. Thanks, Elt—Roshan." I avoided his implied question about why I hadn't been to his class in more than a month. "We missed you at Preston and Caroline's wedding."

He let out a deep sigh and took my mat from me. "It slayed me I couldn't be there. The only thing that could have kept me from it is the conference I went to. It was a once-in-a-lifetime opportunity that took my life-coaching skills to a whole new level." His voice rose to include the yogis in our conversation who were already lying on their mats. "I would love to share with all of you everything I learned. You won't believe the change it will make in your life. Talk about *ommm*-powerment." He laughed at the play on words, and a few of his yogis laughed with him. I assumed they were cemented somewhere below him in the Om-powerment pyramid.

"Sounds interesting," I said, looking for the most noncommittal words I could find as I unrolled my mat. Elton had a gift for inspiring people but also for talking them into buying his products.

"We can talk more after class," he whispered before walking to the front of the studio.

I laid down on my mat and took a deep cleansing breath, letting go of all the negative thoughts I was projecting about the rest of the session being as annoying as the first few minutes had been. But once Elton got out of salesman mode and into yogi mode, his words were exactly what I needed.

"Be present in this moment. Forget what's happening off your mat, and focus on becoming a better you, right here, right now," he began.

I took another deep breath. His words helped clear my head, and it only got better after that. He seemed to be reading my mind when he chanted, "Be grateful for the relationships in your life, no matter how they may be transitioning. Relationships have to grow and change in order to thrive."

His words didn't usually speak to my soul the way my regular instructor's did, but that day he seemed completely in tune with everything I needed to hear. Not only that, but I had a total epiphany while lying on my back in my last vinyasa: Elton would be perfect for Hailey.

Who better to help me help her see and reach her potential? Elton lived to motivate people, and if anyone needed motivation, it was Hailey. He would love her.

I popped up from the floor, ready to put my next matchmaking endeavor into motion and nearly knocked over the very man who'd not only inspired it, but also would benefit from it.

"How did you like it?" he asked, hovering over me as I rolled up my mat.

"It was exactly what I needed today. Thank you so much." I tucked the mat under my arm and stepped around him to walk to the door.

"I know," he said as he walked next to me with his hands behind his back and his chin to his chest, the epitome of a meditating monk. "I could tell what I said really empowered you today. Energy radiated off you in warrior pose."

I laughed. "Maybe I'll have to come more often." His Dalai Lama imitation had me wondering why his room was full of Buddhas but he'd taken a Hindu name. Then I remembered Hailey and banished my negative thoughts. "I actually have a friend I think would love it."

"Bring her. I'll give her a first class free." He led me to the front desk, his fingertips resting on my spine, and handed me a card for a free class.

"Thank you." I took the card from him and slung my mat over my shoulder, knocking away his fingers. "I'll bring her for sure. I think she'll love it, and you'll really like her. She's a sweet girl with a lot of potential. She could use someone like you."

"Can't wait to meet her." He opened the door for me, and I stepped out. "Namaste."

"Namaste."

I walked to my car, smiling. In a little less than an hour, I had gained renewed purpose and clarity. Yoga, as usual, had fixed everything. I could hardly wait to tell Hailey I'd found the perfect guy for her.

I could have texted her, but I wanted to tell her in person, so I waited until she came into work Monday morning. The smile on her face made me even more excited to tell her about Elton, but she had her own news first.

"You won't believe what I did on Friday night," she said, taking Xander out of his seat and handing him to me. My favorite part of every day was when she gave me Xander to cuddle.

"What did you do?" I nuzzled Xander's nose and then blew a raspberry on his cheek that made him giggle.

"Ashton took Xander and me to the park and then out to dinner. You should have seen him with Xander. He was so great. He put him in the baby swing and pushed him, and then he held him and went down the slide. We had the best time. He took us to In-N-Out, and he even fed Xander." Hailey paced, vibrating with energy.

"Baby food?" I asked.

"Yeah, I mean he snuck him a little shake when he thought I wasn't looking." She giggled, but I didn't find anything funny about it.

"Babies his age aren't supposed to have fast food, are they? Weren't you worried he'd choke?" I crawled my fingers up Xander's belly before tickling him into another laugh.

Hailey slowed. "I don't know. I guess he could have."

"As long as you're sure he'll be okay. I know you wouldn't want anything to happen to him." It didn't surprise me Ashton had fed him milkshake. A twenty-year-old man with a *South Park* tattoo obviously didn't have the best judgment in the world.

"I'll make sure he doesn't do it again." Her brow creased. She stopped in front of me and ran her hand down Xander's bare arm. "I was so excited to be out with a guy, I guess I wasn't thinking."

"Was Xander okay on the swing and the slide?" I asked. "I don't know how old babies are supposed to be before they do that stuff."

"It seemed like he really liked it, but I don't know. I probably should check with his doctor." She rubbed Xander's back, and I handed him back to her.

"You can never be too careful with babies, right?" I turned on the computer and pulled up my Taylor's-Wedding spreadsheet. There were a lot of to-dos on it. "Are you going out with him again?"

"I think so. I mean, we just hung out." Her excitement was gone. "It's not like we're talking."

"What?"

"We're just hanging out, nothing serious. We're not *talking*."

"So, you're not dating?" Sometimes Hailey made me feel old. I wasn't sure how the meaning of talking had changed, but apparently it wasn't just about communicating with words anymore.

"Is hanging out dating?" She bounced Xander and hummed a Taylor Swift song.

"Depends on whether he's the only guy you're hanging out with and whether he's the only guy you *want* to hang out with." I stared at her and raised my eyebrows so she'd understand the seriousness of my point.

"I mean, I don't know," she answered slowly. "I didn't used to care who I hung out with until I had Xander. Now I want him to have a dad. Not a bunch of wannabe dads like I had." Xander squawked, and she patted him. "Maybe I shouldn't hang out with him so much . . . should I?"

"I could never make that decision for you, Hailey. You have to decide for yourself who's right for you." I paused long enough to close my spreadsheet and then turned my attention back to her. "But you might want to keep your options open. Anyone you choose to date—or even marry someday—you'll also be choosing for Xander."

"So true." She ran her hand down his head to his back, and he rested his cheek on her shoulder.

"We've got some orders," I said and pointed to the shelf. "Can you hand me one of those large vases?"

"Sure." She moved Xander to her hip to get the vase and then set the vase on the table. "What was the news you wanted to tell me?"

"Oh yeah, I almost forgot." I shook my head. "It's not a big deal, especially if you're really into Ashton." I grabbed a bucket and went to the cooler to get the flowers I'd purchased that morning.

Hailey followed and held the door open while I filled the bucket.

"I'm not that into him," she said, her voice perking up as she followed me back to my work table. "I don't know if I'll even go out with him again."

I set my filled bucket on the table and grinned at her. "Okay, if you're not serious about him, I think I know the perfect guy for you." I knew I'd been right about discouraging her from Ashton. If she was ready to give him up that easily, he wasn't right for her.

"Really?" All her excitement was back. Maybe even more. "Tell me about him."

"His name is Elton—except he goes by Roshan now." I ignored the look she gave me and kept talking. "He teaches yoga, but he's more of a life coach. He even has his own company called Om-powerment."

"Yoga? I've never done yoga." Her enthusiasm went as mushy as a bad wave.

"Now's your chance!" I said to get her pumped again. Even if it meant stretching the truth. "I told him about you, and he wants to meet you. He even gave you a free pass for one class."

"Really? That's cool." She set Xander in his bouncy seat. "I could try it, I guess."

"We can go tomorrow night after work." I pulled Roshan's card out of my purse, realizing for the first time it had his picture on the back. "He's cute, isn't he?" I asked, showing the card to her.

She nodded, a slow grin spreading across her face. "Is this what he wears to class?" She stared at the picture of Roshan in his spandex shorts, lunging forward in warrior one pose. The "sweat" on his skin emphasized each ab in his six pack. "I wouldn't mind looking at that for an hour."

"So, it's a plan, then?"

She nodded but then stopped.

"What should I do with Xander?" she asked. "Do you think he could come? I could leave him in his bouncy seat at the back of the room. He'd be fine."

"I don't think so." I'd forgotten about Xander, who happily batted the toys in his bouncy seat as if to back up his mom. Maybe he'd do that for an hour, but it was probably best to give Elton a chance to get to know Hailey before he met Xander.

"What if Taylor watched him for you?" I suggested. "I could ask her."

Worry replaced the smile that had been on her face. She trusted Taylor as much as she trusted anyone, but she didn't really trust anyone. She chewed her lip and cracked each knuckle while she thought.

"Do you think she would?" she finally asked.

"You know she loves Xander, and she'd do anything for you." I put my hand on Hailey's shoulder. "If she's not busy tomorrow, I'm sure she will."

"Okay, if you really think he wants to meet me." She let out a nervous breath.

"Of course he does!" Even if he didn't know it yet. "I'll text Taylor."

I pulled my phone out before Hailey could change her mind. She'd made the best decision of her life, and I was going to make sure she followed through.

Chapter 8

When I got home that night, Daddy was wrapped up in a blanket on his recliner instead of outside on the patio.

"What's wrong?" I asked, eyeing the stack of wadded-up tissues on the table next to him.

"This cold came on suddenly," he answered and coughed.

"Why didn't you call me?" I rushed to his chair and handed him the box of tissues he was reaching for.

He took a tissue and shook his head while he blew his nose. "It's nothing serious." He coughed again. He'd sounded congested the day before, but I didn't think I'd come home to find him totally sick.

"I'm here now, so let me take care of you." I tucked the blanket around his feet, tipped his chair back, and adjusted the pillow under his head.

He let me baby him—he always did—but shook his head again. "You've got to go to the game with Parker. I can't."

"Me?"

One of the few things Daddy would leave the house for was an Angels baseball game. Not every game—only the good ones. Tonight they were playing the Dodgers. He hated the Dodgers—who didn't? He had to be legit sick to miss a game he'd bought primo seats for.

"I invited him to go with me weeks ago." He sneezed then moaned, reinforcing just how much he needed me to take his place in Angel Stadium. "He won't want to go alone."

And so, an hour later, I climbed the stairs above the garage to Parker's apartment and knocked on the door wearing my Albert Pujols jersey and my Angels baseball cap, with my curls tucked into it as best as I could get them. He opened the door, and his head jerked back with surprise.

"Guess who's going to the game with you tonight?" I popped a bubble and pulled the brim of my hat down.

"Hal's not going?" He stepped back and let me in.

"Nope. He's really sick this time."

"He must be if he's missing the Dodgers." Parker grabbed his hat and car keys. "I bought a car. I'll drive," he said and then changed topic. "Does he still curse like a truck driver when he watches?"

"Yep."

"Hmm." With obvious disappointment, he led me down to the garage. "His insults are the best part of the game."

"I'm pretty good company too, you know," I said, offended. "I can scream and swear with the best of them."

"I'm going to hold you to that." He opened the car door for me, and I climbed in.

Once he got in on his side, I continued. "I know I have disappointed you on many occasions, but I promise not to disappoint tonight," I said with my nose in the air.

"You think you disappoint me?" he asked in a much more serious tone than I'd used.

"Um, yeah." I plugged my phone into his USB and pulled up my playlist, purposely choosing a song I knew he'd hate. "You make fun of everything I do. That's not exactly a glowing endorsement of my projects."

"I don't make fun of *everything*." He quickly tapped the volume button to turn down Taylor Swift as she burst out of the speakers. "Your taste in music definitely disappoints me, but not 'everything' you do does."

I let him navigate to the freeway before I turned up the volume again. Not a lot, but enough. He hit the gas to get past a car changing lanes, and I grabbed the emergency handle.

"Why are you going so fast?" I yelled. He knew I hated it when he sped. I hated it when anyone drove too fast. That's how Mom had been killed.

"Sorry. I forgot." He slowed down, and I checked his speedometer. Sixty-five. Just right.

"I haven't made fun of you for whatever you're doing with Hailey," he said.

"It's called being her friend. I hope even you can't criticize me for that."

"Don't get snarky. Seems like she appreciates your help." He skipped to the next song on my playlist and turned the music up a fraction of a decibel. "See? That's me complimenting you on one of your 'projects.'"

"Hailey's not a project, but thank you." I checked the mirror in the visor and straightened my hat. "How do you know she's grateful?" I would have freshened up my lip gloss, but even without the guidance of a mother, I knew not to reapply make-up in front of a date. Not that Parker was a date.

"I took this car into Tony's place to get it checked out before I bought it. Turns out I know the kid who works there."

"Ashton?"

"Yeah, Ashton Martin," he answered. "I coached his water polo team that year before I moved to Hong Kong. Good kid. Great name."

"What's so great about his name?" I asked and shifted in my seat, suddenly feeling uncomfortable.

"Like the car. Aston Martin." He looked at me, making sure I understood. "His dad is really into cars. I think it's clever."

"You think you're clever, so that's not saying much."

"Ha ha." He shook his head. "Sounds like he's really into Hailey. I told him I found his place because of you, and all he could talk about was her. They hung out last weekend. She told him you helped her enroll in the community college she's going to." He looked at me, so pleased with himself I almost felt guilty.

"Eyes on the road." I pointed to the windshield. When it came to being a passenger, I may have inherited some of Daddy's anxiety about dying a horrible death. "I'm glad he had a good time with her, but he probably shouldn't get his hopes up."

"Why not?"

"She's keeping her options open," I blurted and grabbed the emergency handle to warn him about his increasing speed. "Sounds like she's been in some bad relationships, so I don't think she needs to get serious with anyone right now."

He slowed way down. Like below-fifty-five slow. "*You* don't think she needs to? Shouldn't that be a decision she makes?"

"It *is* her decision." I clutched the handle tighter. Not because I was nervous anymore but because I wanted to give him a good smack. I hadn't told her not to see Ashton again. She came to that conclusion on her own.

"Liza, I know you think of yourself as some kind of matchmaker, but be careful with that. You're playing with people's lives here, not flowers."

"Gee, thanks for the mansplaining, Parker. Anything else you want to tell me about the advice I do or don't give to friends?" I let go of the handle and looked out the window. "Hailey is perfectly capable of choosing who she sees and doesn't see. If she doesn't want to see Ashton again, maybe it has more to do with him than her."

"She could do a lot worse than Ashton," he said.

"Wow." I stared at him. "You think pretty highly of a guy you barely know who's covered in tattoos and piercings and works in a garage. I'm sure he's really going places. Hailey should totally tie herself down to him."

"He's a nice kid." His voice echoed in the tight space of his small car. "He's going to own that garage. What does Hailey have going for her that's better than that?"

"Since when does owning a repair shop mean someone has something 'going' for him?"

"You have no idea how much that place makes."

"And you do?"

"It's not hard to guess, with the cars they had lined up out front and the reviews they've got."

"You know what? I don't want to ruin the whole night, so why don't we stop talking about this."

"Fine with me." He changed lanes and slowed down even more.

I stared out the window, trying not to flinch every time a car whizzed by. Part of me wondered if maybe I'd been wrong about encouraging Hailey away from Ashton. It's not that I didn't like him. He did seem nice. But I doubted he would help her expand her horizons, and that's what she really needed. She had plenty of life experience—more than anyone her age deserved—but not a lot of cultural or educational experience. Ashton wouldn't help her gain that.

Ten minutes passed before either Parker or I spoke. Traffic slowed almost to a stop, and we happened to be within sight of a science museum close to the freeway.

"Do you remember taking me there?" I pointed to the gray building with a giant cube jutting out of its top.

The crease between Parker's eyebrows smoothed, and a smile made its way across his face. "Oh yeah. What were you, ten? Eleven?"

"Probably. The summer before you left for Stanford, when I broke my arm and couldn't go to surf camp with my friends." I stared at the building, remembering how Parker had come to my rescue that day. What other eighteen-year-old boy would take a heartbroken little girl to a science museum to cheer her up?"

"You wanted me to take you to Disneyland, didn't you?" Traffic sped up, and we drove past the museum.

"Roller coasters are more fun than science." I pointed to the top of Space Mountain just before we veered off toward Angel Stadium. "Do you still hate it as much as you did then?"

"Maybe."

"*Maybe?* If you don't know for sure, then we need to go. I could get you to like it. In fact . . ." I bounced in my seat. "That will be my next matchmaking project—helping you fall in love with the Happiest Place on Earth." I smiled wide and fluttered my eyelashes at him.

He laughed, and I knew everything was okay between us again. "Good luck. Are you woman enough for that kind of challenge?"

"Um, yeah! I can hardly wait."

"I didn't agree."

"You didn't disagree either." When he didn't say anything, I decided to press my argument even further. "I can either hook you up with Disneyland, or I can start looking for an actual woman to set you up with."

I said the words without thinking, and then they felt wrong coming out of my mouth. I don't know why, but the thought of Parker dating someone bothered me. Not that he hadn't ever dated anyone—he had. But I couldn't picture him with anyone now. Maybe because he was the closest single friend I had. If he tied the knot, I'd be alone.

He flinched and turned his head for half a second before he focused back on the road. "Let's see how you do with Disneyland before I hand over my entire love life to you," he said with more resignation than I expected.

"If I can convert you to Disneyland, that will be enough for me." The air between us had gone stale, and I fought to make it fresh again. "Once Taylor's married she won't be able to go with me whenever I want, so you're my new ride buddy. I doubt I could find a woman willing to put up with you anyway." I nudged his arm, and he almost smiled.

"I doubt it too. We'll be those old single people who still get together for dinner in fifty years." He smiled at me, and I smiled back, but something weird was going on in my stomach. I kind of liked the idea of us being old together, still teasing each other over prunes and toast—or whatever it was old people ate.

"Speak for yourself. I'll only be seventy-four. You'll be the old one." I sat back in my seat, my anxiety about the traffic and his driving gone. "But don't get any ideas about us making a pact to get married in fifty years if we haven't found anyone else by then."

"Ha! Can you even imagine the two of us married?"

Strangely, I could. But I wasn't about to tell him that. I checked my hat and lip gloss again, sneaking a glance at him in the mirror.

Yeah, I could totally imagine me married to Parker. That is, if I had any interest in getting married.

Chapter 9

I LOVED BASEBALL, BUT THERE was no denying it could move really slow. Like, waiting-for-Christmas slow. So when we got to the seventh-inning stretch, I decided to make things interesting.

"What do you want to bet Trout hits a double?" I asked Parker.

The crowd cheered as the kiss cam circled the stadium, landing on a couple a few sections away from us. "Depends on what you want to lose." Parker leaned against me, which sent a tickle of excitement down my spine. "He always strikes out against Kershaw."

"Not this time. I've got a good feeling." I turned my head before he moved his, putting us well within kissing distance. A distance that didn't go unnoticed by the guy running the kiss cam. The fans around us broke out into louder whoops and pointed at our faces on the JumboTron. Their cries of "Kiss! Kiss! Kiss!" had to be answered, but Parker and I only stared at each other for what seemed like a lifetime but couldn't have been more than a couple seconds.

A tap on my back broke my trance. I looked over my shoulder at the Chris Hemsworth look-alike who'd been flirting with me all night.

"If he's not going to do it, can I?" he yelled.

I didn't hesitate. I nodded and turned my cheek to him, but he planted a big kiss on my mouth before I could point to the spot he was allowed to peck.

"Hey!" Parker jumped up, and my Thor wannabe let me go.

"You had your chance, Dude!" He laughed then held out his fist for Parker to bump. "No hard feelings."

Parker looked like he wanted to make his own fist but not for bumping.

"It's fine, Parker." I grabbed his hand and pulled him into his seat.

"Are you okay?" He leaned forward and glared at my kisser, who was too busying high-fiving his friends to notice.

I was still in shock, but as I watched the replay and saw the surprise on Parker's face, I broke into a laugh. I liked to think if the kiss had been anything more than what it was, I would have decked the guy.

But my gut reaction was, if Thor hadn't reeked of beer, I would have shown Parker what he should have done for that camera.

"I'm glad you think it's funny." Parker glared at the giant screen. "I still want to knock him out."

"Forget it," I said, even though I hoped he wouldn't. I kinda liked this jealous version of Parker. "Back to our bet. Trout's up. If he hits a double, you come to yoga class with me."

"And if he strikes out?" Parker tore his eyes away from Thor and focused on the field.

"I won't use any of my matchmaking charm on you."

"Deal."

No sooner had he agreed than a crack sounded and Kershaw's pitch was headed toward left field while Trout ran for first. The ball dropped, Trout hit first, and the coach waved him to second. I jumped out of my seat, cheering him all the way to base and my winning bet.

I clapped in Parker's face. "Did you see that? I won!" I yelled, hopping up and down. The rest of the crowd moved on to watching the next batter, but I still cheered for Trout. I'd be adding one of his jerseys to my wardrobe for sure.

When I finally sat down, I folded my hands in my lap and very calmly leaned over to Parker and said, "Roshan's yoga class is at six tomorrow night."

"Ro-*what*?"

"Ro*shhhan.*"

"No," he growled. "I am *not* doing yoga, especially with someone named Roshan. That's the stupidest name I've ever heard. It sounds made-up."

"You are doing yoga, and Roshan isn't made-up; it means 'guiding light' in Hindi—or Buddha"—was that even a language?—"and it's only marginally stupid. Besides, you already know him. His real name is Elton Thomas. He was a friend of Preston and Caroline's."

I reached across his legs and removed his drink from the cup holder. I pulled my gum out of my mouth and held it between my fingers while I took a long sip of his Coke. I knew what he was going to say. I could predict that better than I had predicted the last play.

"Elton Thomas?" He took his drink back. "That guy? Of course he changed his name to something stupider than the one he already had. I couldn't stand him ten years ago. There's no way I'm going to his yoga class."

"Then you shouldn't have made the wager." I popped the gum back into my mouth. "You lost the bet, and now you need to man up." I blew a giant bubble in his face, let it pop, and then sucked it back in.

He glowered at me—yes, glowered—then readjusted his hat and sat back with his arms crossed. I loved it when I won.

I was still gloating the next night when Parker met Hailey and me at Elton's studio. He didn't look any more excited about yoga with Roshan than he had when he'd lost the bet, which made my win even more satisfying.

"This is my friend, Hailey, I told you about," I said to Elton as he bowed to us. "Hailey, this is Elton."

"Please, call me Roshan," he gushed as he grasped her hand. "It's so good to meet you."

I could see the sparks between them already as he looked into her eyes, probably reading her chakras.

"And do you remember Parker Knightley?" I hated to distract him from Hailey, but I sensed Parker was about to bolt.

"Oh yeah. Preston's brother. Good to see you again." He pressed his palms together in prayer pose and bowed.

"Nice to see you . . . Roshan, is it?"

"Yeah, it means 'guiding light.'" He gazed thoughtfully past Parker's shoulder. "I chose it after I went through all my enlightenment training. Really, it chose me."

"I'm sure it couldn't have chosen better." Parker pursed his lips, and I knew he was holding back a smile. I elbowed him in the stomach when Roshan turned his back to us.

Be nice, I mouthed, to which he replied with a bow.

We followed Roshan into the packed room and put our mats down. Hailey watched me closely, following my every move, although not before tripping over her mat after she laid it down.

"Are you sure I'll be okay at this?" she whispered loudly, garnering some glares from the people lying flat on their backs.

"You'll be fine. It's all about being in the moment and respecting where you are now. Don't worry about getting everything right; just do your best," I whispered back.

Hailey nodded. Parker scoffed. I pulled a face at him before lying down on my mat and waiting for class to start.

"Is this what we do for an hour?" Parker asked, getting shushed by the woman next to him.

"No, this is *shavasana*, or corpse pose. No more talking." I closed my eyes and tried to channel some zen, but Parker kept moving around.

"Will you please play dead?" I said through clenched teeth after he knocked over his water bottle with a loud clang.

A bell chimed, and Roshan invited everyone to roll over into child's pose.

"Into what?" Parker looked around the room then kneeled with his butt on his heels and his arms stretched forward. On the other side of me, Hailey did the same thing. But instead of keeping her forehead on the mat, she kept looking over at me.

"Om-powerment, or life in balance, happens when your yoga practice and your life goals are in sync. You achieve synergy." Roshan talked quietly while stepping over and around his students.

Our "guiding light" took us through all the poses, encouraging us to "gain clarity" and "be in the present" as we twisted ourselves into human pretzels. It all made sense to me, but every look Parker gave me said Roshan was *exactly* what he had expected, if not worse.

Hailey, on the other hand, concentrated so hard on getting the moves right she was always two steps behind. I doubted she heard anything Elton said, and she was the one who needed it most.

When class ended, Parker popped up from shavasana before anyone else, but I stayed lying on the floor. I wanted to miss the crowd so Hailey could talk to Elton. I ignored Parker's impatient sighs and kept my eyes shut until I didn't hear any more footsteps. Once I was sure everyone else was gone, I got up and gathered my mat.

My plan worked, and Elton stopped us on our way out. "How'd you like it, . . . ?"

"Hailey," I finished for him and nudged her forward.

"Um, I liked it. I couldn't keep up though." She smiled nervously at me and then at Elton.

"You'll get better every time you come." He rubbed her arm, and her eyelids fluttered with excitement. "I have a book you can read that will help you not only in your next class but also in life." He stepped around her to take a book off the shelf.

"Oh, wow. This is what you were talking about in class," she said, reading the title *Om-powerment: Life in Balance* emblazoned across the front right above his name. "You wrote this? Thank you."

"I did." He stuck his chest out and nodded. "You can pay for it next time you come to class. You're going to get a package, right?" He grabbed a brochure from the same shelf. "You can get a series of ten classes that includes one free aura reading, but I always recommend the thirty-class package that includes a weekly reading."

Hailey's smile quickly disappeared as she took the pamphlet and saw the prices. She stared at it as though searching for the words she wanted to say. Finally she found them. "There's no way I can afford that." She shoved the pamphlet back at Elton, who flinched with surprise.

"This is a really good deal. I usually charge fifty dollars just for the reading," he said and put the pamphlet back into its plastic holder.

"Hailey just started working, so she's on a budget," I explained to him then said to Hailey, "What if I got you the ten classes as a kind of bonus?"

"That's too much. I haven't been working for you that long." She looked at the floor and tucked her hair behind her ears. "You should be giving yourself the bonus for hiring me."

"That's silly. You're doing a great job, and you deserve a bonus." I ignored Parker's *Really?* look. I had let slip at the Angels game that Hailey still needed more training. "Plus, who will I go to yoga with if you don't come with me?"

"Not me," Parker mumbled.

"All right, let's get you rung up," Elton said before Hailey had agreed. He led us to the counter then pointed at the little bottles on the shelf behind him. "Can I get you some oils too?"

"No, but thanks," I answered.

Parker let out a snort that was somewhere between a laugh and a cough, and I narrowed my eyes in a question. "What?" I mouthed.

He turned his back on Elton and leaned down to whisper, "He's literally trying to sell you snake oil."

I ignored Parker and handed Elton my credit card. He swiped it while telling Hailey about his "innovative approach to inspiring students to their highest potential." She nodded and smiled but couldn't say a word.

"I'd love to tell you more about it sometime," Elton said, gazing intently at her.

I nudged Hailey to answer, but when she stayed frozen, I answered for her. "That sounds great. When?"

"Stop by tomorrow around ten," he answered and led us to the door while Hailey and I exchanged grins behind his back.

"For sure," Hailey managed to squeak as we passed by him on our way out.

"I'm looking forward to it." He opened his arms for a hug, but she didn't notice. I got it instead.

"Thanks for coming tonight and for bringing your friend," he whispered in my ear.

"Of course," I answered and wriggled out of his embrace. "I told her all about you. I'm sure she loved the class."

"Nice to see you too, Parker," Elton said. He barely got a curt nod in return.

I waited to say anything to Parker until we were in the parking lot. "You liked it, didn't you?"

"I'm not even going to dignify that question with an answer," he answered and then waved goodbye and jogged to his car.

Hailey and I got into my car, and by the time I'd shut my door, we were both on the verge of bursting.

"Did he just ask me out?" she squealed.

"You liked him, right?" I asked and backed out of the parking space. "I told you he would like you."

"Yeah." She sighed. "I mean, he's so different from any guy I've ever met. I don't know. I think I like him. He's definitely cute. I love ponytails on guys. And his body." She sighed again and fanned herself. "I could look at that all day."

"Right?" I interjected. "But did you like all the things he had to say? Wasn't it motivating?"

"Oh, yeah, totally . . . I mean, I didn't catch all of it, 'cause I was just trying to keep up. I kept getting lost. I felt like such a loser." She snort-laughed—not her most endearing quirk—then turned in her seat to face me. "Do you really think he likes me?"

"He invited you to come by tomorrow, didn't he? Of course he likes you!"

By the time I dropped Hailey off, her self-confidence had more than doubled. Elton was legit boyfriend material. Not for me, obviously. But for someone like Hailey who'd never had anyone to encourage her, he was perfect.

They were perfect.

And my matchmaking skills?

On point.

Chapter 10

A FEW NIGHTS LATER, I pulled into my garage and smelled Pedro's Tacos before I even opened the door into the house. It was the perfect food greeting.

Daddy wouldn't have left the house to pick up tacos, so I guessed Parker had. I followed the smell of carnitas to the kitchen to find my guess was spot-on. Parker stood at the kitchen counter, unloading food from a plastic bag.

"Are you eating Pedro's, Daddy?" I asked before kissing the top of his head.

"Goodness no," he scoffed. "My stomach couldn't handle it even if I felt well enough for it. Parker brought me a chicken soup from Gelson's."

"I brought you carnitas." Parker handed me a Styrofoam container. "Pinto beans, right? And I told them extra limes."

"I can't believe you remember my order."

"I figured your favorite hadn't changed."

"You were right. I'm impressed."

"Don't be. You're fairly predictable."

We sat down at the table, and I opened my box, letting out the smell of pork, chile spices, and lime. I breathed it in, expecting to enjoy it as much as I usually did. Instead it smelled too . . . familiar, I guess.

"I am not predictable. Daddy, tell him I'm not predictable." I scooped the meat into a tortilla and went to make a second taco then stopped. I would eat the first taco and then make a second one. I didn't have to eat them the same way I always did.

"There's nothing wrong with knowing what you want and sticking to that thing." Daddy blew on his soup, completely oblivious to the I-told-you-so Parker shot me.

"Is there anything else you'd like to tell me about myself?" I skipped squeezing lime onto my taco before each bite. That would have been predictable, even if my food would have tasted better.

"Your plan to hook up *Roshan* and Hailey isn't going to work." He took a bite of his own taco and seemed to enjoy it a lot more than I enjoyed mine.

"What are you talking about?" I squirmed in my seat.

"Who or what is *Roshan*?" Daddy asked, looking between Parker and me.

"He's an old friend of Preston's," Parker answered. "Elton Thomas. He goes by Roshan now so he can change the world one yoga pose at a time."

"I don't see the connection," Daddy said. "Why does he have to change his name to teach yoga?"

"He doesn't." Parker took another bite of taco and then licked the grease off his fingers. "He was pretentious then, and he's even more pretentious now. Too pretentious to look at someone like Hailey as anything more than a potential customer."

"What's he trying to sell her?" Daddy looked to me for an answer, but Parker gave it.

"Oils and empty promises."

"He's a con man?" Daddy asked in alarm.

"No!" I yelped at the same time Parker calmly said, "Yes."

"He's a life coach, Daddy," I said before sending Parker a withering look. "He's developed a program to help people reach their goals through yoga and meditation."

"People need a coach for life?" Daddy asked Parker. He would always take Parker's side against me. "I don't understand. I've never meditated a day in my life or done yoga, and somehow I've survived. Life isn't baseball. You don't need a coach to learn how to live."

"Exactly," Parker said.

"She doesn't *need* Elton," I protested. "What she does need is more direction in her life. You never did, Daddy, because you had parents and a support system. Hailey has never had that."

I picked up a fork and stabbed at my food before pushing it away. What was so wrong with helping Hailey? Maybe not everyone needed someone like Elton, but he'd done a lot of good for the people who did. Who cared if he made money off it?

Daddy patted my hand. "You're a good friend to her. If you think this is what she needs, I trust your judgement." His brown baggy eyes filled with a mix of love and pride as he defended me to Parker. "She's always wanted to rescue everyone and everything she could."

Parker nodded. "I know. It's her greatest strength."

I sat up straighter. "That's probably the nicest thing you've ever said about me."

Parker pointed to my container. "Are you done?"

I nodded. "I'll save the rest for later."

He closed the lid and carried it to the fridge. "Just remember," he said as he closed his own half-full container. "Sometimes what we want to do for people isn't actually what they need."

I didn't know what that meant. All I wanted to do was help Hailey, which is exactly what she needed. She was a single mother with a messed-up family, who'd never had the chance to go to college. I could fix all those things—I'd already fixed the college part.

"Wanna take a walk?" Parker asked me after he'd shut the fridge.

"Sure," I answered, surprised by his sudden invitation. "Will you be okay, Daddy?" I asked as I went to the closet for a sweatshirt.

"You two go have fun," Daddy answered and settled into his favorite chair. "I've got a book to read."

Parker and I walked the short distance from my house to the beach in comfortable silence. When we reached the sand, we both slipped off our shoes and strolled along the water. I stopped under the full moon and let the ocean bury my feet with wet sand as its watery fingers grasped the shore.

Parker kept walking but turned around when he realized I wasn't behind him. "What are you doing?" he asked when he came back.

"Embracing a moment before it's gone," I answered and pointed to our feet. "Watch your footprint. The ocean may change it a little or completely wash it away."

"Yeah?" He stared at his feet, uninterested in what had me spellbound.

"It reminds me of how quickly moments pass in our lives," I explained. Because, obviously, he wasn't going to get it if I didn't. "Some go little by little—like a baby growing up. Others come and go almost before we notice them. Sometimes you have to stop and look around so you can enjoy all those little moments before they slip away." I wiggled my toes then stepped aside to watch the prints I'd left behind disappear.

"Wow. That's kind of profound." He watched his own set of prints wash away and then walked on.

Of course, I followed, but I walked backward until the sea claimed the steps I left behind for it.

"I wanted to talk to you about something without your dad around," Parker said abruptly when I had caught up to him.

"What about?" A thousand thoughts about what he was going to say flitted through my head, all of them more romantic than what actually came out of his mouth.

"Your books," he said and slowed his pace.

"What books?" I wasn't a big reader.

He stopped and looked over his glasses at me like a stern librarian, reminding me why I didn't like books. "Your financial records."

"Oh," I stammered. He was going for stern accountant, not librarian. Even worse.

"You're not making money, Liza." He took his glasses off and cleaned off the condensation with the bottom of his shirt. "In fact, you're losing money, but I can't figure out some of your expenses."

I shrugged. "I know what they are, so don't worry about it."

He replaced his glasses and rubbed the back of his neck. "Your dad's worried about it."

"I'm not running that shop to make money." I started walking again. "I like what I'm doing, so who cares if I don't get rich doing it?"

"The IRS will care if you get audited."

"Fine, I'll keep better records."

"Do you have any idea where the money is going?"

"Of course I know where the money is going. I'm the one who's writing the checks." I stepped on a rock and yelped.

"Are you okay?" Parker grabbed my arm to help me regain my footing.

"I'm fine!" I shook his arm off and rubbed my foot on top of my other one. It helped relieve the pain in my sole, but it didn't take away the sting of his words. "I'm not dumb, Parker."

"I didn't say you were dumb." Parker stepped back and then followed me as I turned to go back the way we'd come. "I'm concerned. Businesses have to make money to stay open."

"Do you know how much money is in my trust fund?" I wanted to be home and done with this conversation, but my foot hurt, and I could only hobble so fast. "I can put money into that flower shop for the rest of my life if I want to and never turn a profit."

"But you won't be able to live like you do now. Not after your dad is gone." He breathed out the words, like he knew they would take my breath away too.

"I don't care." I stopped and glared at him. "It doesn't matter where the money is going; it's not any of your business. I didn't ask to be born rich, and the millions of people born poor didn't ask for that either. All you need to know about any profits I make is that I'm going to use them the way I want to use them, and it's not going to be to add to my bank account."

He stared at me, and I knew he was poring over every word, searching for his rebuttal. "Okay. Got it," he answered slowly. "Your dad asked me to take a look. I'm only telling you what I found."

We started walking again, but there was nothing comfortable about the silence between us. By the time we got to the stairs leading to the path home, Parker had found the chink in my defense.

"Are you supporting Hailey?" he asked. "I mean, beyond paying her salary?"

I didn't answer. I could have said no and it wouldn't have been a complete lie. Paying her college tuition wasn't necessarily supporting her, in the strictest sense of the word. But I did sometimes buy her groceries and other stuff she needed. She could get the basics with the welfare money she got, but she couldn't buy stuff like apples, which she loved. And she deserved to have some apples in her life.

"I admire your instinct to help . . ." he went on. "But I think it will do more harm than good." His jaw moved back and forth as he worked out what to say next. "She's got to be able to take care of herself and Xander, and she won't learn how to do that if you're giving her everything she needs. Trust me. Helping people become more self-sufficient is what I do."

"I'm not 'giving her everything she needs.'" It wasn't a lie. I was helping her go to school—and yoga, I guess. But I wasn't supporting her like Parker thought I was.

I turned to walk away from him, but he grabbed my hand and pulled me back.

"What about when the next Hailey comes along? Your trust fund won't last forever if you keep giving money away like you are." He held both my hands and looked me in the eye. "I know you don't like to hear this, but your dad isn't going to be around forever. He wants to make sure you'll be okay after he's gone."

"I understand that." I stepped back, and he let go. "I'm not a kid anymore, and you need to quit treating me like one. I know you're trying to help, but don't talk to me like I'm dumb—"

"Then quit doing dumb things," he snapped then took a deep breath. "It's all well and good to enjoy the moment, but you have to plan ahead," he said with a forced calm. "Quit playing with people's lives like you're putting on a puppet show, and figure out your own future . . ." He trailed off.

I forced my mouth to ignore my quivering chin and move. "I can walk the rest of the way myself."

"Liza Belle, come on. I live at the same place," he pled. "Am I supposed to stand here until you get home so we're not walking together?"

"I don't know. Maybe you should have planned that out before you called me dumb," I said over my shoulder then crossed the street in front of a car.

"And don't call me Liza Belle anymore!" I yelled over the car's horn.

Chapter 11

Six weeks passed, and Parker and I barely spoke. Part of it was we were both busy with work. But the other part was we'd let too much time pass after our fight on the beach. We didn't know how to make up.

He came over sometimes, usually when I wasn't home. If he was there when I got home, he left with hardly a goodbye, let alone an actual conversation. I missed him. I could have apologized, but I didn't feel like I'd done anything wrong. I hadn't told *him* how he needed to change *his* life.

Still, I didn't like being mad or dealing with tension. Relationships were more important than being right, and he'd only been trying to help me. And, to be honest, I did need to keep my financials in better order. So, one day at work, I broke down and texted him.

Caroline called. They're coming for Thanksgiving. Dibs on hosting. You can come though. It was sort of a joke. There's no way he'd have room in the apartment to host Thanksgiving.

When I didn't hear back after an hour, I texted again.

Or not. No pressure. You can have Thanksgiving by yourself. I get my sister and Preston.

Another hour passed, and still no response. That's when I got worried. Maybe I'd actually hurt his feelings. I thought back through our entire fight, analyzing every word while I clipped thorns off roses. I couldn't pinpoint exactly what I'd said, but I could pinpoint exactly what I was feeling as I waited for Parker to respond: sadness and loss. What if he didn't want to be friends anymore? What if I had teased and fought with him so much he couldn't stand to be around me? He'd only been back four months, and already I'd driven him away.

My head was in a tailspin when Hailey walked into the shop, rescuing me from my darkest thoughts about Parker. Elton followed behind her, wearing his daily uniform, an Om-powerment tank top and baggy yoga pants.

"Hi!" Hailey had Xander in one arm and a load of books in the other. She'd been in class, so I was surprised to see her with Elton.

"Hi!" I ran to take Xander from her. "Don't you have a backpack?" I shot an accusing look from her books to Elton. He didn't take the hint.

"No, I haven't bought one yet. I thought I could carry everything inside. Good thing Elton opened the door for me." She set her books on my worktable and then took Xander back and nuzzled him.

"You two didn't come together?" I asked, looking between them.

His head jerked from Hailey to me, like I'd asked a ridiculous question. "No. I came by to see you. Hailey walked in at the same time."

"Oh." *Weird.* They were seeing a lot of each other. She went to his classes a couple times a week, and he stopped into the shop every once in a while.

"I'm so glad you're here though," Hailey said to Elton then sat down on a stool, plopped Xander onto her lap, and opened one of the textbooks. "Do you know anything about algebra? I'm so lost, and I can't work up the energy to care about *x*'s and *y*'s."

"Hmm." He peeked over her shoulder. "I don't remember any of that stuff."

I glanced at him to see if he was serious. He'd been an engineer before he went all yogi/life coach.

He walked away from Hailey and closer to me. "Need some help?" he asked fingering the white petals of the roses I was arranging. They'd have brown spots by the end of the day.

"Thanks. I've got this." I moved the bucket of roses out of his reach before he ruined all of them. "Why don't you take Xander from Hailey." He wasn't touching any more of my flowers, but he could probably handle Xander.

He looked at the baby grabbing at Hailey's math pages and back at me. I raised an eyebrow.

"You can put him in his playpen if he gets too squirmy," Hailey said and held Xander out for Elton. He took him and carried him at arm's length straight to the portable play enclosure.

"This thing?" he asked while dangling Xander above it.

Hailey's brows wrinkled, and she nodded before turning back to her algebra.

"I'm so dumb. I don't understand any of this." She blew hair out of her eyes and pushed the book away.

I went around the table and examined the page. They were basic problems, and some of what I'd learned in high school came back to me. I pulled a piece of paper from her notebook and took her pencil.

"Look, start by redistributing . . ." I showed her what I meant and then the next step in the process. I was about to go on when I felt hot breath on my shoulder. I turned my head slowly to see Elton standing right behind me.

"That's right. Good job, Liza," he said and patted me on the back, leaving his hand between my shoulder blades for too long.

"You've got some knots back here, girl." Without warning, he was kneading my shoulders like a German baker with a bread vendetta.

Hailey's eyes widened, and she stared at me as I tried to get away from Elton. Every time I moved he discovered a new knot, his grip got tighter, and the massage got more intense. It lasted maybe thirty seconds, but it felt like thirty minutes before I was literally saved by the bell. Or the ding anyway.

"I think that's me," I said and lunged across the table for my phone. I avoided Hailey's eyes as I escaped Elton's clutches but heard him say something about looking at the next problem with her.

My heart did a funny skip when I saw I had a message from Parker. I walked to the back wall where only Xander could see me read it.

In Hong Kong. It's two A.M. I was asleep. You can feed me turkey to make it up to me. Caroline and Preston are yours.

I smiled and banished all the negative thoughts that had tortured me all morning. He wasn't mad, only asleep. But then the thoughts returned. Why hadn't he told me he was going to Hong Kong? Was he making plans to move back there? Would he tell me if he were?

Only he could answer those questions, so I texted them all.

Why are you in HK, and why didn't you tell me you were going? My thumbs flew across the keyboard, and I expected an answer just as quickly. I hit Send and stared at my phone, hoping the bouncing dots at the bottom of the screen weren't teasing me. I let out my breath when his message finally appeared.

Still two A.M., still sleeping. Be back in a few days. Talk then.

I smiled and tucked my phone into my apron pocket. Then I took it back out because I couldn't resist. He'd ignored me for too long.

Are you sleep texting? I typed.

I'm putting my phone on silent now, he wrote back.

You're literally going to silence me? Good luck.

Shhh, sleeping . . .

I knew you couldn't do it. Good night.

I dropped my phone back into my pocket and returned to Hailey and Elton.

"Worry less about the numbers on this page," Elton said. "And focus more on visualizing the number of correct answers you want to get. Visualize your grade not as a letter but as a percentage." He put his fingers to his temples and closed his eyes. "Put your energy into seeing those numbers, and you'll be fine."

Hailey tilted her head to the side with a blank look on her face.

"Do you see the number you want?" he asked with his eyes still closed.

Understanding dawned. She mouthed *oh* and quickly scrunched her eyes and her mouth shut.

My phone dinged, breaking their concentration. They both opened their eyes, looked at me then back at each other.

"Did you have an image fixed in your mind?" Elton asked her.

"I kind of got distracted by Eliza's phone." Hailey giggled. "Should I try again?"

"Maybe you should focus on the actual material first and then do the visualization," I suggested. I mean, I'm not a numbers girl, but that seemed pretty obvious.

Hailey and Elton gave each other knowing smiles, commiserating over my un-enlightenment, or un-powerment—I think that's what Elton called it when people weren't om-powered.

"You really should come to my seminars." Elton patted my shoulder with a condescension that felt ickier than the massage he'd given me. "Look how much it's done for Hailey."

"Uh huh. I'll think about it." I took out my phone out and saw the text was from Parker.

I'm awake now.

I laughed out loud. We were even.

Elton cleared his throat. "Like I was saying, you wouldn't believe the growth Hailey's achieved. She's so much more aware now than when she first came to me."

I smiled and nodded. The biggest difference I'd seen is she spent a lot of time talking about Roshan. Maybe she had learned a lot. Most of the time I pretended to listen while she rehashed her entire sessions with him. I'd been into Om-powerment, but I could only take so much of it anymore.

"I've got to get back to the studio," he said and walked toward the door.

"I'll see you tomorrow," Hailey called after him, barely waiting for the door to close behind him before the gushing began. "Can you believe all the stuff he was saying about me?"

I nodded but couldn't muster up the same level of excitement Hailey had. Parker's opinion about Elton being pretentious and only interested in making money had been rolling around my brain for weeks. His words had finally landed front and center as I'd watched Elton with Xander. I couldn't deny it. I had overestimated him. If Elton didn't love Xander on sight, he wasn't the right guy for Hailey.

"I've been wondering if he's really interested in me," she went on. "But maybe he is. We talk all the time in class, and he sends me texts to check in on me, but I don't know . . ." Her eyes drifted to Xander, who'd fallen asleep in his playpen. "He took care of Xander. That's gotta be a good sign, right?"

"He picked him up, but I wouldn't say he took care of him." I took a rose from the bucket and picked up my clippers. I couldn't look Hailey in the eye. I didn't want to disappoint her or crush the dreams I'd built up, but I couldn't lie either.

"It's a start, right? Not everyone is good with babies. I mean, Ashton was great with him . . ." She trailed off, and I felt even worse.

"Have you seen him lately?" I asked. I still thought she could do better, but Parker had seen through Elton, so maybe his opinion of Ashton was spot on too.

"Not really. He asked me out a few times, but I turned him down, so he quit texting." She shrugged like she didn't care but then looked up at me with expectant eyes. "I bumped into him the other day, though, and he said to text him sometime."

As much as I hated to admit it, the possibility existed that Parker was right about me trying to run Hailey's life. Why else would she be looking at me like she wanted me to tell her what to do?

"Ashton's a nice guy. If you're interested in him, go for it," I answered and vowed I'd only give advice, not instructions. "My only suggestion is to keep your options open."

I left out the part where I should have told her to give up Elton as one of those options.

Chapter 12

ELTON WALKED INTO THE SHOP again a few days later when Hailey was at school. He waved then walked behind the counter and planted himself across the worktable from me. He eyed the flowers I had laying on the table, and I wondered how I could subtly move them out of his reach before he touched the petals.

"How's it going?" I asked to distract him from my peonies.

"That's what I came to talk to you about." He rushed to my side of the table, taking me by surprise as he stopped inches from the stool I sat on. "I haven't been sure how to say this, but I've got something to tell you."

"O-kay." I set my clippers down and turned to face him, faking a calm I didn't feel. I did *not* have a good feeling about what he wanted to tell me. Not with the half-starved look in his eyes.

"I've wanted to say this for so long, but you're never alone." He set his hand on top of the one I had resting on the edge of the table. "When Hailey said she wouldn't be here this afternoon, I knew I had to come over."

I slipped my hand away and stood. "What do you mean? I thought you liked Hailey."

A crease formed between his eyebrows. "Of course I like her. She's a nice kid, but I don't feel about her the way I feel about you." He reached for my hand again, and I stuck it behind my back.

"Elton—"

"Roshan."

"Whatever." I rolled my eyes. "I think you've got the wrong idea. It's Hailey who has feelings for you, not me."

"I know she does. I'm not interested in her." He took a tentative step forward, and I took a very deliberate step back, putting the stool I'd been sitting on between us.

"You know she does?" I took another step back. "Then why do you keep coming in to see her here?" The fact he didn't feel the same way about Hailey that she felt about him wasn't a complete shock, but his feelings toward me were. The whole situation was even worse than I could have imagined. I'd never be able to explain it to her.

"I come here to see you, not her." He laughed and touched the tip of my nose. "Why would I possibly want to get involved with a nineteen-year-old kid who already has a kid herself? I'm not looking to be some baby's daddy." He stepped around the stool, and I put my hand on his chest to stop him.

"Look, Elt—Roshan, I'm flattered, but I don't feel the same." With each word, I exerted more pressure on his chest to keep him away.

"Liza, I've charted our auras and mapped our energies." He reminded me of my fourth-grade teacher who had thought by speaking very, very slowly I would understand long division. "We're a perfect pair. Our auras complement each other."

I dropped my hand and stood straighter. "I don't even know what you're talking about, and I don't care. The two of us as a thing? That's not happening."

He stopped his advance and stared at me. "But our signs—"

"No."

Long seconds passed before he spoke again.

"You don't know what you're missing," he said finally before storming out. As soon as the door swung shut behind him, I flipped the lock shut and turned over the Closed sign. I didn't care how many customers I lost; I had to think through what had happened. More importantly, I had to figure out how to tell Hailey.

For that, I needed Taylor.

Help! I texted, followed by *911* and a string of ambulance emojis. Within thirty seconds my phone was ringing.

"Are you hurt?" she asked before I finished saying hello.

"No. I've been really stupid, and I'm afraid Hailey is going to be hurt."

"Whew." She breathed a sigh of relief. "Tell me what happened, but for future reference, 911 should be reserved for medical emergencies."

"Fine." I told her the whole story about Elton hitting on me and waited for her advice.

"Oh, that sucks," she said. Which already seemed pretty obvious. "Can I think this over and call you later? Weston just got here."

"Sure," I answered slowly. Weston always seemed to be showing up right when I needed Taylor most. I tried not to be jealous that he got a lot more time with her than I did, but it was hard. I never realized how much I relied on her until I didn't have her anymore.

I hung up even more miserable than I'd been when I called Taylor. The thing with not having a mom is I had to find other women to turn to for advice. Taylor's mom had been that person when I was young, but then she remarried and moved. Taylor and Caroline had taken her spot, but now they were both ditching me for married life too.

I had no one to turn to, and I worried Hailey would hate me once I told her about Elton. The only option I had was to curl up on the sofa next to Xander's playpen and throw myself a pity party.

I tucked my legs under me and was about to bury my head in a cushion when my phone dinged. I held it up to see a text from Parker.

World Series on tonight, but meatloaf is on the menu.

You're back! I texted. Watching game one with Daddy and Parker would cheer me up, but meatloaf was not going to make the day better.

I'll pick up some burgers for us, I added and hit Send, already feeling a little better.

If Parker wasn't mad at me anymore—and it didn't sound like he was—I had someone I could talk to about my Hailey problem. If there's one thing Parker didn't mind, it was dishing out advice. Sometimes, it was even good advice.

I swung by A's Burgers on my way home, hoping the smell of fries would cover the smell of humiliation seeping from my pores. By the time I walked into my kitchen, though, I still reeked of overexuberant stupidity, an odor on the spectrum of embarrassing smells somewhere between a fourteen-year-old boy doused in body spray and a substitute teacher's nervous toots.

Parker got a whiff of it almost immediately. "What's wrong?"

"Nothing." I looked past him to the TV, where the game was already on. "Who's ahead?" I needed food and baseball before I'd be ready to talk about Elton.

"Indians."

I kissed Daddy's cheek and then sank down next to Parker on the sofa.

"You sure everything's okay?" he asked. "You're not your usual cheerful self."

That's all it took for me to spill. "Elton asked me out today."

"Elton? Is that the yoga guy?" Daddy asked without taking his eyes from the game.

"Did you tell Hailey?" Parker asked.

I shook my head. "You were right about him. He thinks he's too good for her. I can't believe I didn't see what a tool he is."

"If it makes you feel any better, I wish I hadn't been right." He pulled me into a side hug and squeezed my shoulder.

"Me too." I rested my head on his chest. "I don't know how I'm going to tell Hailey. She's going to hate me."

"Why would anyone hate you?" Daddy asked, still more interested in the game than the conversation, but at least he tried. "There's no one more lovable than you."

"Thanks, Daddy," I said. "Except your opinion may be a little biased."

He tore his eyes away from the game long enough to give me a stern look. "It's not an opinion. It's a fact."

"Listen to your dad," Parker said and waved his head in Daddy's direction. "Tell Hailey the truth. You're a good friend to her, and it's impossible to hate you. She'll get over him."

"I hope so."

I sat up and ate my burgers and fries. After I'd finished, he motioned me back into his arm where I nestled my head on his shoulder and stayed there. Everything looked better from that angle. Even the World Series without my Angels.

After the game ended, I walked Parker to the door and said goodbye.

"Hey." He paused in the doorway. "Maybe this will cheer you up. I'm starting a legal defense fund for garment workers, so I'm throwing a charity party kind of thing around Christmas to fundraise for it. Can I hire you to do it for me?"

"Really?" I loved my flowers, but I missed the excitement of planning events. "I'd love to!" I shouted and threw my arms around him.

"See? I knew that would make you feel better." He stepped back with a conqueror's smile and his hands still on my waist.

"Is that the only reason you asked me? To cheer me up?" I stepped out of his embrace and back into all the humiliation I'd been feeling before. I didn't need his pity; I needed his confidence.

"Of course not. I'm hiring you because, first of all, I don't want to do it . . ." He moved closer and stared down his nose at me with an intensity I hadn't seen before. "Second, I trust you to do it." He brought his hand close to my face, and my breath caught as I waited for him to touch me. His fingertips brushed my cheek, and time stopped.

Then he tugged the curls hanging in my eyes and asked, "Are you ever going to tame these things?"

The earth started turning again in the same way it always had.

"You'd still find a way to pull them even if I did." I pushed him out the door and went back upstairs.

"You and Parker were pretty cozy," Daddy said when I walked into the room.

"What's that supposed to mean?" I asked and helped him up from his chair. "We're just friends."

"Hmm." A gentle smile spread across his face. "Your mom and I started as friends too." He kissed me on the cheek and walked down the hall to his bedroom, leaving me to think about what he'd implied.

That was the closest Daddy had ever come to encouraging me to date someone. He'd never had much to say about boys I'd dated, other than that he wouldn't give me up to anyone who couldn't take care of me as well as he did (I was fine with him thinking he was the one doing the taking-care-of). Daddy had missed my mom every day since she'd died. It would kill him if I ever left.

But he had me thinking. I always thought Daddy meant he'd only give me up to someone who had as much money as he did, but Parker barely had any money at all. Maybe Daddy meant someone who loved me as much as he did. If any man came close to how much Daddy loved me, I guess it might be Parker, if I was looking for a brotherly kind of love.

Of course, I'd be devastated if Parker really fell in love with someone. I'd already lost most of my support system to marriage. I didn't want to lose him too. That was the problem with people falling in love: they gave up everything for one person. Daddy had pretty much given up his whole life after Mom died. I didn't ever want to love like that.

Chapter 13

It took me days to tell Hailey that Elton had made a pass at me. I used Parker's party as an excuse to put off the long conversation I knew it would start. I only had six weeks to put it all together, and I needed to get invites out quickly. Plus, I still had Taylor's wedding to help plan.

When Hailey came into work with her eyes glistening with tears, however, time was up. My first thought was that she'd found out on her own and that's what her tears were about. When she handed me Xander and collapsed onto the couch, I figured it had to be something else or she wouldn't have let me within ten feet of Xander.

"What's wrong?" I asked and rushed to her side, sitting next to her and planting Xander on my lap.

"Roshan's leaving," she said, lifting her face from the same cushion I'd used to smother my Roshan problems in.

"What do you mean he's leaving? Forever?" I wanted to be disappointed for her, but mostly I was relieved. Maybe I wouldn't have to tell her about Elton.

"No, only a couple of months, but that feels like forever!"

Xander leaned over and patted Hailey's legs. Maybe he sensed she was upset, or maybe he was just doing what babies do, but either way it soothed her enough to sit up and dry her eyes.

"Two months isn't long." I wished Xander would soothe me. I'd still have to tell Hailey about Elton, only now it would add to the blow of his leaving. "Where's he going?"

"To this amazing yoga retreat geared toward visualizing and actualizing your dreams." She rubbed her nose then wiped her hand on her pants. "And then he's going on a speaking tour to all these different places where he'll meet amazing people. I don't know what I'm going to do without him!" Xander took the place of the couch cushion, and she laid her cheek on his head. He squirmed, but she only tightened her hold.

I rubbed my hand in circles on her back trying to find words to comfort her, but all I could come up with was a question. "What exactly is 'actualizing'?"

"You know, when you *actually* make something happen. You make it actual." Hailey paused long enough to set Xander on the rug at our feet.

"It's like my plan to have my own nail shop and do the coolest designs anywhere," she went on. "When school is hard and all I want to do is paint nails, I visualize what my shop will look like so when I'm done with school I can actualize it."

No matter how hard she tried to explain the concept, I didn't get it. Actualizing still sounded kind of . . . made up. More and more, that's how all of Elton's stuff sounded.

"Are you sad he's leaving because he's a sort of mentor to you?" I asked slowly. "Or are you sad he's leaving because you have deeper feelings for him—like romantic ones?" I sent up a desperate prayer that my matchmaking magic hadn't worked on her.

"Well, obviously, I like him as more than a guru kind of guy," she answered too quickly for my prayer to be heard. But who am I kidding? Like that prayer would have worked anyway. I was good at what I did.

"You're the one who told me we'd be perfect together," she added, driving a theoretical knife deeper into whatever organ in the body is responsible for humiliation. "Things aren't going as quick as I thought they would, but I'm cool with that. It's not like I can introduce someone into Xander's life super fast anyway." She touched the top of his head when she said his name, and he banged his plastic ring on the floor in response.

"Maybe what you could focus on while he's gone is finding ways to motivate yourself," I suggested. I had to find some way to undo what I'd done and to soften the blow of what I knew I had to tell her. "You're already so amazing you should have all the confidence in the world.

"In the meantime," I added and stood to pull her up next to me. "Let's get some pizza." The news I had to deliver would be easier to swallow with some deep-dish pepperoni pizza from my favorite pizza place. Sal's made everything taste better.

My plan probably would have worked, too, if Elton hadn't already convinced Hailey to go vegan. No slice of cardboard covered in fake cheese was going to make bad news better. Ever. I tried. I waited until she'd finished half her pizza, but when she cringed through an entire slice from first bite to last, I knew I couldn't put it off any longer. I spilled everything about what Elton had said to me.

"He wants to take you out?" she asked, her eyes already watering. Though, to be fair, that could have been from the pizza.

Either way, I could only nod.

"Of course he does." She set her pretend pizza down. "I knew he was way outta my field. Why would he wanna go out with me when he could have you?"

"First of all," I said and passed her a slice of my pepperoni pizza. "He can't have me. And second, *you're* out of *his* league." I assumed she'd meant league and not field, but I'd wait for another opportunity to fix her mixed metaphor. Instead I listed every talent and good quality she had. There were a lot. By the time I was done, she'd finished my pizza, and I figured she could give up Elton as easily as she had veganism.

Wrong.

The next day the first thing she said to me was, "If I'm all those things you say, why doesn't he want me?" Her lip quivered, but Xander beat her to the tears.

The day after that the bells at the door chimed, prompting a deep, jagged sigh. Apparently they reminded her of the last time Elton had come in to see her. Except now she knew he'd been coming in to see me.

A couple days later I said something about yogurt, and her chin started quivering. "It sounds so much like yoga," she cried. She didn't have to explain. She couldn't have anyway. She'd flown to the bathroom, wiping at her eyes as she went.

After two weeks whatever punishment I thought I deserved had been served up in heaping spoonfuls of sighs and hidden tears. I hated myself for ever thinking Elton would be right for her.

The only thing that kept me from running away was the fact my sister would soon be home for Thanksgiving. Most days when Hailey wouldn't stop talking about Elton, wondering where he was and what he was doing, I focused on planning everything I would do with my sister during her visit.

She and Preston arrived the day before Thanksgiving. Even though Caroline and I talked at least once a day, I hadn't seen her in five months. As soon as I walked in the door from work, I ran into her arms. After weeks of comforting Hailey, I needed some comfort of my own.

Parker came in five minutes after I had and shook Preston's hand before pulling him into a hug and asking, "How's married life?"

Preston slapped him on the shoulder. "You need to find someone like Caroline."

"There's only one Caroline." Parker broke away from Preston to hug my sister. "And you took her. I'm resigned to bachelorhood."

"You're right." Preston took Parker's place and wrapped his arms around Caroline's waist, pulling her close. "There is only one Caroline." He bent down and kissed her. Not a peck. A good long kiss. Long enough for Parker and me to glance at each other then quickly glance away.

"There's always Liza Belle," Preston said breaking away from Caroline to hug me. "She's a close second."

I winced and inched out of his hug. I didn't mind being compared to my sister. It had been happening most of my life. I was used to it. It just got old always coming in second.

"Preston!" Caroline smacked his arm. "She's not a cheap knockoff. She's an original." She put her arm around my shoulder and squeezed. "An original who has no interest in getting married. What would Daddy do without her?"

I didn't respond. I'd said the same thing about myself at least a thousand times, so there was no reason hearing her say it should make my chest close up tighter than the sea anemone I used to poke when the tides were low. But there I was, pretending I wasn't gasping for breath.

"Where is Daddy anyway?" I asked.

"He went for a walk on the beach," she answered.

A walk on the beach meant he was having a good day. I should have been thrilled. Daddy was feeling well enough to do the thing he loved most, and Caroline was home, but all I could think about was why I suddenly didn't like the idea of *not* getting married.

"Let's see if we can find him," Caroline said to me and grabbed Preston's hand. "I could use some beach time anyway. It's been too long." She and Preston headed for the door, expecting us to follow. I glanced at Parker, who motioned for me to go first.

"For the record," he said in a low voice as I passed by him. "I don't think you're second to Caroline. If anything, you're first among the Woodhouse sisters."

"Thanks." I smiled.

Not everyone would understand all my complicated feelings toward my sister. I worshipped her, but it wasn't always easy measuring up to her straight *A*'s, her UCLA undergrad degree, and her USC master's degree. Or her perfect smile, size-four figure, and long list of accomplishments that had nothing to do with her looks. It was hard to compare myself with her and not feel second-best.

Somehow Parker got that without me ever saying anything about it. The longer he was back, the more grateful I was for his friendship—even when it came with a healthy dose of "advice." I slipped my arm through his, and we followed Preston and Caroline into the sunset, so comfortable in our familiarity that we didn't need to say anything at all.

We kept a few paces behind Preston and Caroline, and for the first time since Elton had ruined my matchmaking plans for Hailey, my world seemed right again.

Chapter 14

The beauty of Daddy having a chef is that all I had to do for Thanksgiving dinner was put the premade food into the oven at the right times to warm them up and then set them on the table for everyone to eat. Once dinner was over, I didn't even have to wash dishes since Caroline and Preston insisted on doing them. They wouldn't let Parker help either, so he followed me to the couch, where we both collapsed, and I handed him the remote.

Since I'd ceded control of the remote without a fight, I deserved to sprawl across the couch, claiming most of it for myself.

Parker didn't agree. "Don't you have a party to plan?" He asked and pushed my legs off the couch before turning on the game, but fair is fair, so I put them right back where they'd been.

"Two parties. Which is why I'm taking a day off," I said and pressed the soles of my feet into his thighs.

He pushed them away a few times, but I kept putting them back until he gave in. I may have won a battle of wills, but more likely he was slipping into a food coma like I was. With my head on a pillow and my feet in his lap, it didn't take long before I was asleep.

I woke up an hour later to Beyoncé belting "Single Ladies," my ringtone for Taylor. I still hadn't changed it. I had until February.

"Hey!" she yelled in her one-too-many-glasses-of-wine voice. "Blake's here. Can we come by and introduce you?"

"Weston's brother?" I asked. "Yeah, come on by."

We said goodbye, and I sat up. I wasn't really in the mood for guests, mostly because I'd have to brush my hair, but Taylor had been dying to introduce me to Blake ever since she'd found out he was coming for Thanksgiving.

"Who was that?" Parker asked as I stretched my arms over my head. "By the way, you snore."

"It was Taylor, and shut up." I let my arms drop, smacking him on the head. "She and Weston are coming over to introduce me to his brother."

"He has a brother?" Caroline asked from the kitchen. "Does he look like Weston?" She wouldn't say it in front of Preston, but she thought Weston was hot.

"Half-brother," I answered, ignoring whatever she was trying to imply. "Weston barely knows him. His mom didn't let him see his dad much after they got divorced because his dad married a Mormon and moved to Idaho."

"Ooh, family drama," Caroline said. "I like it."

"I don't blame her. Martha's ex-daughter-in-law was a Mormon too," Daddy said from the kitchen, where he was scrubbing his hands. "I wouldn't want you girls hanging around them, let alone marrying one."

"Daddy! I've had lots of Mormon friends, and they're just like anybody else." I stood and moved my head side to side to work out the kinks. "Besides, you don't have to worry about me marrying anyone, Mormon or not. Blake's staying with Weston for a while, so Weston wants him to have some friends." Taylor had said something once about us being sisters-in-law if Blake and I hit it off, but I'd given her a look to remind her that marriage was not my jam.

"That's a relief." Daddy walked into the family room, rubbing his hands with enough hand sanitizer I could smell it from ten feet away. He planted a kiss on Caroline's cheek and then did the same to me. "Say hello to Taylor for me. I'll see you in the morning." He went down the hall to his room, where I knew he'd read and watch TV. It was too early for bed, but it was too late for him to muster up the energy to meet someone new.

Thirty minutes later, Taylor and Weston arrived with their very special guest. Taylor didn't wait for me to answer the door, but instead walked right into the living room. I muted the show Parker, Preston, Caroline, and I were watching, while Taylor introduced Blake. Before she got past me he interrupted her, looked me straight in the eye, and said, "You know they're trying to hook us up, right?"

I burst out laughing. "Oh, I know." I stood and shook his hand. "Nice to meet you finally. Are you hungry? I can heat up some leftovers."

Blake put his hands on his chest and fake collapsed. "That's all you had to say to win my heart."

I laughed again and led them into the kitchen. I already liked Blake. It wasn't hard. I would have liked *looking* at him even if he hadn't made me laugh. He had dark hair, blue eyes, and a chin so chiseled it could—I don't know—chisel whatever needed chiseling?

"I hope we didn't crash your party," Taylor said as I opened the fridge and passed the containers of leftovers to her. "Blake couldn't wait to meet you."

"Please tell me they've talked about something besides me." I closed the fridge and faced Blake. "Because, *boring*."

"They've found a few other things to talk about, but I keep asking about you," he answered. Then he put on a British accent and added, "I find the topic endlessly fascinating."

"So, pray tell." I tried an English accent of my own, but it sucked, so I dropped it. "What have they said?"

"You have a flower shop, and you're the best florist in the entire continental United States. There's not a flower you can't name or tame. You're fabulously wealthy but unpretentious—"

"Blake!" Taylor gave him a good smack that only made his smile stretch wider.

"I would tell him to stop, but he's already told me there's no keeping him in line." Weston's grin matched his brother's, the only distinguishing feature they shared, although Blake was just as good-looking as his brother.

"Well, I'm out," Parker interrupted from the doorway. Until then, I hadn't noticed he'd followed us to the kitchen.

"You don't have to leave," I said, suddenly feeling hurt he was bailing even though he'd been there all day.

He answered with a wave goodbye and left without giving me my usual hug.

"And you surf." Blake picked up where he'd been interrupted, and I turned my attention back to him. "Which is perfect because I'm looking for someone to teach me. I figure it can be part of the terms of our arranged marriage. I've already asked Taylor to put it in the contract." Blake took a roll from the basket I'd set in front of him and popped a piece into his mouth.

"You've never surfed?" I asked, smothering my laugh so he'd understand the seriousness of the situation. "That could be a deal breaker."

"Of course I've surfed . . ." He shifted his eyes back and forth guiltily. "What Idaho boy doesn't surf? I only need you to help me tune up my skills."

"Oh, well, in that case," I said with the innocent enthusiasm of a twelve-year-old girl going to her first middle school dance. "Meet me here at seven, Saturday."

"Seven? In the morning?"

"Surf's up early," I said. "Of course, you already know that. Being from Idaho and all."

"Of course. Seven it is." He swallowed hard.

Yeah, I liked him. He was fun.

Blake scored more points when he showed up Saturday morning with coffee and my favorite donut. Taylor and Weston were with him, so I suspected Taylor had something to do with it.

"Did you tell your brother to wear something under his swim trunks?" I asked Weston and took a bite of my apple fritter.

"I need something under them?" Blake asked.

"You can't wear a wetsuit over them," I answered.

"You can slip 'em off at the beach," Weston said. "That's why I brought you a towel."

"I'm getting naked at the beach?"

"Only if the towel falls," I said.

"I really don't wear anything underneath the wetsuit?" Blake asked, looking less sure about his surf lesson by the second, and we hadn't even made it to the water.

"Not if all you've got are board shorts." I picked up my board and headed toward the beach. "I'm not gonna lie though, you'll probably be a little rashy this time."

I turned around when the sound of his flip-flops slapping the concrete stopped.

"Rashy?"

I pinched my fingers close together and held them in front of my face. "Little bit. It'll be worth it," I said and continued on my way. Seconds later I heard the *thwack thwack* of rubber hitting cement.

Once we got to the beach and Blake had successfully navigated changing behind a towel into a wetsuit, he was a lot more comfortable with the prospect of catching some waves. Maybe not physically comfortable, but at least mentally.

"Is it supposed to be this tight?" he asked, pulling on the neck of his wetsuit.

"It'll be better once you're in the water," I answered. "Stop fidgeting and watch your brother."

Taylor and Weston were already paddling past the break. We stayed on the sand and watched them get set up for their wave. When it came, Taylor popped up first with Weston right behind her.

"Is that all it takes?" Blake asked.

"First of all, they make it look easier than it is," I said. "Second, don't get discouraged if you can't get up. It takes a long time." I started toward the water and waved him to follow me. "And last, when you do get up, don't ride someone else's wave unless they want to share."

"Are we going all the way out by them?"

"Not today," I said, wading into the water. "You've got to master the little waves first. Staying upright is going to take more than one lesson."

And then I ate my words.

It took him two tries to get up. On his third time, he stayed up all the way to shore. And he liked it so much I couldn't get him out of the water. Taylor and Weston had to leave, but we stayed until the wind changed and the waves got mushy.

"Are you impressed?" he asked as we walked back to my house with our boards tucked under our arms. "I feel like you should be. I don't know how long it should take to learn to surf, but I think I won at it today."

"You definitely won. You even conquered the wet suit part." I patted his back. "You're almost ready for a big-boy board."

He stopped in the middle of the sidewalk. "What do you mean 'big-boy board'?" He untucked the long, wide board I'd loaned him, nearly dropping it. "I had the biggest board out there," he said once he had it rebalanced under his arm.

"Yep. And when you're ready to surf with the big boys, you can try one of these." I held up my much slimmer, lighter board. "You've passed the first test to becoming a full-fledged San Clemente resident. Well done."

"Nice." He nodded. "What's the second test?"

"Purchasing your first pair of Rainbows."

"I've always wanted to buy a rainbow."

"Different kind of rainbow," I said. "I'm talking about flip-flops."

"You mean—"

I held up my hand to stop him. "We never call them thongs. Ever." Plenty of tourists made that mistake. "And I know what you're thinking about now."

"How do you know what I'm thinking about?" He leaned his board on the side of my house then took mine to stand next to it. "Why wouldn't I be thinking about footwear when you say the word *thong*?"

"Because you're a man." I raised my eyebrows and waited for a response. He was less than a foot away and moving closer. For one exciting split second, I thought his comeback would involve lips rather than words.

"Hey," a voice called behind me. A very familiar but unexpected voice.

"Hi." I turned to face Parker. A memory flashed in my mind of the time he'd caught me pilfering some of his Halloween candy, and the same feeling of guilt I'd had then swept over me. Guilt over what I didn't know. There wasn't any candy in sight. Although, technically, Blake counted as eye candy.

"What's going on?" His eyes bounced from me to Blake and back again.

"I taught Blake how to surf." I wagged my head toward Blake. "He said he wanted to learn, so we went out this morning. The waves were awesome. He's a natural—" I winced as Parker's face clouded over.

"Eliza is an awesome teacher," Blake interrupted and stepped closer to me. He shook the water out of his shoulder-length hair and pulled it back.

"Is that right?" Parker looked like he hadn't had his morning coffee. He was testy. "Let me guess what she told you: 'Enjoy the moment; live in the wave.'"

Blake laughed. "Yeah, something like that. It worked though. I didn't worry about wiping out; I just went with what was happening with the water around me."

I grabbed Blake's arm and shook it in victory. "See? He totally gets it! I told you he's a natural."

"That's great." Parker's "great" wasn't very convincing. He was only getting grouchier. "You working today?" he asked.

"Yeah. How late is it?" I'd lost all track of time. I usually only opened for a few hours on Saturday, but with holiday shoppers out downtown, I had planned on working most of the day and having Hailey come in for a few hours.

Parker checked his watch. "Nine forty-five."

"Oh! I've gotta go! I'll have to ask Hailey to open."

"Can I catch a ride with you since mine left?" Blake asked. "I can hang out at the shop for a while if you need me to."

"Sure. Let me take a quick shower." I typed in the garage code and the door went up. "Come inside. Parker can keep you company."

"Uh, sure," Parker answered and then picked up my board without my asking and put it away.

I yelled my thanks then ran upstairs to the shower. When the warm water hit me and blood started flowing to my brain again, I wondered why Parker had come by. We'd spent most of Friday together with Caroline and Preston before they'd left early this morning for San Fran. I hadn't expected to see him again until Sunday.

Maybe I'd done something wrong the day before. That would explain his surly mood. I replayed everything I'd said but couldn't figure out what I'd done to upset him, so I let it go. Whatever it was, he'd be sure to let me know.

Chapter 15

The Sunday after Thanksgiving is always reserved for our annual leftovers feast. Daddy had been hosting it ever since Caroline and I were little girls. As he got older and became more and more reclusive, Caroline and I had insisted on having it, even if the list of people he invited had shrunk. It was good for Daddy to have some connection to his past life before his compromised immune system and his tendency toward hypochondria led to a never-ending tug-of-war between his thinking he was sick and his actually being sick.

Parker was the first to arrive that night—no surprise since his definition of punctual meant fifteen minutes early. I didn't mind. I needed an extra hand anyway. As usual, I'd underestimated how long the food prep would take.

"Make some gravy magic happen," I said, handing him a whisk and pointing to the pot on the stove.

He looked in the pot then back at me. "Do you mean warm it up?" He turned a knob with a click, and whoosh—a fire ignited under the gravy. "Is that the magic you were looking for?"

I lowered my chin and raised my eyebrows. He pushed his glasses higher on his nose and responded with an unrepentant grin.

"Just stir." I went back to scooping my reheated sweet potatoes into the serving dish that matched my mom's china.

Parker was about two minutes into his gravy stirring assignment when the interrogation I should have expected began.

"Seems like you and that Blake guy really hit it off," he started.

"Yeah, he's a nice guy."

"How long is he in town?"

"I don't know." I nudged him away from the drawer with my hot pads in it.

"Does he have a job?"

"He's thinking about it."

"Thinking about it?" Parker stopped stirring and took the gravy off the stove. "Must be nice to 'think about' having a job. What does he do?"

"I don't know." I shrugged and opened the oven to check on my turkey casserole. We always served it, but this was the first year I'd made it. It had always been Caroline's job, and before that, Daddy's.

"Hmm." Parker leaned against the counter and crossed his arms.

"What else do you want to know?"

"What makes you think I want to know more?"

"Your 'hmm.'" I took the casserole out of the oven and scooted around him to set it on a trivet. "That's what you always do when you're thinking about how to phrase your next question or piece of advice."

"Is it?" He *hmm*ed again. "Anything else I should know about myself?"

Before I could answer with my long list of Parker-isms, the doorbell rang.

"You answer the door," I ordered. Because sometimes it was nice to boss the guy who thought he was the boss of me. "I'll get Daddy."

He pushed away from the counter and grabbed my wrist as I walked by. "I know your heart's all aflutter for this Blake guy, but I hope you won't ignore Jami."

His words rushed out barely above a whisper. His grip was light, but I was intensely aware of his fingers wrapped around my wrist and his arm pressed against mine. Our faces were close enough I could see where he'd nicked himself shaving, and I wondered if it had hurt.

I breathed in a cacophony of smells. Cinnamon and garlic, yeast and onion; but also the clean, crisp scent of him. It reminded me of sitting on Daddy's lap, resting my cheek on his freshly laundered shirt as he read to me before going to work. It brought out a longing in me I didn't know existed. A longing to be safe and loved. A longing to have a turn being taken care of instead of always being the caretaker.

I pulled my arm back, and he released me. "There it is," I laughed, pushing away my ridiculous memory-induced emotions.

"There what is?" He stepped back.

"What you've been waiting all day to say to me." I brushed by him as I walked to Daddy's room, snapping, "And my heart is not all aflutter."

I helped Daddy down the hall and got him settled into his chair while Parker showed Martha, Nancy, and Jami in. The too-skinny, buck-toothed ten-year-old I remembered had grown into a tall curvy woman with dark hair spilling down her back. I took the dish she'd brought, and we exchanged an awkward hug, politely acting like our childhood friendship had been strong enough that we were excited to see each other again.

"How long are you in town?" I asked Jami after I set the dish on the table and we'd all taken a seat in the family room.

"At least a few months, if Grandma and Aunt Nancy will have me," she answered, glancing at the two women seated on either side of her, both glowing with admiration.

"We'll keep her forever if we can." Nancy took off talking, and I prayed we were in for a sprint, not a marathon. "We only need to find somewhere for her to work. She's a school teacher, you know. She's so good with children. Any school would be lucky to have her. Even a preschool. Or a high school, although you probably wouldn't want to teach there, would you?" Nancy patted Jami's knee.

"I don't have the right credentials to teach anywhere in California right now," Jami answered.

"She wants to go to grad school, but it's too expensive, and she hasn't passed the test yet to get in." Nancy patted Jami's knee while Jami's cheeks matched the tomatoes in my fruit bowl. "We would have paid her tuition if we could have, wouldn't we, Mother?" Nancy raised her voice to get her mother's attention, but Martha only nodded. "College is so expensive these days. I'm not sure how anyone goes . . ."

Every conversation with Nancy was like déjà vu. She talked so much I could never remember what she'd said, but it always felt like I'd heard it before. When the doorbell rang, I rushed to get it, as much to escape Nancy as because I knew it had to be Blake.

I opened the door to find him laughing about something with Taylor and Weston. I didn't know what it was, and it didn't matter. Hearing them reassured me we were in for a fun night that not even Nancy could ruin with her babbling.

"Come in!" I kissed them each on the cheek, even Blake—that's how excited I was to see him—then handed the dish to Weston that Taylor had carried in so I could stick my arm through hers. "Martha and Nancy are already here," I whispered to her. "I was seconds away from slipping into a coma before the doorbell rang. Jami isn't any better than the two of them."

"Be nice," she whispered back.

"I'm trying. It's so hard."

We walked into the family room, giggling like we were fourteen again, which, for some reason, elicited a glare from Parker. Blake and Weston were behind us, and I happened to glance at Jami, whose eyes rested on Blake. I looked at him in time to see his eyes meet Jami's. A flicker of recognition passed between them, which I brushed off until I introduced him to her.

"You look familiar." He stuck out his hand for her to shake, which she did reluctantly, but her face didn't register any emotion. "Where are you from?"

"Utah." The two syllables came out curt and short.

"Did you go to BYU–Idaho?" He still held her hand, which she jerked away.

"Yeah." She tipped her head to the side and set her mouth in a straight, serious line. "Did you?"

"Just graduated."

"Wow." I moved between them. "What are the odds?"

"I think I remember you now," Jami said, ignoring me. "You hung out with the bros who were always too loud in the library, right?" There was no teasing in her tone, and the air in the room went tight. I stepped out of her line of sight, not wanting any shade thrown my way.

"Bros?" He stared down at her, and there was something in his eyes that sparked a moment of jealousy in me. "Yeah, that sounds right." He laughed, and the rubber-band-stretched tension snapped.

"What a coincidence! Can you believe it, Mother? Jami has a friend here . . ." Nancy launched into a new monologue, and everyone's eyes moved from Blake and Jami to Nancy.

"How crazy is that?" Taylor whispered to me.

"Unbelievable," I whispered back. My eyes were having a hard time leaving Blake. "How did he even remember her? She barely says a word." I watched the two of them carefully while Nancy asked question after question about where and when Blake had seen Jami, not waiting for answers. Blake nodded politely, occasionally stealing a peek at Jami.

"The world is a smaller place than we realize," Daddy said. "Even smaller now with all this Internet stuff." He moved his hands as though waves of information were floating there waiting to be captured by the World Wide Web, a thing that still mystified him despite his computer proficiency. His comment, though, had finally shut Nancy up.

"Are we ready for our leftover smorgasbord?" I seized the opportunity to get a word in while I had it. My stomach was growling, and if Nancy started talking again it might be another hour before we ate. I motioned everyone toward the table and told them where to sit.

Parker was supposed to sit by me, but he took the seat next to Jami instead. I saw Jami's first and only smile of the night as she talked to him, which sent a wave of nausea over me. It didn't feel like when I'd seen Blake look at her, so it couldn't be jealousy, but I didn't have a name for whatever it was.

"I can't believe you know Jami Fairfax," I whispered to Blake, who had followed directions and sat next to me.

"Barely," he answered. "The Mormon world is a small one."

"What do you think of her?" I knew I shouldn't ask, but she'd just refused the scoop of mashed potatoes Parker had offered her. Who does that?

"Undecided." Blake answered, his breath hot on my neck.

"I thought Idaho was the potato state. Why isn't she eating mine?" Technically they weren't *mine* since I hadn't made them, but that wasn't the point.

The real question was, why did I even care? Why did I feel like I was in a competition with her and she had the upper hand? It made no sense.

"Maybe they're too exciting for her."

I giggled loud enough for Parker to reprimand me with a deep crease of his brow, which only made me giggle again.

Before I could take the first bite of my food, the doorbell rang.

"That must be Hailey and Xander," I said and pushed away from the table to go let them in.

"I'm so sorry I'm late!" were the first words out of Hailey's mouth as I answered the door. Xander, on the other hand, squealed with delight when he saw me.

I took him from her as a burst of laughter from the dining room floated toward us. "I'm not good at meeting new people," she said, pausing mid coat removal.

"You don't need to be. Everyone's going to love you and Xander."

"I wish Elton was here. I need some breathing tips." She finished taking off her jacket and clutched it in her arms. "I've been trying not to think about him, but I can't help it."

"It's only been a few weeks." Closer to a month, but who was counting? Me, obviously. But only because I was hoping she'd be over him by now.

I guided her to the table and introduced her. She mumbled hellos to everyone and then sat down and filled her plate to overflowing, which meant she probably hadn't eaten much that day. Money was always tight by the end of the month, even when she stuck to the budget I'd made for her. Of course, budgeting wasn't my greatest talent. Lately I'd been considering asking Parker to help her, but I was afraid he'd take it as an open invitation to tell me what I needed to do differently too.

I sat down with Xander on my lap so Hailey could eat. I tried to take a bite of my already-cold food, but he kept sticking his fist into my mashed potatoes. I laughed, but I really wanted those potatoes. The third time he did it, nearly knocking over my drink, Jami stood and held her arms across the table.

"I'm finished. Let me take him."

Parker looked up at her with a smile that made me want to say no, but the hunger pains in my stomach were more persuasive.

"Are you sure? He's squirmy," I said, handing him to her before she could change her mind.

"I can handle squirmy." She wiggled her fingers in Xander's face, and he flapped his chubby arms in return.

"If you're positive." I glanced at Hailey, seated next to Nancy, to make sure she was okay with it. She was too overwhelmed by Nancy to do more than blink at the barrage of questions coming at her. She didn't even notice me hand off Xander.

"How old is he?" Jami asked as she moved behind her seat to bounce him up and down. She was more relaxed than I'd seen her all night.

"Six months or so." I couldn't remember exactly. I probably should have, considering how much time I spent with him.

Within minutes Xander had settled his head onto Jami's shoulder and looked ready to fall asleep. She reminded me of the perfectly backlit moms in diaper commercials who didn't look anything like the frazzled ones I saw in real life. She'd probably be one of those ad-ready moms someday, with a perfect, blond-haired, blue-eyed, Warby-Parker-glasses-wearing husband by her side. There was a candidate in the room who, a quick glance told me, was watching me watch her.

I tore my eyes away from Jami before I was tempted to walk further down Comparison Lane and turned my attention back to Hailey. Her red cheeks and eyes tipped me off that something was wrong. It only took a few seconds to determine the something threatening to make her cry was Nancy.

"Seventeen is so young," Nancy said. "Why didn't you give him up for adoption? Are you still together with the father? Or was it a one-night thing? Your son must look like him; I don't see much resemblance to you. Do you get welfare? I know a lot of single mothers have to be on welfare to take care of their babies . . ." Nancy's questions came one after the other, with barely a breath in between. Not that Hailey would have wanted to answer them anyway. She looked to me for help, but before I could say a word someone else did.

"Hailey, tell us about school. You've been taking some classes at Saddleback, right?" Parker's voice boomed across the table, silencing Nancy. Hailey's face flooded with relief, and after a deep breath she answered him.

"I'm taking a math class and an intro-to-business class. Those are both pretty hard, but I like my English class." She attempted a smile.

"She's doing so well," I said. Nancy's mouth had opened. I had to spit words out before she did. "I can't believe all the stuff she tells me."

"I'm not surprised." Parker had skills when it came to making people feel comfortable. He'd only talked to Hailey a few times, but her shoulders relaxed as he spoke. "If you need some help with your math and business classes, let me know. Those are my specialty."

"Thanks. I will." Hailey took her first bite of food and even smiled at Nancy, who had started talking again.

Daddy got up from his chair and patted his stomach. "Delicious, Eliza."

"It wasn't only me. Everyone brought something."

"But you planned it, and it's been excellent." He padded over to Nancy and held his arm out. "Why don't you join me in the other room if you're finished eating. I could use some good conversation," he said to her then gave me a wink.

That was why he was the best. Sometimes I wondered if he noticed anything beyond his newspaper, but then he would do something so thoughtful and remind me why I'd never find anyone who could live up to him.

I went back to eating my dinner, looking around the table and into the living room. Parker had taken Nancy's spot and was talking to Hailey about her business class. Nancy sat next to Daddy in the other room, telling him a story he'd probably heard a million times, but he smiled and nodded like he'd never heard it before while Martha sat silently by his side, her mouth occasionally curving into a half smile. Jami still held Xander, who slept on her shoulder, but Blake had moved closer to them and ran his fingers over Xander's pudgy fist. Jami didn't look entirely comfortable with him that close, but she didn't look as uncomfortable as she had at the beginning of the night.

The fire flickered behind Daddy. The lights were low, and the smell of cranberry drifted through the air. With a room full of old and new friends—even those who talked too much—and the sounds of conversation filling the room, I couldn't help but feel content. I had a perfect life, and I didn't want to change a thing about it.

Chapter 16

My leftover feast was such a success that those of us under the age of fifty decided to keep the party going and take it to the waves Monday morning. The forecasted weather was in the low seventies, and the wave report was even better: offshore winds and four-foot waves.

"Do you surf, Jami?" I asked when we met up bright and early before work.

"It's been a long time since I tried, but Parker offered to teach me." She smiled up at him as he handed her a board. One of his favorites. He'd never even let me borrow it, and I knew how to surf.

"How nice," I said to him, ignoring Taylor's raised eyebrow.

"Just following your example." He smiled.

"Hopefully you're as good a student as Blake," I said to Jami. Parker's mouth switched directions, and his eyes wandered to Blake.

"I'll probably spend most of my time on shore," she replied. "I told Hailey I'd watch Xander for her."

"Oh." I hadn't thought to offer that. "Let me know if you need help."

On cue, Hailey pulled up in the ancient Honda Civic that Ashton had found for her and got running again. Once she parked and had Xander and all the baby stuff that went along with him out of the car, we all headed toward the beach.

Parker and Jami walked ahead of everyone else. He not only had his board tucked under his arm but Jami's also since she'd offered to carry Xander so Hailey could carry the board I'd loaned her. They were so busy talking they completely ignored the rest of us. I wasn't jealous or anything—Blake was fun to talk to. It was just weird not to have Parker to myself, since I usually did. I guess I was used to him being around all the time. He didn't even line up next to me in the water like I thought he would. We always had our best conversations waiting for waves. It's the only time he ever chilled out.

Suddenly things had changed. Every time Jami went in to watch Xander—which was a lot since she didn't have much success getting up on her board—Parker went with her.

"I think he's into her," Taylor said when she caught me watching them instead of looking for my next wave. Bobbing up and down in the water usually soothed me, but not that day.

"Maybe. I don't know." With each rise of the ocean, I'd catch a glimpse of Jami and Parker playing in the sand with Xander, laughing and smiling like they were a little family. With each dip, I'd lose sight of them at the same time my breakfast tried to make its way out of my stomach. "She doesn't seem like his type," I said, more for my benefit than Taylor's.

I lay down and slowly paddled to meet Blake. The waves were bigger than what he'd surfed his first time, but he seemed confident he could handle them. I hoped he was right and his glances back to shore weren't out of regret or, worse, fear. He definitely didn't look stoked to be out there.

I gave him some tips then watched him get worked by a wave before I caught my own and rode it in to shore. I paddled out again and encouraged Blake to give it another go. And another . . . and another, but he kept wiping out and getting angrier each time he did. Finally he paddled in, carried his board out of the water, and plopped down next to Jami.

I rode a few more waves but wasn't really feeling it. I was about to head in when I saw Parker paddling toward me, taking advantage of the lull in the waves.

He lined up next to me, sat up, and swiped the hair out of his face. He'd never looked *bad* in a wet suit, but I'd never noticed how good he looked in one. Especially the one he'd chosen this morning, which hugged his shoulders and chest in a caped-crusader kind of way.

"What's up with Blake?" he asked.

"I don't know." The bobbing ocean wasn't making me sick anymore. In fact, my stomach had a nice roller-coaster tickle going on. "He got raked over. He's probably thrashed."

"Yeah, maybe." He started to paddle, and I followed, but our wave went mushy on us, so we sat up to wait for a better one.

"You and Jami looked like you were having fun." I checked the swell behind me, mostly to avoid his gaze. I'd said the words, but I didn't really want to hear they were true.

"Yeah. She's nice. You should give her a chance."

"What do you mean give her a chance? I invited her here, didn't I? I've talked to her. What else should I do?"

"Technically I invited her. You say the bare minimum to her." He looked over his shoulder, and I followed his glance. The water was flat. "You've gone out of your way to welcome Hailey into your life, so why not do the same for Jami? Their stories aren't that different."

He glanced over his shoulder again then paddled hard to catch a sick wave. He took the drop and then did a bottom turn. It was a cool trick, but there was no beauty in his form. He surfed to conquer a wave, to achieve something, not to be a part of it. That's what always bugged me about watching him.

I was doubly bugged now because of what he'd said. He lobbed me a major "do this better" and then sailed off to punch his surf clock. *Lecture Little Liza Belle,* check. *Ride wave,* check. *Go do all the things for Jami that Eliza should be doing,* check.

Plus, I'd missed the best swell of the day because I'd been too busy stewing over what he'd said. I caught the next wave and showed Parker how to really enjoy surfing. After taking the drop and doing my own bottom turn, I carved the face, anticipating where the wave would go next and following it to its end and my happy place. I hopped off when my board hit the soft sand, and then I walked up the beach to where everyone else was sitting. Parker clapped, and the rest joined in, so I stood my board up, stuck my right foot behind my left, and curtsied.

They showered me with compliments, but the only one I heard was Parker's.

"It's always an experience watching you ride a wave like that," he gushed.

I didn't like that he was sitting by Jami again, but I'd take the compliment and try to forget his advice about her. A task easier said than done.

I got some help forgetting about Jami when a bigger problem reappeared a few days later, when Hailey dragged into work as sad as a kid who'd lost her brand-new puppy. "He's back," she said. Then she tossed her diaper bag onto the couch and crumpled next to it, cradling Xander close to her chest.

"Who?"

"Elton," she mumbled. "Who else?" The week she'd gone without mentioning his name had given me hope she was over him. I had to force back a sigh and an eye-roll before answering her.

"How do you know?" I picked up a sunflower and cut its stem with more force than necessary.

"I saw him walking out of the studio." She laid her cheek on Xander's head and held him tighter to keep him from wriggling out of her arms.

"I thought you were ready to move on." I stuck the sunflowers into a vintage-looking jar, giving the simple arrangement all the attention I should have been giving Hailey.

"I was . . . I am." She set Xander on a blanket with some toys and joined me at the table. "I just want to make sure . . . I don't know. I guess I hoped maybe he'd change his mind while he was gone."

"Change his mind about what?" My arrangement didn't work out like I wanted, so I took them all out and started again.

"Like, maybe he'd decide I really am awesome, like you keep saying I am." She bit her lip, and all the insecurity I'd been trying to help her overcome was back. "Like, I want him to see me and regret not taking the chance when he had it."

On first thought, staying as far away from him as possible seemed like the best move, but then I reconsidered. "You could go to a class and show him you're not embarrassed to be around him and you're only interested in him as an instructor."

"Oh yeah, that would be a total burn—showing him I'm only into yoga now." She stood taller with each word until she came to the last one. Then her renewed confidence slipped, threatening to pull her back into the depths of despair. "Will you go with me though?" she pleaded.

I rearranged my sunflowers and thought over her question even though I knew I had to say yes. I didn't want Elton to think I'd changed my mind about anything. But I did want to support Hailey, and I wasn't going to throw away all the money I'd spent on yoga packages just to avoid him.

"Okay." I stuck in the last sunflower and stepped back to assess my creation. "And only so you can know for sure you're over him. You really can do better. Take all the good stuff you've learned from him and use it, but forget about him."

"Deal." She forced a smile. "Can we go tonight?"

The last thing I wanted to do after a busier-than-usual day at work was see Elton, but it was better to rip the Band-Aid off sooner rather than later. So I agreed, and within a few short hours I found myself lying on my mat, forcing myself to stay awake.

"Namaste, fellow yogis." Elton's voice brought me back from the pleasant half-sleep I'd drifted into. "I'm glad to be back with you after so many weeks gone, and I have some good news to share with you, my most ardent supporters."

My eyes were still shut, but that didn't stop me from rolling them.

"I know you were sending me good thoughts while I was away, and I received them." His voice came closer, and I opened one eye to see him standing at my feet. "Your wishes for me and my dreams for myself have been actualized."

I played dead hoping he'd move on. He didn't.

"I met someone," he said. Even with my eyes closed I could tell his words were directed right at me, but it was Hailey who gasped. I opened my eyes, catching the frown he directed at her.

"She's moving here next month to teach and coach with me as we start our life together," he said while finally moving away. "I know you'll find her as motivating and inspiring as I am—maybe even more so."

I didn't have to look at Hailey to know Elton's words were stabbing her in the heart despite the soft, gentle voice he used. I peeked anyway. My worst fears were confirmed. Tears ran down her cheeks, sliding off her face as she stayed on her back even after Elton instructed us to move into child's pose.

The class had to be the longest of my life and the total opposite of what yoga was supposed to be. Instead of releasing anxiety, it increased mine by about a hundred times. I couldn't keep my eyes off Hailey, and she couldn't keep from tearing up every few minutes. Instead of focusing on any postures, my attention was on Hailey and how to get her out of class. I mouthed, "Let's go," but she shook her head.

I finally convinced her before the last two-minute *vinyasa* was over. We were headed out the door when Elton called my name. I pretended not to hear, but he caught up to us, stepping in front of me to block our exit.

"Hi!" He leaned against the open door, making an escape impossible. "I don't know if you heard what I said about Erica, but I'd love for you to meet her when she gets here."

"Um, sure." I blinked. Had he forgotten the last thing he'd said to me? The thing about our stars being "totally aligned" or whatever?

"You two will connect." He went on, not even acknowledging Hailey, even when I moved so she was directly in his line of sight. "You have the same kind of energy—similar auras."

"Similar auras?"

"Yeah. Red." He waved his hands around me, like he wanted to pet whatever colored magnetic field surrounded me.

"Okay." I had no idea what he was talking about. I looked terrible in red.

"I want to hire you to do a meet-and-greet kind of thing so my friends and clients can get to know her. You can invite your friends, too." He didn't even crack a smile, even though he had to be joking. "I know you don't really do that anymore, but I figured you'd do it in return for all the help I gave Hailey."

I looked behind me expecting to see Hailey, but she'd slipped out—likely through the back exit. Smart. I turned back to confront him. "I paid you for those classes."

"I gave her a lot of free sessions because she's a friend of yours and because we've known each other for so long." His voice had an innocent tone to it, but there wasn't any innocence in his manipulation. "I know you had ideas about me being more than a mentor to her, and I'm sorry I didn't feel the same, but I gave her something better than my heart. I gave her my soul. She's come a long way."

I fought back a gag. No way would I let him take all the credit for getting Hailey to enroll in school or set some high goals. That was me. But, at the same time, I couldn't deny he had helped her. So, I decided to be gracious rather than argue an inarguable point.

"Fine." I smiled through gritted teeth. "Let me know when you want to do it, and I'll plan it at a discounted rate." As though I didn't already have enough to do with Taylor's wedding and Parker's party. But once it was over, Elton and I would be even—as far as I was concerned, anyway—and I would never again feel any obligation to attend his yoga class instead of the one I actually liked.

I left without saying goodbye and met Hailey at my car, where she was leaning against the door, waiting for me to unlock it. She turned her face to dry her tears, but I saw them before she could.

"I'm glad that's over," she said after she'd climbed in and shut the door. "It totally sucked, but I think I'll be okay now. I can face him and pretend nothing ever happened." She took a cleansing breath and let it out.

"Good." I stopped myself from pointing out nothing had ever happened between them. I also stopped myself from telling her about Elton's party. I'd break the news to her before I sent the invites so she wouldn't be shocked when she got it, but hopefully by then she'd really be over him.

In the meantime she had no shortage of tears between the time I pulled away from the studio until I dropped her off at Taylor's to pick up Xander and her car. By then, I'd almost vowed never to play matchmaker again.

Chapter 17

Even if I had wanted to play matchmaker, I didn't have time. Between my actual job at the shop and planning three major events, I had too much on my plate to manage other people's love lives for them. Parker's party alone had me under enough pressure to make breathing hard some days.

Party was the wrong word to describe what he wanted to do. He didn't care about the party part at all. His goal was to raise money to take on big name-brand manufacturers who used smaller companies to do their work and then paid them so little that those smaller employers often hired immigrant or undocumented workers and way underpaid them. He wanted to fight for fair wages for those workers.

But getting people to fund his fight had to involve some entertainment and fun. Enter: me, the party girl. The flip side of bringing the fun, though, was feeling like I couldn't breathe some days. I wanted everything to be perfect. Which is why I recruited help in the form of Daddy and Jami.

Daddy was sponsoring the event, and Jami . . .

Well, Jami's job was to do the grunt work for Elton's party so I could focus on Parker's and to ease my conscience. Parker's reprimand about not reaching out to her had been echoing in my head for months. Elton's demand for a party gave me an excuse to offer her a job and a way to avoid dealing with Elton. Plus it would make Parker happy. It was a win-win for everyone.

The guest list for Parker's event included every philanthropist within a fifty-mile radius plus anyone else Parker thought might donate to the fund. Even Blake was on the list. I set up a silent auction and got some great donations as prizes, but there had to be some entertainment.

Since I'd gone with a Japanese theme for the decorations—lanterns, mini bonsai on the tables, arrangements of mums and apricot blossoms (cherries weren't in season)—it seemed obvious what the entertainment should be:

karaoke. And obviously Parker would be participating. I was even willing to do a duet with him.

I told him my very good idea as I stood outside his door one rainy afternoon, and I got the exact reaction I expected.

"What makes you think karaoke is happening at my party or that I'd be participating in it if it were?" He stepped aside to let me in.

"Of course you'll have karaoke. The party will be boring without it." I squeezed my damp hair then walked past him into the family room and sat down. "Can we watch something besides soccer?"

"Liverpool is playing. And karaoke is not a prerequisite to making a party fun." He sat next to me and took the remote out of my hand before I could change the channel.

"Why do we care about Liverpool, and why are you talking like a professor?" I reached for the remote, but he held it away from me.

"We care about Liverpool because they're the best soccer team in the U.K., and I'm not talking like a professor. I'm talking like a grown-up."

I sat back to fool him into believing I wasn't interested in the remote anymore. It worked, and he lowered his arm.

"Well, *Professor*, karaoke *is* a prerequisite to party fun. If you had thrown a party before, you would know this. But you haven't, so you don't, which is why you hired me. Remember?"

"Oh, I remember." He sat back and crossed his arms, clutching the remote in the hand closest to me. "You can get your friend Blake to do it."

That was all the yes I needed. "I'm sure he'll be happy to." I scooted closer, targeting the remote. "Because he's fun."

"Are you saying I'm not fun?" He narrowed his eyes. "That's original."

"I'm saying you'd rather tell me what, when, and how to do something than sing with me, even though I know you like to sing and, in fact, have a very good voice." I narrowed my eyes back at him and crossed my arms, all while keeping the remote within my line of sight.

"I've never claimed to be fun." He shifted his weight away from me and turned the volume up on the TV. "You'll have to go to Blake for that."

"I'm only teasing." I hadn't meant to hurt his feelings. "You don't have to sing. And you're fun in your own way." I squeezed his arm and then seized my opportunity to grab the remote from him and hold it above my head.

"Hey!" He leaned over me to grab it, but I dug myself into the corner of the couch, holding the remote high with one hand and pushing him away with the other.

"Let me watch HGTV, and I'll tell you something you'll be happy to hear."

"I'd rather take my chances overpowering you." He poked my side right in my most ticklish spot. I tried to squirm away, but I'd backed myself into a corner. Literally. "Odds are in my favor right now," he added as I tried not to let my hand down while also trying to maneuver away from his wiggling fingers.

By the time he got the words out, he was close to getting the remote from me. Which meant he was close. Very close. As in, his arms and hands and were wrapped around my waist. As in, his face was inches from mine, our lips close enough to touch. Kiss even.

Our eyes locked and everything stopped, except his chest, which moved in and out with each breath he took. I suppose mine did too, but I didn't want to breathe. Breathing meant moving, and any movement might put distance between us, and suddenly I didn't want any distance between us. Even those few inches felt like miles.

And I thought he wanted to close the gap between us. I could have sworn he leaned forward before I closed my eyes, waiting, wanting . . .

But then he cleared his throat and said, "Okay, tell me."

I opened my eyes. He sat back and ran his hands through his hair, the muscles in his biceps flexing as he did. The heat of the moment was gone, leaving only a cold space between us. Blood rushed to my cheeks as the weight of what had almost happened hit me.

Kissing Parker would be like kissing a brother. *Wouldn't it?* I'd never had a brother and wouldn't want to kiss him if I did have one, but kissing Parker definitely would have changed our relationship. One make-out session could ruin a lifetime of friendship.

"Tell you what?" My mind had gone blank.

"The thing I'll be happy to hear." He rubbed his legs and kept his eyes on the soccer game.

"Oh yeah." I handed him the remote and tucked myself back into the corner—as far from him as possible—with my legs curled under me. "I've been thinking about Jami's story being like Hailey's." I hazarded a look at him. "You were right. I wasn't giving her much of a chance, so I hired her to help me out with this little party I'm planning."

"Really?" He turned his head toward me. His ears were red. "That's very grown-up of you."

"Thanks." I let the tip of my mouth curve into a sarcastic grin. "Maybe I'm ready to use big words now too."

He laughed. "No, really. I didn't mean to be condescending. I think it's great you're reaching out to her. She needs it." He handed the remote back to me. "Now tell me about this party you're planning."

I turned off the TV and turned to face him. "Well, first, as much as I hate to admit it, you were also right about Elton . . ."

I explained all about Elton coming back from his yoga adventures with a girlfriend and how he'd hired me to plan a meet and greet for her.

Parker scrunched up his face then laughed. "You've got to be kidding me. Like a reception or something?"

"I guess. I don't know." Now that he was laughing, I could laugh at the whole situation too.

"And you agreed to do it?"

"I couldn't say no!"

"Yes, you could. You just don't know how. Practice it with me." He reached over and grabbed my chin, moving it up and done while he said, "N-o. No."

I swatted his hand away and laughed again. "That would have been helpful when he asked me. It's too late now."

He shook his head but let a smile play at his lips. I could still feel his fingers on my face even though he wasn't touching me.

"The point is, I hired Jami to help me plan it." I cocked my head and gave him a satisfied grin. "Are you proud of me?"

He looked more shocked than anything, but in a happy way. "Yeah. I think she'll like that. It's a nice thing for you to do."

"I do a lot of nice things, FYI." I uncurled my legs and planted them on his lap. "Plus, I couldn't exactly ask Hailey to help me, and I don't have time to do it alone."

"You do, do a lot of nice things," he said and grabbed my big toe.

"You said doo doo." I snorted then broke into full-on laughing.

"Just when I thought you were a grown-up . . ." He shook his head sadly, but I caught his smile.

We hung out for the rest of the night, eating Cheetos (the Trader Joe's kind, because maybe they paid their employees fair wages) and going back and forth between the soccer channel and HGTV. The next day, though, I put Jami to work finding tents, tables and chairs, and a caterer for Elton's party while I kept working on Parker's.

Most of the big details were taken care of, so the next item on my agenda was finding dresses for Hailey and me. She wouldn't let me buy a dress for her, and she was too little to fit into anything I already had, so that left consignment stores. I'd never bought a used dress before, so I was stoked when we both found designer dresses with tags still on them at a quarter of the price.

"I can't believe someone would spend this much on a dress and then never wear it!" Hailey said when she saw the original tag.

I hadn't really thought about that before. I probably had three or four dresses in my closet that I'd bought then changed my mind about and never returned. I had a lot more than three or four of other things I'd never worn that still had tags on. It wasn't the first time Hailey had reminded me how much I took for granted. She'd say something about never doing or having something, and suddenly I'd recognize how much I'd always had.

She did it again the night of the party. As soon as she saw Parker in his tuxedo, I thought she'd never stop talking about how good he looked. It's not that I'd never noticed he was good-looking, I just hadn't noticed how straight-up handsome he was until Hailey couldn't stop gushing about him.

"Seriously, he looks like he walked out of a movie or he's on his way to some award show. I'd marry him in that tux right now if he asked. No question," she whispered as he walked toward us.

I nodded and smiled and tried not to laugh out loud when she fanned herself, but she opened my eyes. The black jacket tapered at his waist, emphasized his shoulders, and his crisp white shirt highlighted his naturally tan skin, making his blue eyes look even darker. The memory of how close his lips had been to mine a few weeks before came rushing back, and my heart stopped.

I mean, not literally. But by the time he made it all the way to us, my palms were sweaty, my mouth was dry, and I couldn't think of anything to say to him. For the first time in my life, I had no words for Parker.

"You look beautiful," he said and craned his neck to give me a kiss on the cheek without touching me anywhere else. A disappointing development because all I wanted at that moment was to feel his arms around me. He gave Hailey a hug when he kissed her cheek, so I didn't understand why he hadn't done the same for me.

Then he did the same thing to Jami, who walked in behind us, except her hug was even longer. And I got that heavy feeling in my gut followed by a tightness in my chest that were becoming all too familiar every time I saw them together.

"Want me to get a table?" Hailey asked, and I nodded, regretting my decision as soon as she walked away because there was nothing to distract me from watching Jami and Parker.

Fortunately Blake walked in soon after Jami, and while he didn't look as devastatingly handsome (as they say) in his tux as Parker did in his, he looked good enough to distract me from the craziness going on in my stomach and my chest.

"What do you think those two are talking about?" Blake asked, leaning close enough for me to hear him over the guests talking and music playing, directing my attention to Jami and Parker, whose heads were inches apart. Their mouths moved and they were both smiling, but it was impossible to hear what they were saying.

I put my hand on his shoulder and whispered in his ear but kept my eyes on Parker. "I don't know. Should we have our own whispered conversation and try to make them jealous?"

Blake put his hand on the small of my back. "Let's." I liked the feel of his arm around me, but there was something missing . . . "Where do you think she got that dress?" Something warm . . . "It looks expensive."

"It is." I took my hand off his shoulder. "I can tell by the beading."

"Maybe she has"—he put on a French accent—"a mysterious benefactor." Then he added in his regular voice, "She couldn't have bought it herself."

Even as I laughed, I wondered if Parker would do something like that for Jami. He'd invited her, after all. He had to have known she wouldn't have a dress or the money to buy one.

I watched him rub her arm. Her bare arm, because of course the dress would be sleeveless. She giggled and covered her mouth. Why was it the only time she smiled was when she and Parker were together?

The better question was why did seeing them together bother me? That question took some self-examination I didn't want to undertake, and fortunately Taylor and Weston walked in before I had to. Blake shook his brother's hand, and they immediately started up their never-ending football conversation. Taylor left Weston's side to stand by me but did the exact opposite of take my mind off Parker and Jami.

"Those two are awfully chummy, aren't they?" she asked, wagging her head toward them.

"Yeah, I guess so."

A waiter came by with a tray of appetizers. I popped a crab puff into my mouth as an excuse not to say anything else. Taylor, however, was allergic to shellfish and had to occupy her mouth by continuing her train of thought.

"I don't know. You know him a lot better than I do, but I think he's into her."

My eyes couldn't help being drawn to them again. They were both looking at Parker's phone, scrolling through something as they stood side by side, arms nearly touching and heads tipped toward each other.

"Parker's not interested in anyone, especially not her." I narrowed my eyes, willing something—anything—to put some space between them. It didn't work.

"What's wrong with Jami? They're kind of cute." Taylor grabbed a crostini from another waiter passing by, picked the olive off, and stuck the cracker into her mouth.

"Nothing's wrong with her; she's just not Parker's type." I would have handed her the whole tray of appetizers if I'd thought eating them all would have kept her from talking about Jami and Parker. Since that wasn't an option, I headed to the bar.

"You know Parker's type?" Taylor asked, following me.

"I just know she's not it." I walked far enough ahead of her to make it impossible to hear anything else she had to say over the music. I asked the bartender for a sparkling water then found the table Hailey had saved for us. I should have told her not to take one in the corner, where I knew Parker wouldn't sit. He'd need to be in the middle of all his guests and wouldn't be able to sit by me.

Blake, Weston, and Taylor followed me, and Taylor took the seat next to mine, sipping her drink and staring at me until I finally met her gaze. "You know what I think?"

"Do I want to know?" I replied.

"Probably not, but I'm going to say it anyway. I think you're worried about losing Parker to someone else." She tipped her glass and rotated it in a circle.

"I can't lose something that's not mine. We're just friends." I pressed my hand to my breastbone to relieve the sudden tightness.

"And if he finds someone, he'll want to spend his time with her instead of you. He might even marry her. No wife is going to want her husband hanging out with the beautiful next-door neighbor, teasing her and answering her every call." She raised her eyebrows and squeezed her mouth into a tight line, daring me to contradict her.

I couldn't. In fact, I couldn't say anything. The pinching in my chest had turned to a painful squeezing. I'd been tiptoeing around examining my feelings, but Taylor had come in with a scalpel and laid them all bare. I had no other option but to examine them.

Once that started, it didn't take long for me to talk myself into a funk that lasted through dinner. It didn't help that Parker had Jami sit by him. Blake was in his own kind of sour mood, so he didn't even try to get me out of mine. We both poked at our food, occasionally saying something about the potatoes being too cold or the meat too done. They probably weren't. I just had a bad taste in my mouth.

"Where's Xander tonight?" Taylor asked Hailey, who sat on the other side of me.

"My friend Ashton is watching him," she answered, and I perked up again. I didn't know they were close enough for her to trust him alone with Xander.

"How's school going?" Taylor asked.

Hailey moved the chicken around on her plate before answering without looking at Taylor. "It's okay." She set her fork down and looked up. "I got all *C*s, so that's good."

Taylor gave me a look. She was the only person who knew that Hailey's "scholarship" was coming out of my pocket. And Hailey hadn't even mentioned her *D* in basic math. I thought with all the studying she'd done her grades would be higher than *C*s, but I was sure next semester would be easier for her. Hopefully.

"I need to use the bathroom." Hailey stood abruptly and bolted for the ladies' room.

"Do you think she's okay?" Taylor asked.

"I hope so." I watched her retreat and hoped it was the questions she was running from and not something worse. "I'll check on her in a minute."

"So, does she like school?" Taylor asked, and I was tempted to bolt to the bathroom too to avoid answering her.

Every time Hailey had to go to class, she got this sad look on her face. She'd never said she hated it, but she for sure didn't enjoy it. For a few weeks, I'd blamed her reluctance to go on being sad over Elton. But two months had passed, and nothing had changed. If anything, she disliked it more each day.

"I think she does." I faked a smile, but Taylor's stern look made me change my answer. "I don't know."

"Would she be happier doing something else? College isn't for everyone." Taylor prodded gently, forcing me to face questions of my own I'd been hiding from.

"Maybe. But she'll have so many more opportunities with a degree." I'd poured my heart into helping Hailey. If all my efforts didn't work, what would she do?

"Maybe." Taylor's noncommittal answer didn't help resolve any of the questions she'd forced me to confront. Things only got worse when she turned away from me, took a bite of potatoes off Weston's plate and then leaned in for him to kiss her.

Seeing them so in love was another reminder that I'd not only pushed Hailey toward college, but I'd also pushed her toward a guy who was totally wrong for her. That thought spiraled into another about my relationship with Taylor. We would always be best friends, but our relationship would never be the same. From there I spiraled even further down, into depressing thoughts about Parker.

Parker had filled the empty spaces Taylor had left, but if he got involved with someone, it would be even worse than losing Taylor to Weston. Taylor may not have had a lot of time for me anymore because of Weston, but at least he didn't feel threatened by me. I didn't know *any* woman, though, who would be okay with her husband having another woman as his best friend. There's no way Parker and I could stay as close as we were if he fell in love with someone.

His amplified voice brought me back to the present, putting a stop to my journey down the path of self-pity that could only end at Eliza, Old and Alone. He was on the makeshift stage, and I turned my chair around to face him.

"I had a special request from Eliza Woodhouse to include karaoke at this party tonight." He scanned the crowd, and I sank into my chair. My party mood had evaporated, along with any desire to karaoke. "She told me it wouldn't be a party without it. I'll take her word for it while I cheer her on. Eliza, come on up."

Light clapping and laughing was followed by an uneasy silence as I sank deeper into my chair, and Parker kept looking around the room for me.

"Eliza?" He said into the mic, color rising to his ears. Then, to my side came loud clapping and a cheer of, "Yeah, Eliza!"

I turned toward the cheering to see Blake standing with his hand out to help me out of my chair. Blake, who could always make me smile. Better yet, he could always make me laugh. Why was I worrying about Parker when I had someone else right in front of me willing to cheer me on instead of lecture me?

With Blake, I had nothing but fun. We lived in the moment, just the way I liked it.

I broke into a smile, mentally tucked away Parker and Jami, and took Blake's hand. Taylor and Weston joined in the cheering, and pretty soon the rest of the room joined in too. Blake walked me to the stage, and I waved to my adoring fans before taking the mic from Parker.

"What's it going to be?" he asked.

"'Last Christmas'. Obviously."

"Really?" One eyebrow went up. "'Wham'?"

I responded with my own eyebrow maneuver, and seconds later synthesizer sounds filled the air while Parker tried to make his escape.

"You're staying up here with me, right?" I said into the mic.

He shook his head and backed away from me despite the boos he got from the audience.

My cue came, and I belted out the first words to him before he could get off the stage.

Parker's guests cheered and laughed as I moved toward him, and he quickened his retreat. His lips fought a grin, but his cheeks were bright red. If the stage had been any longer, he would have broken into a run to get off it, but he reached the step before I could serenade more than the first few lines to him.

When the song ended, cheers erupted and calls for an encore put the final nail in the coffin of my bad mood. I loved to sing, I had a pretty decent voice, and there was a microphone in my hand.

"Okay, one more, but I need a partner." I glanced at a terrified Parker, who shook his head. I rolled my eyes. Like I'd choose him.

"Blake." I held the microphone toward him, and it took all of five seconds for him to join me on the stage.

"What are we singing?" I asked.

"'Baby, It's Cold Outside'," he answered with a strange smile on his face.

I didn't know it very well, but I found it on the list and started it. Once the words started scrolling, I understood the smile he'd given me.

"Wait a minute!" I shouted when I saw the questionable lyrics.

Blake kept singing the given lines, but to make the song less creepy, I threw in a line about #MeToo and then scurried away when the lines said something about scurrying.

Blake chased me then stopped and laughed. "I guess I'm singing both parts now," he said and finished the song while I bolted for my seat.

"You were right to run, Eliza," he said once it ended and I'd retreated back to my seat. "That song ain't right."

The crowd laughed, and he took a bow. "Do I get to choose my replacement up here?" The audience whooped their permission. I figured he'd choose Weston and Taylor, so his actual choice shocked me.

"Jami, come on up." He held the mic out, and all eyes followed until they landed on her. Even with the lights as low as they were, I could tell her cheeks were nearly the same color as her wine-red dress. She shook her head with a slight, horrified movement, but he kept the mic pointed in her direction.

Some of the less-sober guests began chanting her name, and Blake motioned them to chant louder. I almost felt sorry for her, but I also knew she had a beautiful voice. Nancy had told me on more than one occasion about Jami's performances in church choirs and other events. She may have been nervous, but her shy act could only go so far.

But when Parker leaned over and whispered something in her ear, which she responded to with a nod, I wished I hadn't joined in the chanting. He stood up and held out his arm. She slipped hers through it, and they walked to the stage.

Hailey returned from the bathroom and asked, "Are they a thing?" before sitting back down next to me. I didn't answer her, but the words *I hope not* trumpeted through my brain.

I swallowed hard as Parker deposited Jami next to Blake on stage but then stayed.

"Parker says he'll sing with me," she said into the mic. The smile on Blake's face disappeared, even as the crowd broke into a cheer.

"'Walking in a Winter Wonderland'?" she turned to Parker and asked. He nodded, and then they sang. Beautifully.

So beautifully they put Blake and me to shame. It was like following up a high school musical with an original cast performance of *Hamilton*. And they just got up and did it. They hadn't practiced beforehand; their harmonizing came naturally. Like they were meant to be together.

I clapped with everyone else as Parker and Jami walked off the stage hand in hand, but I didn't cheer. The thought of losing Parker had taken a step closer to becoming reality. I knew we would always be friends, but that didn't feel like enough anymore.

Chapter 18

I LEANED DOWN TO ADJUST the strap on my shoe, buying myself enough time to fight back the emotions trying to gnaw their way out of the corner where I'd carefully but unfairly kept them locked up. They were wrongfully convicted prisoners demanding to be set free, but I wasn't ready. Not there, not then. But with each passing second, I came closer to letting my guard down and letting my feelings out.

I picked up the clutch I'd set by my chair and stood at the same time Blake returned to our table. "I'd better get home to Daddy," I said to everyone.

Too many crazy thoughts were playing tag in my head. I kept picturing walking over to the apartment to watch an Angels game with Parker only to have Jami answer the door and tell me to go away. Or inviting Parker over for dinner and having him tell me he couldn't because he and Jami already had plans. Scenario after scenario popped into my mind, but they all ended in the same way: Parker choosing Jami over me.

"We can take Hailey home if you want," Taylor offered without even trying to convince me to stay longer, a clear sign that at least one person could see through my happy façade.

"Can I get a ride with you?" Blake asked. "I'm ready to go too." He popped out of his chair before I could answer. Even if the others had been ready to leave, I would have volunteered to take Blake. I needed some cheering up, and he was the guy to do it.

"Sure." I gathered my wrap in my arms, too hot to put it on. I knew what I had to do next, and it was going to be uncomfortable. "Let me say goodbye to Parker first."

I wanted to talk to him about as much as I wanted to see him and Jami up on stage again, but obviously I had to. My anger toward Parker made no sense. But it would make even less sense for me to sneak out without saying goodbye.

He and Jami were deep in conversation as I approached their table with Blake in tow. "You two were great up there." I bent down between them, talking loud enough they could hear me but not loud enough to interrupt the lady on stage.

"Are you leaving?" Parker asked.

I answered with a nod. "Daddy needs me. Your party was great."

"You deserve all the credit. Karaoke was an excellent idea." Parker held out his hand to shake Blake's, but Jami kept her eyes up front. I didn't know if she could hear us over the music, but she sure acted like she couldn't.

"No hard feelings?" Blake nudged Jami's arm. Until that moment it hadn't occurred to me he had to have known she could sing. Why else would he have called her up on stage?

Jami let her eyes drift to Blake long enough to shake her head and then focused back on the fifty-year-old Madonna wannabe. The shoulder she gave him was so cold it was full-on glacial. Global warming couldn't touch it.

Blake sucked in his lips then let them out like he wanted some words to follow them, but none came. When Jami didn't look at him, he walked away. I hugged Parker goodbye and then followed Blake, waiting until we were out of the room before I asked the question that had been bothering me.

"How did you know Jami could sing?"

"I heard her at school once. She was kind of a big deal there." He shrugged off the info he'd dropped like it wasn't mind-blowing, but he wouldn't look at me.

"Really?" If I hadn't seen Jami on stage fifteen minutes before, I would have never believed she was a star. A star in *Idaho*, but still . . .

"How big of a deal?" I asked. She definitely had stage presence, but lots of people had that. I'd even had someone tell me I did.

"I didn't know a guy on campus who didn't want to take her out after he saw her sing." He stuck his hands in his pockets and didn't offer any more info, including whether or not he was one of those guys.

We stepped into the cold night air heavy with the smell and feel of the Pacific. I handed my tag to the valet, and we waited in silence for him to bring my car around. I wondered if I'd made a mistake agreeing to take Blake home, but by the time the valet returned, so had Blake's smile.

"So, I've got a great idea," he said as he opened my door for me.

"What is it?" I slid into the car and then had to wait for his answer until he'd climbed in the passenger side and buckled his seatbelt.

"We're throwing a party." He clapped his hands and rubbed them together like a master plotter.

"We?" Generally, when people wanted to throw a party *with* me, that meant they wanted me to throw a party *for* them, for free.

"Okay, so mostly you," he confessed. "But I think you're going to want to do it."

"What kind of party, and who is it for?"

"A wedding party thing for Taylor and Weston." He beamed.

"I'm the wedding planner, so trust me, it will be a party. How many more parties do they need? " Despite my semi-protest I was already mulling over his idea, so I didn't sound very convincing.

"I know, but Taylor's mom is stressing her out about the whole destination-wedding thing." Blake didn't know me that well, but he knew exactly what to say to convince me of his idea. "She wants her friends to see Taylor get married, but they can't go to Hawaii. We'll have a party for them before they go."

"Like a pre-reception?" Any thoughts of telling him no disappeared. "That's a great idea." I couldn't believe I hadn't thought of it, and now that Parker's party was over and I had Jami helping me with Elton's, I had time to plan something for Taylor.

I was too excited to drive anywhere, so I pulled up ten feet out of the way of the valet. "We're planning this right now."

"Like, right now, now?"

"We only have six weeks." I reached across him to get my iPad out of the glove box.

"Whoa."

"What?" I sat back and turned on my tablet.

"Nothing." He snorted and shifted in his seat.

I set my iPad down and looked at him. "Tell me."

A smile stretched across his face. "I thought you were going to kiss me."

"Why did you think that?"

"I don't know. You were pretty excited, and then you leaned toward me—"

"I was getting my iPad!"

"I know that now!" He laughed. "You can't blame a guy for hoping though. Let's talk about something else. I'm embarrassed now."

I shook my head and turned my focus back to party planning.

Sort of . . .

He had hoped I would kiss him? It wasn't like the thought had never crossed my mind; it just hadn't at that moment. It was sure crossing it now though. I mentally calculated the last time I'd really been kissed. It nearly took an algebraic equation to figure it out, that's how long.

I scooted my seat back and turned to face him, fluttering my eyelashes. "I can't believe you thought of a pre-wedding party before I did. I'm impressed."

If Parker and Jami were kissing—if they hadn't before, they would be after tonight's performance—why shouldn't I kiss Blake? The correlation between the two was pretty shaky, but it made sense to me. Parker shouldn't be the only one kissing someone.

"Don't be too impressed," he answered and relaxed into his seat. "I overheard Taylor say her mom wanted to have a small reception here."

"I love Patty, but she'd go way overboard and make it more formal than Taylor would ever want it." I rested my arm on the console between us, in case he felt like holding my hand or something.

"You just repeated everything Taylor said almost word for word. That was eerie." He moved his arm, bumping mine in the process, and I thought for sure he'd reach for my hand, leading us to the first step of kissing time. Instead he apologized and turned on the radio. "Do you mind if we have some music?"

"Not at all." Music would set the mood.

Except maybe not the '80s rock channel he chose.

"Okay, let's plan this thing." He leaned his seat all the way back and put his hands behind his head. I didn't know if that was some kind of signal or if he just wanted to be more comfortable. I decided to play it safe and go with the second, even if he was in a perfect position for me to plant a kiss on his perfectly full lips.

Soon enough, however, I'd forgotten those lips and thrown myself into the thing I loved almost as much as flowers: planning a good party. We chose some dates to check with Taylor and Weston and threw around some ideas for food and venue. With the heat on in the car and the wet air outside, it didn't take long for the windows to steam up. In the back of my mind, I thought about how that might look to anyone passing by, especially because Blake had his seat down. But I brushed aside any concerns I had when he drew a tic-tac-toe board in the windshield and challenged me to a game.

"My only request is for dancing," he said and put an *O* in the bottom left-hand square. "We need a DJ and a dance floor. Nothing else matters."

"You don't think that will be too formal?" I put an *X* in the middle, but my mind focused on what kind of flowers would be best to use to keep everything from looking too fancy. "Taylor wants it casual. It can't feel like a formal reception."

"Make it a luau, and tell everyone to come in Hawaiian shirts. That will keep it *tooootally* casual," he offered then put an *O* in the bottom right-hand corner.

"Okay. That's actually a pretty good idea." I typed it into my iPad, waving off my irritation with him for coming up with all the good ideas. I made my next move and put an *X* in the top-middle box.

As soon as I did it, I realized my mistake. And what a dumb one. Blake put his *O* in the bottom middle square, and the game was over.

"You want to try again?" he asked, and his mouth curved into a grin as he traced a new grid onto the steamy window then laid back down in his seat.

I was ready to make my first move when a knock at the window made us both jump. We laughed when we saw it was Taylor and Weston, and I rolled down Blake's window.

"What's going on in here?" Taylor asked, her words more of an accusation than a question.

"Nothing!" My face prickled with heat despite the cold air that hit it.

"Uh huh." She looked between Blake and me, unconvinced.

"I swear! We've been planning your pre-wedding reception."

"It's true," Blake broke in. "I'll vouch for the fact that, though she was sorely tempted, Eliza behaved herself as a perfect lady and never laid a hand on me." Blake put his hand over his heart as proof of his honor.

"Too bad," Taylor said.

"What's a pre-wedding reception?" Weston asked at the same time Jami and Parker walked up with Hailey.

"I thought you left." Parker eyed me in the same way Taylor had but without any humor. Hailey's face broke into a sly grin that she followed with waggling eyebrows.

The moment Blake saw Jami, he bolted his seat upright so fast I thought it might launch him out the windshield.

"We started planning a party for Taylor and Weston and never made it out of the parking lot." I shrank from Parker's questioning look. I had to prove my innocence to him, and I didn't know why. "The party's not over, is it?"

"No. Jami's ready to go, so I'm walking her to her car." He waved his head at the car the valet had pulled up behind mine. I recognized it as the old company car Jami's grandpa had driven while he still worked for Daddy. It was so old, every time it started had to be counted as a miracle. "For being out of the party-planning business, you're spending a lot of time planning parties."

I laughed, even though he didn't. His sarcasm didn't override the happiness I felt that Jami was going home without him.

"Text me," I said to her. "Let's finish planning Elton's meet and greet."

She gave me a slight nod but didn't make eye contact with me or Blake before Parker led her to her car. I understood why she might be mad at Blake, but I didn't know why I deserved her cold shoulder too. The only reason I'd asked her to help me with the stupid meet-Elton's-girlfriend reception (the unofficial title we'd given the event) was to make Parker happy. If she was mad at me now, the whole thing would be even more unbearable.

Parker shut her car door and waved goodbye then walked back to us.

"See you later. Thanks for coming," he said then shoved his hands into his pockets and walked toward the club with his head down.

"You're really planning a party for us?" Taylor squealed.

"How does a luau sound?" I tried to match her enthusiasm, but I was still watching Parker.

"I love it!" More hooraying followed.

I leaned on the steering wheel so I could see around her dancing until Parker disappeared inside. "It was actually Blake's idea, but I should have thought of it a long time ago."

"You two are the best," she gushed. "Aren't they the best?" she asked Weston and Hailey over her shoulder.

"They are, but I'm freezing. Let's go." He took her by the hand and waved to us. Taylor blew me a kiss as Weston pulled her away.

"You have to let me help," Hailey said before she followed Taylor, waving goodbye and grinning with the same accusatory smile she'd had since she saw me with Blake.

"I guess I could ride with them instead of making you go out of your way." Blake opened his door and slid out before I could protest. "I'll talk to you tomorrow. We can figure everything out then." He slammed the door shut, gave me a wave, and hustled to catch up with the others.

I watched him go and with him any chance I had of being kissed that night. But somehow it was okay. I didn't have any feelings of regret. Maybe I should have since a part of me had hoped we would, but after Jami left without Parker, everything seemed a little brighter, even without a kiss.

Chapter 19

Blake had plenty of other chances to kiss me over the next week as we planned Taylor and Weston's party. Their wedding in Kauai was set for Valentine's Day, so we didn't have a lot of time to get the invites out. Plus, Blake was leaving for two weeks, which meant two days before Christmas, when I should have been finishing my shopping, we were sitting in my TV room trying to nail down party details before he left.

At least, one of us was trying. Blake's ideas went as far as suggesting we have the party. Beyond that, he wasn't very . . . how should I say it? Detail-oriented.

"We still need to choose the invites." I took my laptop off the coffee table and opened it, clicking on the website I'd been looking at earlier.

"I'm no good at that sort of thing. I'll leave the foofy stuff to you." He stood and stretched. "I'd better get back to Weston's and pack."

"Foofy?" I raised my eyebrows. "And why haven't you packed yet? Your plane leaves in . . ." I checked the time on my computer. "Four hours?! You'd better get on it!"

"It's just throwing clothes into a bag. It'll take about a minute."

I set my laptop beside me and followed him to the door, where he stopped with his hand on the knob. He faced me and opened his mouth, shut it, then opened it again, clutching the doorknob with the same intensity of a surfer riding out a choppy wave.

"There's something I've been meaning to ask you," he said finally. "Or tell you . . . or, I don't know . . ." He opened the door and stepped outside and then looked back at me. "You probably already have an idea of what it is, so maybe I'll wait till I get back."

"Okay . . . ?" I had no idea what he wanted to say to me, but he'd brought back to mind all the questions I'd had the night of Parker's party. *Was Blake into me? Did he want to kiss me?*

He stepped back inside, and I thought maybe I'd get a definitive answer when he wrapped me in a bear hug, but it fell somewhere between awkward and awesome and only increased my confusion. He released me then grasped my forearms. "I'll see you soon."

I thought maybe a kiss was coming, but no. He let go and jogged to his car, yelling, "Merry Christmas!" and waving before he pulled away from the curb. I tried to work up some disappointment that, once again, he hadn't kissed me, but within half an hour I was back to planning Taylor's party and had forgotten all about him.

The following day Caroline and Preston arrived from Arizona, where they'd spent a few days with his parents, and Parker came over for Christmas Eve. Between my shop and planning two parties, I'd barely spoken to Caroline over the past week and I hadn't seen or heard from Parker at all. In fact, I'd been so busy I could hardly keep my eyes open after we finished dinner.

We had a family tradition of watching *Scrooged* on Christmas Eve—Daddy preferred funny over sentimental and Bill Murray over Jimmy Stewart—so I put on my Christmas pj's—another family tradition—and curled up on the sofa to watch. Parker sat next to me, wearing the matching Christmas pj's Caroline had bought him and Preston and insisted, amid much protest, they wear.

"Tired?" he asked.

I nodded and forced my eyes back open. "I was slammed at work this week, and every spare minute I've had I spent with Blake trying to plan this luau."

I closed my eyes again, hoping he wouldn't ask about Hailey. Part of the reason I was so busy at work is because she hadn't shown up the past two days. Xander had a cold and she didn't want to take him outside even though I said I didn't mind her bringing him in.

In the end it may have been better that she hadn't come in. Having twice the work to do on my own was almost easier than having to fix her mistakes. It was definitely cheaper since I didn't have to throw out any ruined flowers. Hailey had been working for me for six months but still didn't have the hang of flower arranging or even managing orders while I was gone. I hoped she'd pick things up soon. I had more orders coming in every day, and I really needed someone who could run the shop while I was gone over Valentine's Day for Taylor's wedding, or I'd have to hire a contract florist.

I realized my thoughts had drifted to Hailey, and Parker hadn't said anything, so I opened my eyes again. He was staring at me with a look I couldn't figure out.

"Sounds busy," he said and shifted away from me.

The tightness in his jaw and my own exhaustion kept me from asking what was wrong. Obviously it was something I'd done, but I didn't have the energy to pull from him what it was. Instead I focused on the movie while my eyelids drifted shut. I forced them open again and again until I couldn't fight the heaviness anymore.

I woke up hours later to Parker covering me with a blanket.

"What time is it?" I mumbled.

"Late," he whispered. "Everyone else went to bed, but we couldn't wake you up."

I took a deep breath and prepared to sit up but snuggled into the fuzzy blanket instead. "I think I'll sleep here and wait for Santa."

Parker sniggered and then leaned down and planted a kiss on my forehead. "Merry Christmas, Eliza."

The smell of bacon and the sound of pans clanging roused me the next morning. I rolled off the couch and stumbled into the kitchen to find Preston making breakfast.

"Where's Caroline?" I asked.

"Still in bed. She's not feeling great," he answered while flipping the bacon. He didn't seem too concerned, but before I could ask any questions there was a knock at the door and Parker let himself in.

I'd never worried too much about how I looked in front of Parker, but I was suddenly very cognizant of the fact I was in pajamas, had no idea what my hair looked like, and without a doubt had stinky breath. I tried to escape to my bedroom, but there was no way I could get there without passing him.

"Good morning!" he chimed when he saw me.

"Merry Christmas," I replied and ran my fingers through my hair. They got stuck, which gave me a pretty good idea of the rat's-nesty condition of my curls. "What's in the bag?"

"Get dressed, and I'll show you," he ordered.

I lifted my chin and drew a bead on him. "What if I don't want to?" I really wanted to change out of my pj's and run a comb through my hair, but I also really didn't want to take orders from him.

He shrugged his shoulders. "I'll probably still show you."

I took two seconds to consider his reply before saying, "I'll be right back" and retreating to my room.

I passed Daddy on the way, gave him a hug, and wished him a merry Christmas. I paused outside Caroline's door and thought about checking on her but decided sleep might be the best thing for her. Then I caught a glimpse of myself in the hallway mirror and decided a shower was *definitely* the best thing for me.

By the time I showered, put on full makeup, and found something cute to wear—none of which was necessary for a small family gathering—everyone else was at the table eating, including my sister. I hugged her then sat next to Parker. I looked around the table at all the people I loved and had the same feeling I got when a peony was in perfect bloom. I knew it wouldn't last forever, but I was grateful I got to witness something so beautiful.

"Tell me what's in the bag now," I demanded of Parker as I put a Swedish pancake on my plate.

"Presents." He passed me the lingonberries before I asked for them. "Eat, and then I'll give you yours."

I thought about defying him again, but I was too hungry. Plus, I didn't want to take any chances he'd make me wait to open my gift.

As it was, he did make me wait, even after I gave him my gift. He passed out his presents to Daddy, Preston, and Caroline and let them open theirs first. He gave Daddy a cashmere lap blanket to keep him warm while he watched the sunset then gave Preston and Caroline a Chinese teapot that was mostly for Caroline, but Preston didn't seem to mind.

Finally he gave me mine. The other presents had been prettier on the outside, but mine was obviously hand-wrapped. The red paper was slightly wrinkled and bulged at the corners where he hadn't quite got them tight. A wide silver ribbon topped it, not quite a bow but close enough. I held it to my ear and shook it, but he grabbed my hand.

"It may not be in one piece anymore," he said, so I stopped and tore the bow and paper off to reveal a box with Chinese characters on the outside.

"You brought me something from Hong Kong?"

He answered with a quick nod.

I wasn't surprised he'd put so much forethought into my gift, especially after I'd seen how spot-on he'd been in choosing his gifts for Daddy and Caroline, but I was still touched.

I took the lid off the box and parted the tissue paper to reveal a vintage lightbulb with flowers painted on it. I pulled it out of the box by the ribbon attached at the top and let it spin in front of my face.

"You got me a Christmas ornament." The bulb had a white background with delicate red blossoms and bamboo shoots covering it.

"You still collect them, right?" He cleared his throat and picked a piece of lint off his pants.

"I love it!" I jumped up to hang the ornament on the tree, finding the perfect spot right in front. When I sat back down, I wrapped my arms around Parker and kissed his cheek. "Thank you."

"I wanted you to have a little piece of Hong Kong since you never made it over while I was there," he said, holding me a heartbeat longer than he needed to.

I pulled away. "I can still go."

He cocked his head to the side and considered my words. "I always thought traveling was more of a dream than a reality for you. Like when you were four and wanted to be a woodland fairy when you grew up."

"And now I play with flowers all day, so I guess maybe I know how to make my dreams come true." I jutted my chin at him then tucked it away again before he could say anything about my stubbornness.

"You've got me there." A slow, maddening smile spread across his face. But there was something different about it. It lacked his usual big-brother arrogance, and it did something to me that his smile had never done before. It gave me the same feeling I got riding a wave all the way in. A combination of anxiety and excitement with a sprinkle of pure contentment thrown in.

"I know I do." I put my chin out again and moved back to the arm of Daddy's chair.

"When you're ready to go, let me know," Parker said, his voice a white flag. "I'll tell you all the places you have to see."

I was ready to go now, but I didn't want Parker to tell me what places to see. I wanted him to show me. I wanted him to show me all the places I hadn't been. My world had always felt like a cozy blanket on a cold day, and I'd never wanted to leave. Now it was suffocating me. All I wanted to do was get out from under it. I wanted to see the shores of a different ocean, meet people who didn't know who I was, eat foods I'd never tried, do things I'd never done. And, suddenly, Parker seemed like the perfect person to go with me.

"You should go on a trip." Daddy patted my back. "I'd be okay without you. I'd worry, but I'd be okay. You shouldn't waste your whole youth taking care of an old man. I'm sure Caroline could do it for a few weeks while you see the world."

Daddy had never said anything like that before. I looked down at him. It's like he sensed my sudden claustrophobia, which left me feeling both grateful and guilty.

"Really?"

Before he could do more than nod, a heaving sound came from the other side of the room. I turned my head toward my sister just as she jumped off the couch with her hand over her mouth and ran to the bathroom. Seconds later the sounds of retching filled the air.

Preston stood and then took his time walking toward the sound of his wife's vomiting. "Are you okay, Hon?" he yelled down the hall. Caroline answered him with more retching.

"Should I go check on her?" I asked Parker.

"I don't know. Do you want to check on her?"

I shook my head as the sounds of barfing filled the air, followed by groans.

Ten minutes passed, and Preston came back into the room, supporting Caroline around her waist.

"Taking care of Daddy may be a little rough over the next few months," she mumbled but with a smile. "And after that I'll have someone else to take care of."

I was running to her before she even got the words "I'm pregnant" out of her mouth. I threw my arms around her neck and rocked back and forth, finally letting go when she threatened to puke again if I didn't stop trying to make her seasick.

Parker hugged Preston then Caroline, and Daddy sat in his chair clapping.

"Did you hear that?" I said to Parker. "We're going to have a nephew!"

"Or a niece. It could be a girl." He moved close like he was going to hug me.

"It's a boy. I can tell already," I said, hiding my disappointment when he didn't follow through on his hug. There was also the disappointment of my trip. That wasn't going to happen now.

But I was going to be an aunt, and Parker was going to be an uncle. We would be even more connected with a baby to spoil with love. I smiled at him and then directed my gaze at my ornament. He'd given us all perfect gifts, and I couldn't imagine a Christmas without him. He knew us so well. Knew us and loved us. It would be a hard day if Parker got married and couldn't spend as much time with Daddy and me.

I pushed that thought out of my head before it could ruin my perfect Christmas Day, but it was still there, waiting for the right time to shake up my perfect world.

Chapter 20

Caroline wasn't due for another seven months, which seemed like a lifetime. On the other hand, I wished I had to wait a lifetime for Erica and Elton's reception. Unfortunately it was fast approaching, and he hadn't stopped putting pressure on me to make it spectacular. Or, in his words, "a positive energy experience where everyone's auras will connect with hers."

Whatever that meant.

Choosing a flower that evoked "positive energy" was no easy task, especially in January. So I was pleasantly surprised when Jami came up with the perfect suggestion while we were planning all the details.

"What about chrysanthemums?" she asked as we scrolled through Pinterest for vegan recipes while we sat in my favorite coffee shop. "They're a happy flower."

"That's not a bad idea." The more I got to know Jami, the more I realized she rarely did have a bad idea. "They're cheap, easy to find, and even easier to arrange. I'm feeling more positive about this whole thing already."

Jami let out a laugh, the first one I'd ever heard in response to my snarky comments. And there had been a lot of those over the past few weeks as we'd planned. Especially when I'd given Elton the guest list for his approval—which I'd stacked with my friends—and the only name he'd crossed off was Hailey's. His excuse was that she'd probably feel uncomfortable. True, but he still could have invited her. I knew she would feel snubbed when she found out, and I would have to be the one to tell her.

"Sorry. I really need to quit saying rude things about Erica." I glanced at Jami, hoping she'd disagree, because I doubted I'd be able to stop. "She's probably not as bad as I think she's going to be."

"I don't know. She *is* vegan. Odds are you're right about her."

Now it was my turn to laugh. Jami continued to scroll through recipes but with a hint of a smile on her face. A comfortable silence fell between us—the first we'd ever shared—and I decided I liked her. I liked her, and I liked hanging out with her. Especially since Taylor cancelled our plans more often than not the closer we got to her wedding.

We were interrupted by a buzzing from Jami's phone. My eyes were involuntarily drawn to it laying on the table between us. It buzzed again, and Blake's name, picture, and number came up. She must have seen my surprise because she grabbed the phone and jumped up.

"I'm sorry, but I'd better take this." She pushed the Receive button but waited to say hello until she'd stepped out the door.

Obviously I watched her. How could I not watch her, with questions racing through my head about why Blake would call her? Was it a church thing? I knew they went to the same meetings every Sunday, so it had to be. He'd barely texted me since he'd been gone, and Jami got a phone call? That didn't seem right.

It also didn't seem right that I wasn't more upset about it. Definitely curious, but not upset. I'd missed hanging out with him, but not as much as I should have if I'd actually been into him. In fact, most days I had enough to do that I didn't have time to think about him.

It looked like Jami had been thinking a lot more about him than I had. I caught the hint of a grin when she'd answered, but she kept her back to the window she stood in front of. The call only lasted five minutes, and the blank look on her face didn't reveal anything when she came back inside.

"Sorry about that. Where were we?" She sat down, keeping her eyes focused on the hot chocolate in front of her, despite my hard stare. When she didn't offer up any info on her own, I resisted the temptation to dig for it.

"I'm not sure. Vegan menu, I think," I said slowly, with my eyes boring through her, still hoping to root out what I wanted to hear.

"Right. Vegan menu." She faked a smile. "Cardboard sandwiches with some kale on the side? Something like that?"

I blinked and let another few seconds pass before forcing my own smile and answering, "Something like that. Maybe we can do some research on our own and meet up again in a couple days."

"Yeah, let's do. Unless you can think of any other details we need to hammer out . . ." She trailed off and glanced at her phone. I could think of a million details I wanted to "hammer out" with her, but none of them involved Erica's party.

"No, I think we've got it. I'd better get back to work anyway." I stood and pushed in my chair. "Have I told you how much I appreciate you helping out with this thing when you don't even know either one of them? Which, by the way, you should be grateful for—the not knowing them, not my appreciating your help."

"I knew what you meant." She gave me a real smile. "And it's been fun. It reminds me of when we were kids and we used to play together." She slipped her purse over her shoulder and handed her cup to the waiter who'd come to wipe down our table.

"You remember that?" I figured she'd forgotten. It had been so long since we'd talked, let alone been friends, I was surprised she had any memories of me.

"Of course. You were nice to me when things weren't so good at home." She opened the door, and we walked out together.

I didn't recall being kind, but all of my memories of her were wrapped up with the nights I'd spent listening to Nancy rehearse over and over the long list of Jami's accomplishments. Maybe I'd always thought she was boring because I was so bored listening to everything about her rather than getting to know her. Maybe I actually liked her. In which case, Parker had been right and now had one more thing to gloat about.

"I'm glad you remember when we were kids," I said and pulled my wrap tighter even though it wasn't that cold. "I'm afraid I haven't been very nice since you've been back."

She lifted her shoulder slightly, not disagreeing with me but not agreeing either. "You gave me a job, and it's been fun planning this party with you."

We reached the door to my shop, and I didn't know whether to wave goodbye or go for a hug. She solved the problem by opening her arms and wrapping them loosely around me. Not quite a bestie squeeze, but definitely a friend hug.

We broke apart, and I waved goodbye. I watched her walk to her car and mulled over her call from Blake, wondering what was going on, searching deep for some reaction other than curiosity.

There was nothing. No hurting heart, no feeling of emptiness, no spilling of tears or any other romantic cliché I'd read about broken hearts.

"I guess he's just a friend." I shrugged then glanced side to side to see if anyone had seen me talking to myself. I stepped inside my shop and continued the conversation, but in my head this time. *Maybe this is why I don't have any interest in getting married. Maybe I'm incapable of love.* That didn't seem quite right either. The more I saw Caroline and Taylor with their "soulmates," the more I envied them. To be honest, part of me even envied Elton and Erica.

Now that Caroline was having a baby, I spent a lot of time wondering if being an aunt would be enough for me. Would I want kids someday? The more I pictured myself as a mom, the more I liked the idea. But no way would I do it alone. I'd seen how hard it was for Hailey.

An even bigger reason for my not wanting to ever be a single parent was my own experience. Most of the time I didn't miss my mom because I'd never known her, but every once in a while, I had an overwhelming feeling of emptiness. I couldn't figure out where it came from, but the thing that made it go away was looking at old pictures of Mom. If I ever had kids, I didn't want them to have that same aching for a parent they'd never know.

My thoughts about Blake and Jami and my own future were taking up so much of my attention I didn't even notice Parker behind the counter holding Xander.

"Hey." His voice brought me back to the present, and seeing him bouncing Xander up and down brought an involuntary smile to my face.

"Hey. What are you doing here?" I held out my arms for Xander, but he snuggled closer to Parker, burying his face in Parker's shoulder.

"He likes me better." A smug grin spread across Parker's face.

"Traitor." I patted Xander's back as I called him out for refusing me. I looked behind Parker to where Hailey was curled over her books, her face scrunched up with frustration.

"Homework?" I asked as I set my wrap and purse on the seat next to her.

"Yeah. Parker came to help." She glanced at him, and her face smoothed over.

"Oh . . . that was nice of you." I followed her gaze back to Parker. He hadn't come to see me. He'd come to help her with her math. I wasn't sure how I felt about that. But I felt something. Something like what I'd expected to feel when I saw Blake's number come up on Jami's phone.

"How was your meeting with Jami? Got everything planned?" Parker handed Xander back to Hailey and leaned over her shoulder to check her homework.

"What are you planning?" she asked.

I hadn't told her about Erica's party yet, and I'd hoped to put it off a little longer. Or not at all, since she hadn't been invited. I glared at Parker, who didn't take any notice of his screw-up.

"I've been trying to figure out how to tell you this." I took a deep breath. "Elton hired me to plan a reception thing for Erica."

Her face went white, and she clutched Xander tighter.

"I knew you wouldn't want to help me with it, so I hired Jami. I really don't want to do it, but he kind of suckered me into it." Words sped out of my mouth but not fast enough to keep her chin from quivering and her eyes turning watery. "I'm so sorry."

"It's fine." She sucked in her lips then shook her head violently enough to make Xander whimper. "I'm over him." She set her shoulders back and tossed her hair. "I'll go, and I'll act like there was never anything between us. I'll be fine."

I clamped my teeth together but then forced myself to say what I really didn't want to say. "You're not invited."

Her eyes grew to the size of sand dollars.

"I put you on the list, but he took you off," I hurried to explain. "I told him he should invite you, but he thought you'd be uncomfortable—"

"*I'd* be uncomfortable?" She rolled her eyes. Hard. "He's the one who pretended to be into me to get me to buy all of his crap." She marched to the back of the store and set Xander in his playpen. "I am so over him. What a—" She stopped herself. She knew my feelings about cursing in front of babies.

I breathed a sigh of relief and glanced at Parker, whose thoughts were so obvious he could have had "I told you so" tattooed to his forehead.

He kept it to himself, though, and directed his comments to Hailey instead. "You did pretty well on most of these," he said, pointing to her book. "I made some notes. Try them again, and I'll take another look tomorrow."

Tomorrow? How often were they getting together?

"I've got to run." He closed the pencil he'd been using inside her book.

"Thank you so much! I don't know what I'd do without you." Hailey held out her arms for a hug, and Parker hugged her. Parker wasn't a hugger. I mean, he hugged me, but he'd known me forever. He'd known Hailey for, like, a couple months.

"I'll see you later," he said to me, without a hug.

"Yeah. Come by for dinner if you want." It had been a while. I'd been so wrapped up in planning Erica's party and Taylor's reception, I hadn't really noticed. But now that I thought about it, I didn't think he'd been over since Christmas. Two weeks was a long time.

"I've got plans, but thanks." He opened the door and walked out, leaving me to wonder what kind of plans.

"He is so awesome," Hailey said once we couldn't see him through the front window anymore, although she kept staring like she might conjure him up again.

"You'll never believe what happened," I said to break her trance.

"What?" She tore her eyes from where Parker had been and looked at me.

"Guess who called Jami while we were having coffee."

"Who?"

Now I had her full attention.

"Blake."

"What?" Her brows went up into sharp peaks that nearly reached the top of her hairline. "You're kidding me!"

I shook my head and recounted the whole story. She listened and let out all the right exclamations at all the right places, and I was sure she wasn't still thinking about Parker. I just wished I wasn't either.

Chapter 21

The day of the dreaded party arrived, and, despite my best efforts—or really because of them—it was beautiful. Elton had insisted we have it on the beach. I didn't outright nix that idea, but I wasn't doing it either. Setting up tables and decorations in the sand sounded like about a thousand times more trouble than I was willing to go to for Elton. I opted for a park overlooking the beach.

Jami and I decorated the large white tent with the sprays of chrysanthemums and roses we'd made (I gave Hailey the day off, for obvious reasons). We kept it simple but elegant, and every guest who arrived complimented us on how pretty it looked. Every guest except for the guest of honor.

I hadn't met Erica before, but I could have picked her out of a crowd as Elton's fiancée. Her white bohemian skirt and khaki-green tank top with *Om-power-ment* emblazoned across her very artificially enhanced chest would have given her away even if she hadn't been holding his hand when she walked in.

Her eyes moved from one side of the tent to the other, and as they took in all of the details Jami and I had so carefully planned, she loosened her grip on Elton. I would have taken it as a sign she was feeling more comfortable if not for the way her mouth sank and her eyes narrowed. I imagined there would have been a vertical line between her eyebrows if not for the tell-tale signs of Botox on her plastic-smooth forehead.

"Do you like it?" Elton asked and reached for the hand she'd taken from him.

She ignored his reach, touched her lip, and then chewed on the tip of her manicured fingernail before she answered, "I do." She surveyed the tent with another quick glance. "I do like it . . . it's just different from what I pictured. I hoped we'd be right on the beach."

Elton shot me an accusing look.

"It's really hard to set up a tent this large or tables on the sand. They sink and aren't very stable," Jami answered with the words Elton should have said.

"You must be Eliza." Erica plastered a smile on her face and stuck out her hand to Jami.

She shook her head. "I'm Jami," she said then pointed toward me. "This is Eliza."

"Oh, you're Jami! Roshan told me about you! You are so sweet to do all this for me." She pulled Jami into an awkward hug, and Jami's eyes darted to mine, both of us too surprised to say anything.

Elton cleared his throat. "Eliza also helped."

Erica let go of Jami and looked at me before sticking out her hand. "It's so nice to meet you. Thank you for helping with everything."

"You're welcome," I said when I'd recovered from the shock of being slighted by someone I'd never met before. "Elton has been so excited to introduce you to our little community, we wanted to do something nice for you."

"It's darling. So different from anything I've seen done in L.A. Everything there is so over-the-top expensive. It's nice to have something so cute and homey." She squeezed her shoulders forward with the word *homey*. For a split-second I thought she was going to boop my nose too. "It looks like you found everything in your grandma's attic. So vintage," she said to me then turned to Elton. "I'm so glad you didn't go to a lot of expense. I know you could have, but I don't need anything ostentatious." Then back to me. "I'm all about finding fulfillment through my connections with people, not things. It's the thing people like the most about me."

Once she'd finished her decree and stopped waving her hands, she picked up a petit fours from the dessert table behind her. After a thorough inspection, she nibbled a corner. "Mmm. Homemade?"

"No, I ordered them from the French bakery in Newport," I said through gritted teeth. "It's been on the Food Network."

And was not cheap, I didn't add.

"Really?" She took another, smaller, bite. "They're almost as good as the petit fours from this little bakery in Santa Barbara I love. Do you remember that bakery, Roshan? The one featured on *Oprah*?"

"I do, Lovie," he answered. "That's why I asked Eliza to order your favorites from our little bakery. Of course, we don't have the same resources here that you've always had . . ."

I looked around to double-check I was still in Orange County. Elton talked like we were in the middle of Nowhere, North Dakota, instead of a county with a greater population and more money than entire states. We *had* resources.

"Oh, I know, Sweets." She patted his arm, and he smiled. "I'm really not into *stuff*," she said to Jami and me, her hand still on his arm. "So many of my friends are wrapped up in what kinds of cars they drive or clothes they wear." She brushed her arm through the air. "I've never been interested in any of that, so I'm perfectly happy being here with Roshan, growing his little business and living a simpler life."

Was it terrible to hate someone the first time I met her? Because I hated her. I'd never hated anyone, but I hated her. If Elton was shallow enough to pick someone like that over someone like Hailey, he deserved her. And his soul ran even shallower than I'd realized.

"I hope you'll be happy here." I forced a smile. "It looks like we're running low on the mini éclairs. I'll go get some more." I stepped around her, and she grabbed Jami by the hand, leading her away, exclaiming, "You are the cutest thing. We need you on our team. You're exactly the kind of person we've created Om-powerment for."

The tent was only ten by thirty feet, and the extra food was hidden under the tables directly behind Erica. It's not like I could escape anywhere far from her. But I would crawl under that table and stay hidden by the tablecloths if it meant avoiding her for the rest of the afternoon.

Fortunately she and Elton wandered far enough away that if I kept my back turned, I didn't have to face them again. I lifted the tablecloth and opened the cooler where the desserts were stored and took out a tray of them. I was transferring the éclairs to the platter on the table when I felt a hand on my back and heard someone whisper.

"What do you think of her?" Parker's breath tickled my ear, and its warmth sent shivers down my spine.

I leaned into his hand and whispered over my shoulder, "Do you want a polite answer or the truth?"

"I think we both know the truth." He reached around me, grabbed an éclair, and popped it into his mouth with a smile.

"She's awful!" I loud-whispered. "We talked for thirty seconds, and I loathe her. *Loooathe,* Parker! I don't loathe people. I love people. How can I loathe someone after only thirty seconds?"

"Because she's loathsome." He glanced at the table where Erica and Elton had Jami cornered, and I followed his gaze. Erica's hands were flying, her bracelets clanging, and even with thirty people squished into the tent, all talking, I could hear her say, "aura . . . positivity . . . red."

"Oh, she is not a red," I said.

"I have no idea what that means," Parker answered.

And then the room went quiet, but Erica didn't, and I heard her say, "There's too much negativity surrounding her. You need better friends." Jami glanced at me, and I knew exactly who Erica meant.

I turned around quickly. "Did she just accuse me of having too much negativity?" I asked Parker, not even trying to be quiet. *"Me?"*

"I think so." He attempted to hold back his smile. It didn't work. "Consider the source, and don't feel bad."

"Easy for you to say. There's nothing wrong with your aura." I brushed past him and stomped out the door—or opening. Or whatever it is you stomp out of in a tent.

I made it about three feet before running into Blake. Literally, I ran right into his chest.

"Blake!" I exclaimed before hugging him. "When did you get back?"

"A few hours ago." He glanced at the tent and back at me. "Where are you running off to?"

"Not to. From." I wagged my head in the direction I'd come from and caught a glimpse of Parker walking back inside. "I had to get away from there." Except suddenly I didn't want to run away. I watched Parker skirt around guests lingering near the dessert table then disappear into the crowd.

"I thought this was your party," Blake said, and I turned my attention back to him.

"It is. I guess. And Jami's."

"So, shouldn't you go back in?" He looked over my shoulder, zeroing in on something. Or someone. "Jami's still there."

I followed his gaze to where Parker stood next to Jami's chair, his hand on her back as she stood and said something to Elton and Erica before turning around and walking toward the dessert table with Parker. She stopped when she saw Blake and me, and I remembered I'd seen his name come up on her phone. I glanced at Blake, who stared at Jami.

The smile on Parker's face as Jami turned away from Blake's gaze and leaned in to whisper something in Parker's ear stirred up something in me. Maybe it was jealousy. I'd rarely had anything to be jealous of before, so I wasn't sure. I only knew I felt a sharp pain in the general vicinity of my heart.

"Well, I just wanted to stop by and tell you I was back." Blake's voice reminded me I wasn't alone. He stepped close, his chest out and a flirty smile playing at his lips. "We should do something tomorrow."

"You're going to leave me here alone?" I moved in closer, unable to resist some return flirting, ignoring the thought that flitted through my head about hoping Parker was watching.

His eyes roamed to the tent, and his smile momentarily faded before returning with his wandering eyes. "I think you can handle it."

Another step, and his hand was on my shoulder and running down my arm. "Surfing tomorrow?"

My heart skipped at the thought he might kiss me, because . . . *kissing*. But, once again, the moment passed without any lip-to-lip contact, and somehow my mouth didn't mind.

"Meet you there at seven?" I asked.

He nodded, and with one last glance at the party, turned and left. I watched him go, wanting to feel something more than appreciation for the nice view, but . . . nothing.

Chapter 22

After what seemed like years but was really only a few hours, the guests finally left. All except for Parker, who stayed to clean up, and the guests of honor who also stayed to "help," which in their case meant enlightening Jami through the power of *om* for the low, low cost of three thousand dollars or ninety-nine dollars per month over a period of thirty months.

"Poor Jami," I said to Parker as we folded chairs to stack on the rental truck. "Do you think she'll buy into it?"

"No. She's too smart." He took the chair I held and walked it to the truck, leaving me empty-handed but also empty inside. His comment stung. Did he remember I'd once been om-powered? Not only that but he'd shut down all my other attempts at conversation and would barely look at me.

"Hey!" I said when he came back inside, determined to give it another go. "Do you want to go surfing tomorrow? The wave report looks good . . . better than good."

He stopped folding the chair he'd grabbed and looked at me. "Who else is going?" His eyes bored into me, and I felt my cheeks flush.

"Well . . ." I swallowed. I'd forgotten I already had surf plans with Blake. "Blake's going too."

He answered by squinting his eyes then dropping the chair and picking up another to fold. "Sounds great. I'll invite Jami too. She was just saying she wants to give it another try." He slammed the chair closed, picked up the one he'd dropped, and brushed past me toward the truck.

A double date with Parker and Jami wasn't exactly what I'd had in mind when I'd invited him, but I couldn't back out of it now.

I could, however, invite Hailey to come along. Jami liked babies. Maybe she'd be motivated to sit on the beach with Xander again, especially when she saw the size the waves were predicted to be. I'd put Hailey in charge of teaching Blake how to master real waves, and maybe I'd get a little alone time with Parker to figure out why he was avoiding me.

The five of us met on the beach the next morning. Hailey's car was in the shop again, so I picked her up, noticing right away her mascara. Not just the mascara but also how her hair was pulled back in a cute twisty braid thing that looked a little too fancy for the waves. She was trying to impress someone. Parker was way too old for her—and so not her type—so it had to be Blake.

That's when it hit me that Blake would be perfect for her. He was fun, he liked Xander, he had a college degree, he had a job—or at least he would have one soon . . . Probably.

He'd be perfect for her.

"Those waves look bigger than last time." Jami interrupted my thoughts, worry emanating from her voice and her face.

"They are pretty big." I answered then let a smile spread over my face. Jami had given me a perfect way to get Hailey and Blake out into the water. "Why don't you and I watch Xander while Hailey shows Blake how to conquer those waves."

"I don't think I'm man enough for those beasts." Blake shot down my idea and held his arms out for Xander at the same time. "I'll stay here with Jami. You pros can show us how it's done."

I expected Hailey to protest. Instead she handed Xander off to Blake with a thanks and grabbed the board she'd stuck in the sand. "Let's go, Parker!"

She ran toward the ocean with her tiny little body in her tiny little wetsuit. Her hair came loose and bounced up and down. She glanced and waved Parker to join her, and I swear she looked like she'd run right off the pages of a *Hollister* catalog.

"Do you see your mommy?" Blake cooed to Xander. Which meant he was watching Hailey. "Wave to her," he added and moved Xander's arm up and down. He was so good with him. And Hailey was comfortable leaving him with Blake. They were definitely perfect for each other, and I couldn't believe I hadn't thought of it before. My matchmaking skills were rusty. But at least they were still intact.

"You coming?" Parker asked me and gave his wetsuit zipper a tug before heading toward the water.

"Of course." I zipped my wetsuit and picked up my board then hustled to catch up with him.

"Is she going to be okay out there?" he asked when I caught up. The water licked our toes, but Hailey was already sitting up on her board waiting for us.

"Why wouldn't she be? She knows how to surf." I waved to her then jumped on my board, noticing for the first time the patches of murky water indicating riptides.

"The water's pretty rough. Be careful." Parker paddled past me toward Hailey.

I paddled harder but didn't get to them before they caught their first wave—a big one I had to duck dive under. I came up from it in time to see Hailey get rolled at the tail end of her wave. Her board popped up before she did, and I could see she'd lost it. I remembered the leash was shot on the board she'd borrowed from me, but I also knew she could swim. At least, I thought I knew she could.

I checked the water behind me. A swell was coming, and I could either paddle and take the wave, or it would take me. But I was too late. I got raked over. By the time I popped out of the water and got on my board, I expected to see Hailey back on hers.

Instead her board was headed toward shore, and Hailey was waving her arms and being pulled in the opposite direction. That's when I knew she'd been caught in a riptide. Riptides aren't that big of a deal for people who know what to do in them. It's basic. Stay calm and float parallel to the shore until you can swim out. People only drown when they waste energy waving their arms and trying to swim out of the riptide. Hailey should have known better, but she was doing exactly what she shouldn't.

I paddled toward her, knowing I probably couldn't reach her before things got really bad. Parker would have to do it, but I didn't see him anywhere.

"Are you okay?" Parker called, and I looked to my right to see him paddling toward me instead of Hailey.

"I'm fine!" I yelled back and pointed to Hailey. "Hailey's not!"

He looked in Hailey's direction then paddled hard. I joined him but stopped when, out of the corner of my eye, I saw something black darting toward the water.

It was Blake. "Darting" may be too generous a description when it comes to running in a too-tight wetsuit, but even with his awkward run that should have been a dive into the water, I could tell he'd be able to get to Hailey before we would.

Parker saw it too and sat up on his board. He cupped his hands around his mouth and shouted to Hailey, "Stay calm! Swim with it!"

Her head dipped momentarily under the water, and Parker let out a curse as Blake swam straight for the riptide. "We're going to have to rescue them both!" He dropped back to his board and paddled so fast there was no way I could keep up with him.

As it turned out, I didn't need to because Hailey figured out what she needed to do even before Blake reached her. Maybe it was Parker's yelling or maybe it was seeing Blake swimming toward her, but she finally calmed down and swam with the current instead of fighting against it until she was able to get out of the rip and swim for shore. In fact, it was her warning that kept Blake from swimming directly into it.

He turned back once he saw she was safe and then met her in the knee-deep water where he wrapped his arms around her waist to help her the final few feet to shore. She laid her head against his chest until they made it to Parker, who had paddled in. They both helped her to our spot on the beach, where she unzipped her wetsuit and rolled it to her waist before collapsing on the sand.

By the time I joined the group, Jami had a towel and her arm wrapped around Hailey, with Blake sitting next to her wrapped in his own towel. Parker stood behind them, bouncing Xander, trying to get him to stop crying. He kept reaching for his mom, who sat cross-legged with her head bent forward and her hair hanging in long, wet tendrils in front of her face. Her back moved up and down in slow arcs with each breath she took.

I squatted in front of her and tucked her wet hair behind her ear. "Are you okay? You scared me to death!"

"I scared myself." She took a deep breath and blew it out before lifting her head to look at me. "I panicked and forgot what to do. I'm so dumb."

"Stop that!" I squeezed her arm and then plopped down cross-legged in front of her so our legs touched, and I could put my hands on her knees. "Anyone could make the same mistake. I'm just glad Blake was there to help you."

"I know. Me too," she said, glancing at him with a shy smile. "And Parker too. I never would have remembered what to do without him."

She popped up, fully recovered from her ordeal, and took Xander from Parker. "Thank you so much. For everything." She gave him a warm smile and squeezed her squirming baby close to her chest.

"You were so amazing!" I said to Blake, thinking maybe Hailey hadn't seen what he'd done for her. "Did you see him swimming straight into the riptide to help you? He didn't hesitate—"

"Yeah, talk about dumb," Blake interjected. "I didn't realize it was there. Someone would've had to rescue me too."

"That's what makes it even more courageous, right, Hailey?" I nudged her, and she stopped kissing the top of Xander's head. "You were willing to risk your life without even thinking about it." I nudged Hailey again because she'd gone back to kissing Xander. How many kisses did he really need?

"Yeah, totally," she answered then held Xander's naked belly up to her mouth and blew a raspberry on it. He squealed with laughter, so she did it again, and suddenly everyone's attention was on the giggling baby instead of where it should have been: encouraging the budding romance between Blake and Hailey.

"It's getting late," Parker said and cleared his throat. Hailey paused mid-raspberry, and everyone turned toward Parker who cleared his throat again. "I'm going to hit a few more waves before I head home."

"I'll go with you if you want," I said and stood. A little alone time on the water with Parker would make for a pretty perfect morning.

"Do whatever you want." His answer felt like the time I'd gotten stung by a jellyfish. Only worse.

"I'd love to give it another go too," Hailey said and handed Xander to a surprised Jami, who barely had enough time to stick her arms out before the baby was dropped in them.

"I actually need to head home." Jami passed Xander to Blake and then stood and brushed the sand off her butt. "I've got a bunch of job applications to fill out."

"I'd better go too." Blake swung Xander into the crook of his arm and pushed himself up. "Are the jobs around here?" he asked Jami, who shook her head.

"I need you to open the store at ten," I said to Hailey. "I don't think you'll have enough time to go out again. Maybe Blake could give you a ride home." I dug through my bag and handed her the fob to my car. "Hide this under the wheel after you get Xander's seat out."

A fast-moving cloud passed by the sun, casting a shadow over all of us. At least, I think that's why Hailey's face looked the way it did. Blake interrupted before she could answer.

"I smell poop." Blake held Xander out to Hailey and turned his face away from the odor of rotten eggs that filled the air as the sun peeked through the clouds again. "I'm happy to give you a ride once that's taken care of."

"Okay." Hailey took her baby back, but there were no kisses or raspberries. Not even a smile. Just a slow dig through her beach bag until she found the diaper and wipey things she needed.

"Ready?" I asked Parker. His eyes narrowed in an unasked question. Or maybe it was an unspoken lecture. Whatever it was, he kept it to himself and only gave me a small nod, which somehow filled me with more guilt than his words ever had.

"I'll see you in a little bit," I said to Hailey and reached down to lightly piano-tap her shoulder.

She nodded and smiled. "I'll have the shop ready." Despite the smile, her voice came out high and tight.

"Okay. Thanks." I waved goodbye to Blake and Jami and expected to see Parker behind me, but he was already in the water.

I grabbed my board and ran to catch up with him, but he didn't wait.

Chapter 23

I DIDN'T CATCH PARKER UNTIL he got to the lineup. In the time it'd taken to rescue Hailey and make sure she was okay, a dozen other surfers had shown up. We'd be waiting a while for our turns to catch a wave. Which was fine. I'd paddled hard to reach him, and I needed a few minutes to catch my breath before I'd be ready to take on the larger-than-usual waves T-Street was spitting out that day.

"This will have to be my last," Parker said after I sat up on my board. "Too much of a lineup now."

"Wave period's pretty short though." I was hoping for a little more time with him than the quick waves were going to allow. A couple of surfers in front of us had already dropped and were riding a pretty sweet wave. "I bet we could get one more in."

"Some of us have to work for a living. We can't hire people to do our jobs for us." He squinted at the sun, and I winced.

"You think it's a bad thing I hired a single mom who needs a job?" I pushed back the lump rising in my throat. All I'd wanted to do was spend time with him, and now he was being mean to me. It was bad enough Taylor kept ditching me for Weston. If Parker didn't want to hang out with me anymore, Hailey and Jami would be the only friends I had left, and who knew how long Jami would be here.

"I think you could have watched Xander to give Hailey some time out here," Parker answered in a gentler tone. "You can surf any time you want. How often does she get a chance?"

I thought that over. He was right, but it didn't make me any less hurt by what he'd said. And then another thought hit me, and it was even more right than what he'd said, "You know, you could have offered to do the same thing." I raised my eyebrows while his mouth fell open with the weight of an answer he didn't have. Seconds passed, and I waited for him to reply, but then my board dipped. I looked over my shoulder to see what kind of swell was coming. A good one. And I was going to break every surfing etiquette rule in the book and snake it from Parker.

I dropped to my belly, paddled to the crest of the wave, and popped up. I rode frontside, running my fingers through the wave and forgetting about Parker, Hailey, and everything else that didn't have to do with that moment. That's what I loved about surfing. It took all my focus, leaving no room in my head for the stupid things people said.

When I hit the flats, I tried to cutback in order to catch more of the wave, but I had to bail to avoid a total wipeout. I let the rest of the wave go over me before I popped out of the water to see where Parker was. I spotted him riding with his back against the inside of a wave. He rode goofy-footed, so he was always easy to spot. When he got to the end, he kicked out of the wave, making a much more graceful exit than I had.

I hoped he'd change his mind and paddle back out, but when he hit knee-deep water, he picked up his board and headed to shore. I debated whether to follow or catch another wave. I'd burned him pretty bad, though, by snaking his wave, and with things already being rocky between us, I decided I'd better apologize.

"That was a pretty nice ride," I said when I got to the spot on the beach where he was drying off.

"Not as good a wave as yours." His eyebrows moved just enough to let me know he wasn't happy about me burning him but he also wasn't mad about it. "Too bad you couldn't take the whole thing."

"I always do." I grinned. "Even when I don't."

"That makes no sense." He peeled his wetsuit down to his waist, and I enjoyed watching every second of it—even though I probably shouldn't have.

"It makes total sense." I unzipped my suit and stuck my hand out for him to hold the sleeve while I tugged my arm out of it. "You've got to find a way to enjoy every moment, even when that moment isn't what you wanted." I held out my other arm and he grabbed the other sleeve. "I rode as much of that wave as I needed to. I'm not going to waste time thinking about how it could have been better."

He let out a laugh. "I guess that's one way to get everything you want." He pulled his board out of the sand and tucked it under his arm. "Maybe that's why things always come easily for you."

I blinked as I processed what he'd said. "You think things come easy for me? Like I don't ever work hard for anything?"

"It's not that you don't *want* to work hard. You don't ever *have* to." He slung his towel over his shoulder and headed for the stairs.

I thought about how much I'd studied to get into San Diego State. Sure, it wasn't Stanford like him or UCLA like Caroline, but if I'd wanted to take harder classes in high school, I could have gone to those schools too . . . probably.

So maybe that wasn't the best example. But I had a better one.

"What about my shop?" I grabbed my board and followed him. "That hasn't been easy. How many twenty-four-year-olds do you know who have their own business?"

He slowed down enough for me to walk next to him and looked at me. "About as many as I know who have fathers willing to bankroll them."

I stopped. "Why are you being so mean to me? Did I do something to you?"

He stopped too, with a look of genuine surprise on his face. "I'm not trying to be mean, Liza—"

"Then what are you trying to do? Everything you've said to me today has been some kind of criticism." Wind stung my eyes, but that's not why they watered.

"Look, don't cry—"

"I'm not crying!" I wiped my eyes with the end of the towel he held out to me. "I have sand in my eyes."

I let go of the towel and walked around him.

"Eliza, I didn't mean to be rude." He ran ahead of me and blocked the path. "I'm sorry. And you're right. I could have offered to watch Xander so Hailey could surf. It was really sexist of me to think you should be the one to do it."

I met his gaze and let my lips pull into a tight smile. "It was really sexist. You're showing your age, Old Man."

"Now who's being mean?" A grin spread across his face. He stuck his board in the sand and took mine to plant next to it. Then he pulled the towel off his shoulder and laid it on the sand before dropping to the ground and taking my hand to pull me down. "Sit down for a second."

I dropped down next to him, and he let go of my hand. "Think about your life for a minute compared to Hailey's." He took a breath. "Do you know why she was in foster care?"

I blinked and shrugged. Taylor had told me enough to know Hailey's life had been rough, but I'd never asked Hailey for details. "Do you?" I asked, not sure I wanted the answer.

He shook his head. "I know how bad things have to be for a parent to lose custody though."

"Yeah . . . so are you saying I should ask her?" I scooped out the sand trapped between my toes and kept my eyes pointed at my feet.

"No." He took a deep breath. "What I'm saying is . . ." He touched my hand. "Be careful about making her a project. She doesn't need someone to run her life. She needs a friend she can rely on. Someone she can trust, who won't hurt her."

Heat crept up my neck. Maybe from Parker's touch but mostly from embarrassment. Had I treated Hailey like a project? Someone for me to fix?

"All I wanted to do was help a girl who wouldn't be able to go to college on her own." I pulled my knees up to my chest and wrapped my arms around them.

Parker moved like he was going to touch me again but then rested his hand behind me and leaned back. "I'm not saying giving her a job and encouragement isn't generous, but even with financial aid, anything beyond community college is going to cost her more than she can afford. She'll have to take out loans for living expenses, and she may never have a job where she'll earn enough to pay them back. Not everyone is cut out for college. After helping her with basic math, I think she may be one of those people."

I whipped around to face him. "First of all, she doesn't need financial aid or loans. Second, how is my believing in her worse than you basically saying she's too dumb to go to college?"

Parker sat up. "I didn't say she was too dumb. Don't put words in my mouth."

"You said she's not cut out for college."

"Plenty of smart people don't go to college," he shot back. "There are a lot of trade schools she might be better suited for, not because she's dumb but because she's got a huge educational deficit to overcome."

"How do you know what she's got to overcome?"

"Because I've listened to her. Do you know how many high schools she went to?"

He didn't wait for me to answer. Not that I could have anyway. "Ten. In four years. That's just high schools. How many middle and elementary schools do you think she went to?"

I had no idea, which made heat creep back up my neck and settle into my cheeks. They felt hotter than the time I'd thought I didn't need sunscreen on a cloudy day and I got more burned than I'd ever been before.

"She didn't have the opportunities you did that made college easy for you." He'd taken a gentler tone, but there was still a hardness in his voice. "Why not encourage her to do something she can be successful at?"

"That's what I'm doing!" I jumped up. I didn't know what else to do. I only knew I needed to be able to look down on him instead of the other way around. "I'm paying for her college so she can have her own nail business someday. She wanted to just work in a nail shop. I got her thinking about owning her own business instead of making money for someone else."

"You're paying for her college?" Parker asked as he pushed himself up from the ground. So much for me looking down on him. And so much for me keeping my "scholarship" fund secret.

"Yes." I tilted my head up to look him in the eye.

"Is that why the shop's not making money?" His brow wrinkled, and his gaze penetrated through me.

I nodded.

He pulled me back from the path as three surfers walked by us. Once they'd passed, Parker spoke. "Does she know?"

I shook my head. "I wrote a check from the charitable organization I set up to pay her tuition." Not that it was any of his business, but I'd already spilled my secret, so there was no reason not to tell him everything.

"Why?"

"Xander." I shrugged. "She needs a way to take care of him."

"That's really generous." He laid his hand on my shoulder. "You're very generous."

"Thanks." I smiled, thinking I'd won him over, but with Parker there was always more.

"But are you sure you're not giving someone a pair of shoes when what she really needs is food?" He let his hand drop, and his eyes pored with meaning I didn't understand.

"I don't know what you're talking about." With each word I lost confidence I'd won our argument. Or debate. Or whatever it was. "Why would I give her my shoes? Her feet are smaller than mine."

"It's an analogy." He picked up my board and handed it to me then grabbed his own before wagging his head toward the stairs. "Remember those trendy shoes everyone bought because the maker donated a pair to kids in need for every pair bought?"

"Toms?" I hoisted my board higher, securing it under my armpit, and followed him.

"Yeah." He nodded. "You probably had a closetful."

"Have." I'd possibly provided shoes for half of sub-Saharan Africa.

"A reporter went with him for one of his deliveries." He stepped aside and let by a couple coming down the stairs. "Know what she saw?"

"A guy passing out shoes to kids who needed them?" I started up the cement steps first.

"A guy passing out shoes to hungry kids who were wearing brand-new Converse." His voice echoed against the metal caging surrounding the staircase, reminding me of the preacher with a wireless mic and a primo sound system at the megachurch I'd gone to once. The loudness of the message had made the whole thing seem impersonal to me.

"What's your point?" I glanced over my shoulder at him. "They didn't need two pairs of shoes?"

"My point is they didn't need what Tom, or whatever his name is, thought they needed, but he was hailed as this great philanthropist by all the people buying his shoes who thought people who'd never worn shoes would need footwear more than they needed food."

"People need shoes."

He stopped at the top of the stairs next to me. "People only need three things: food, shelter, and—"

"Love?" I don't know why that popped out. It sounded right in my head, but once my ears heard it, I knew it was wrong.

He stared at me, tilting his head in a question. "Clothing . . ."

"Oh, yeah." My ears burned. "That's what I meant."

"Sure." He nodded like he believed me but kept staring like he had mind-reading powers he was secretly using on me.

I hoped he didn't because I *really* didn't want him to know I was thinking about those blue eyes flecked with gold. My face grew hotter just thinking about anyone, especially Parker, knowing how those eyes broke down my defenses. If anyone else had talked to me the way Parker had—and did—I would have pushed him down and kicked sand in his face. Parker made me stop and think about whether I could do better. Whether I could *be* better.

I readjusted my board and stepped in front of him. "What does any of this have to do with Hailey?" I asked as I walked ahead of him.

In two quick steps he was by my side. "If you want to give her something, give her what she needs, not what you think she needs. Otherwise she's your project, not your friend."

He tossed me that grenade like we were playing a game of touch football and not talking about saving a young mom and her son from a life of poverty. Every good thing I thought I'd been doing for Hailey exploded in my face.

I'd tried so hard not to treat her like a project, but maybe I had. Maybe I'd needed something to do without Taylor and Caroline around. I thought back through the past six months with Hailey. I'd helped her get into school, I'd taken care of Xander when she needed someone, I'd encouraged her to find the kind of guy who deserved her. Those were all good things. Right? And maybe she had been a kind of project, but was it so bad to make someone a project if they came out better in the end? Wasn't that a kind of friendship?

Parker walked ahead of me while I thought through the questions tornadoing through my brain. He glanced back once and asked if I was coming. I shook my head.

"Go ahead." I told him. "I'm wiped out." Which wasn't a lie, but his words and the chain reaction they'd caused, not the ocean, were the cause of my exhaustion.

Luckily once I got in my car I could have driven home blindfolded because I didn't pay attention to anything around me. The only thing I could focus on was Parker and everything he'd said about my relationship with Hailey. I finally landed on the one question I had to find an answer to: Did I want a friend, or did I want a project? Because Hailey couldn't be both.

Chapter 24

The answer should have been easy, but by the time I put my board away, stripped out of my wetsuit, and wrapped up in a towel, I still hadn't come up with one. I climbed the stairs to find Daddy right where I knew he would be, sitting at the kitchen table with the *Los Angeles Times*, toast, and oatmeal laid out in front of him.

"There's my girl," he said and held out his cheek for a kiss. "How was the surfing? The wave report said they were big. I was worried."

I put my arms around his neck and kissed his cheek. "You worry too much. I can handle the waves."

"You can handle anything," he said.

"Hmm. I'm glad you think so." I broke away and handed him the business section he pointed to.

"I know so." He put his glasses on and spread the paper open, ready for his morning routine: sip of coffee, bite of toast, spoonful of oatmeal, check the headlines, starting with the business section. He liked his mornings predictable and quiet, but I needed his advice.

"Daddy, what do you think makes a good friend?" I asked as I walked into the kitchen to make my breakfast. I could always count on my dad to build me back up when I was feeling down about myself.

He set the paper down and took off his glasses. "Hmm. I suppose a good friend is someone who shares the same interests you do and someone you can rely on." He put his glasses back on and picked up the paper. "That's an interesting question. What's prompting it?"

"I don't know." Not entirely true, but his answer hadn't really done what it was supposed to. Now all I could think of was how few things Hailey and I had in common. And she could for sure rely on me, but did I consider her someone I'd call if I needed something?

I opened the fridge and pulled out all the fixings I needed for a smoothie. Then I got to the kale and changed my mind, opting for something that would cheer me up. All the healthy stuff went back in the fridge, and I grabbed the milk instead. I hip-bumped the fridge door shut and got my Lucky Charms out of the pantry. Grabbing a bowl and spoon, I carried everything to the table and sat down next to Daddy.

By this point he'd forgotten about my question and was engrossed in his paper. The problem was, I still didn't feel any better.

"Parker said something that made me think maybe I haven't been a very good friend to Hailey," I blurted. I had to say something to really get his attention. "I guess that's what made me ask the question."

"Parker hurt your feelings?" The paper went down again. Daddy looked like he'd been slapped. He may have thought I could do no wrong, but Parker walked on water. "What did he say?"

"It's not that he hurt my feelings, he just said some things that made me think I could be a better friend to Hailey." I patted his hand then filled my bowl.

"How could you possibly be a better friend to her?" His voice registered as much shock as his face had. "You've taken a girl who had no prospects in life, given her a job, helped her with her baby, encouraged her to go to college, invited her for dinner . . . What more could you do for a girl in her circumstances?"

"I don't know, Daddy." I blinked and stared into my bowl. He made Hailey sound an awful lot like a project. "Maybe I should treat her like someone I can rely on instead of like someone who can't take care of herself."

The marshmallows floating in my already discolored milk didn't seem so appetizing anymore. I pushed the bowl away, no longer hungry but more than ready for a hot shower and some beats to drown out the voices in my head.

Neither one worked, but listening to all the voices actually helped me work some things out. But it also meant I got to the shop later than I'd planned. Promptness may not have been high on my list of personality traits, but usually when it came to work I could make it on time. Not today. Not when I had a long list of apologies and making up to do with Hailey.

When I finally walked in, I was relieved to see her with a customer. As much as I wanted to get "the talk" I needed to have with her over with, I was grateful for the few extra minutes.

I shut the door behind me and flipped the sign from Closed to Open. I guessed she'd forgotten to do that. Again. Any other day I would have been annoyed, but not that one. The voice of the customer sounded familiar, and judging by the conversation going on between them, she definitely knew him.

He leaned over the counter on one arm with the sleeve of his dark-blue work shirt rolled up to his shoulder.

"It looks good," Hailey said, rubbing her hand over his bicep. "Oh, hey, Eliza!" she said and jumped back from the customer. "You remember Ashton?"

He turned around, smiled, and stuck his hand out. "Good to see you again."

"He was showing me the tattoo he just got." Hailey's voice bounced nervously as I shook Ashton's hand.

"Oh, that's nice." *And weird. He just popped in to show off a new tat? Like he doesn't have an armful already?* I moved my head half a millimeter to shake loose the negative thoughts. If Hailey liked this guy, I needed to be supportive. He wasn't Blake, but maybe Blake was more my pick than hers.

"Can I see it?" I plastered on a pageant-winning smile and looked at the spot Hailey had been ogling minutes before.

Ashton turned his arm toward me and whipped up his sleeve to show off a molar with a nail sticking out of the top of it that covered his whole bicep. His face beamed with pride.

"That's nice work." I'd heard other people say that about tattoos. I hoped it was the right thing to say then because I had no idea why someone other than a dentist would get a giant tooth permanently inked onto his arm.

He looked at it and lovingly rubbed his hand across it a few times. "I got it because I'll fight tooth and nail for what I love—my family, my business . . ." He glanced at Hailey. "My friends."

"Oh." *I guess that makes sense.* "But . . ." I almost stopped myself from asking the question burning my tongue, but sometimes my brain has little control over my mouth. This was one of those times.

"Doesn't that mean tooth and *finger*nail? Not"—I made a hammering motion—"nail?"

Too late, I realized I'd done it again. I'd been totally judgmental. Who cared if he'd tattooed the wrong nail on his arm? Wasn't it more important he'd defend who and what he loved? That kind of devotion was admirable. And, unless I was wrong, Hailey was on his list of loves. Or at least likes.

"Yeah, I know." His smile widened. "But a nail"—he pointed to his tattoo—"looks a lot cooler."

I laughed with him. "It really does." I liked him. I liked anyone who could laugh at himself and, more importantly, had permanently inked his commitment to loyalty and love on his arm for the world to see. I leaned closer for a better look. "It's cool. And very cool you'll fight for what you care about."

"Thanks," he said and snapped his fingers. "Which reminds me why I came here in the first place. I need flowers for my mom."

"You came to the right place, then, right, Hailey?"

"More like you came to the best place," she answered. "Eliza can do anything with flowers."

"That's sweet, but you should make an arrangement for Ashton," I answered and walked behind the counter. "Show him how good you are now."

She nodded okay, but when she didn't move, I pulled out a receipt pad to write down what he wanted.

"First of all, what's the occasion?" I asked him and picked the pencil with the sharpest point from a cup on the counter.

"No occasion. Just to tell her she's the bomb." His eyes wandered to Hailey, but not to see if he'd impressed her. I think more because he couldn't help it. Her eyes did some wandering over to his too, but not with the same intensity.

"That's really sweet," she said then dropped her head.

"It is," I nodded. "So we want to make it special. What kind of flowers does she like?"

"I don't know." He looked in the cooler at some of the prepared arrangements we had. "She likes pink. I think she likes roses."

"Everyone likes roses," Hailey interjected. "Mostly because that's what they know. They used to be my favorite until I started working here. Then Eliza showed me all kinds of different flowers I'd never even heard of. And there's about a million shades of pink."

"That's true." I'd said what I had about her being good with flowers to be nice, but obviously she'd learned something. I just wished she was learning things faster. A lot faster. But I figured Ashton would like whatever she did, so I'd risk letting her do the arrangement for his mom. "What kind of flower reminds you of a bomb?" I asked her. "Something that looks like it's exploding."

"Oh! Those flowers you used for Parker's party and for Elton's thing!" She waved her fingers back and forth searching for the name.

"Yes! Mums! That's perfect. I've got some in the cooler." I headed to the back of the shop, passing a sleeping Xander on my way. When I got there, I decided to give Hailey and Ashton some time alone. If she liked him, I wasn't going to interfere. I'd misjudged him the first time around.

More than misjudged. I'd been a snob about her dating a mechanic with tattoos. But he seemed like a good guy, so why get in the way of her happiness? And she must have been happy, because she'd mentioned Elton without tearing up.

I slipped on the sweater hanging next to the cooler and pulled open the heavy steel door. A dozen different scents hit me as I walked into the cold. I closed my eyes and breathed in the gift my flowers offered and thanked them for it. Every living thing deserved gratitude.

My eyes popped open as I realized I'd never thanked Hailey for everything she did to help me in the shop. One more thing to add to my growing Ways-to-Be-a-Better-Friend list.

I took my time finding exactly the right flowers for Ashton's mom, carefully inspecting each petal on the pink chrysanthemums to make sure they didn't have any brown spots. After I'd found the perfect blooms and some interesting greenery to go with them, I figured I'd given Hailey and Ashton plenty of time alone. Plus, my sweater had fallen down on the job of keeping me warm. My teeth were starting to chatter.

I cradled the flowers in my arms and walked carefully to my work table, expecting to see Hailey and Ashton still talking. Maybe even flirting. That would have been okay. Instead Hailey was on the computer.

"Hey, where did Ashton go?" I set the flowers in a bucket of water then looked over her shoulder at the computer.

"I told him it would take a while, so he's going to come back in an hour." She stared intently at the Saddleback College website, her leg bouncing up and down.

"Oh. He could have hung out here."

"Why?" she continued to scroll through the website without looking at me. "He had stuff to do."

"I don't know . . ." I hesitated, not wanting to be nosy but also not wanting to miss the opportunity of telling her I thought Ashton was a good guy. "It seems like you two are kind of into each other."

Suddenly Hailey jumped out of her seat with a cheer. The metal folding chair hit the floor with a loud clang, startling Xander out of his sleep. His crying didn't stop Hailey's cheering, which had gone from a simple "Yahoo!" to full-on jumping up and down and dancing.

"I passed!" she yelled over and over, bouncing her way to Xander's playpen and picking him up.

"Passed what?" I shouted over Xander's wails.

"My math test! The one Parker's been helping me study for!" She spun around with Xander in her arms, which only made him cry harder.

"That's fantastic!" I rushed to the Pack 'n Play and tossed Xander's blanket to Hailey then grabbed his paci and stuck it in his mouth. "I'm so proud of you." I side-hugged her as Xander nestled his head into her shoulder and blinked slowly.

"Isn't it amazing? I never thought I'd pass that test. But I got a sixty-eight percent! A sixty-eight!"

I stepped back, opened my mouth, then shut it, then opened it again because words needed to come out. "That is great . . . and you're sure it's passing?"

"Professor Bryan said I only had to get a sixty-five. I scored two points higher than I had to!"

"Three." I smiled. Her eyes narrowed, and she tilted her head to the side.

"Three points," I repeated.

Her eyes and mouth ahhed open. "Right! Three! That's even better. I can't wait to tell Parker."

"Yeah. He'll be so impressed." *Maybe.* He might have expected a better result than sixty-eight after all the studying they'd done for a remedial math test. "It's too bad Ashton's not still here too. He's going to be really proud of you."

She gave me the same confused-at-math look she'd given me seconds before. "Why would he care?"

I sensed I'd waded into uncertain waters, but I didn't quite know how to get out of them. "I thought you two were, you know, kind of . . . talking. Or something." I pressed my lips tight and let my eyes wander to the floor.

"Well, yeah, we talk, but it's not like we're *talking*." She drew out the word talking to emphasize just how much they weren't doing what I thought they were doing. I still wasn't quite sure I knew what the difference was.

"You said I could do better than Ashton." Hailey boosted Xander back onto her hip as he tried wiggle his way to the floor.

"Did I?" I walked past her, avoiding eye contact and pulled a vase from the shelf. "I didn't mean to give you that impression. He seems like a really nice guy."

"He is." She bounced Xander, who clearly didn't want to go back to sleep. "But I've set my sights higher, like you told me to. I'm not settling for someone whose only goal in life is to work on cars."

"Hmm." I was tempted to tell her how wrong I'd been, but then I reminded myself that I wasn't getting involved in her love life anymore. She was my friend, not my project. If she didn't like Ashton anymore, then maybe I'd been right all along by not encouraging her. "Have you got someone in mind?"

The sparkle in her eye returned, and she broke into a grin.

"Anyone I know?" I hoped it was Blake. And asking her who she was into wasn't "getting involved." Girlfriends talked about boys. It was one of the three pillars of true friendship, along with clothes and makeup. I mean, Taylor and I talked about a lot more than that, but she was a bestie. Besties were special.

"You want me to tell you?" she asked. As if to get in on the excitement, Xander yanked the paci out of his mouth and threw it on the ground with a smile that matched his mom's.

"Yes!" I set the vase down ready to rush to her, but then came to my senses. "I mean, no."

"Oh. Okay." Her shoulders slumped, and she bent down to retrieve Xander's paci.

"It's not that I don't want to know." I fumbled to explain. "I'm dying to know! But I gave you the *worst* advice about Elton. Maybe it's better I don't know until we see how things go."

"That makes sense, I guess." She let Xander grab the paci. He waved his arms up and down like a sumo wrestler attempting a sit-up, and the pacifier flew across the room. "Ugh, this kid's making me crazy."

"Here, let me take him." I held out my arms. "You work on Ashton's arrangement. I'll hold him."

She passed him off to me, and I wished Parker had been there to see me recognizing she needed a break from the baby sometimes. I was already making progress in being more aware.

Hailey went to work on the arrangement. And "work" is really the only way to describe what she was doing. There was no flow to her process, only brute force. She'd forgotten the number-one rule I'd taught her: beauty can't be forced. I focused my attention on Xander to keep from cringing or, worse, correcting her.

"You know, you could give me a clue about who it is." I had to think about something besides the damage being done to my chrysanthemums. Arranging flowers is all about picturing where they should be before placing them. Hailey didn't have the hang of that. After stuffing all of the flowers into the vase, she took them all back out again to start over.

"Who, *who* is?" She bit her lip and jammed a rose into the middle of the flower arrangement.

"The guy you like. Or you're talking to. Or whatever it is you call it." Xander squirmed in my arms, determined to get down. I carried him to the playpen, set him in it, and arranged toys around him. He protested being left, but I ignored his squawks. My flowers needed rescuing.

"Oh yeah." She giggled and handed me the mum she had in her hand before I even asked. "I don't know if we're really *talking*, but he did rescue me. I wouldn't have survived without him."

"I knew it!" I squeezed my fist in victory and almost jumped up and down, nearly dropping the flower I'd saved before regaining my composure. "I mean . . ." I took a deep breath and smiled wide. "I think I know who it is, and I think he's perfect for you!"

She'd fallen for Blake without me even suggesting it. And his playing the hero that morning was exactly the catalyst they'd needed to get together. I couldn't have planned it any better. I almost felt guilty taking credit for being their matchmaker.

"You do?" She clasped her hands together then released them and rescued Xander from his imprisonment. "That means so much to me, because he is *yum* and so good with Xander. I think he could be the one."

I hadn't seen Blake with Xander much, so I'd have to take her word for it. Although, I didn't know when he would have spent time with Xander. And it was a little early to be making long-term plans, but not out of the realm of possibilities.

The thing I knew for sure though? I could hardly wait to tell Parker I'd been the one to get Hailey and Blake together.

Chapter 25

WITH ERICA'S PARTY OUT OF the way, I was able to focus on the event I really wanted to plan: Taylor's reception. Having Blake back in town made the luau a lot easier to put together—not that he'd been super helpful, but he was good at taking directions. He made all the calls I asked him to make and even had a pretty good eye when it came to making decisions about decorations. All in all, we were spending a lot of time together. More than I wanted to, but it did give me plenty of opportunities to bring up Hailey.

I suspected he was into her because he always had a lot of questions when I brought her up. But my suspicions were confirmed one night when we were sampling different caterers for the party.

He'd been much quieter than usual, which, for Blake, meant only interrupting every third sentence or so. When I'd been able to finish an entire five sentences without any interjections from him, I couldn't take it anymore.

"Are you okay?" I asked as we pulled up in front of our second caterer.

"Yeah, why?" He backed into the spot, executing a perfect parallel park without cheering or bragging about it afterward. Totally abnormal.

"You seem kind of down." I pulled my wallet out of my purse and counted out coins for the meter.

"I'll get it." He pushed away the handful of quarters I offered him. "Keep your change."

"I don't want it." I offered them to him again.

"Those machines always eat half of what you put in." He pushed my hand away again but less playfully than before. "I'll use a card."

"Fine." I stuck the coins back in my wallet, trying not to be offended by his brusqueness. "But only if you tell me why you're ticked."

He snorted and turned the car off. "Fine." He wrapped his fingers around the door handle but didn't pull it. "Maybe you can help me. There's this girl who's driving me crazy."

"And it's not me?" I figured it wasn't, but maybe a little part of me hoped it was. I think that part is called the ego.

He laughed again and shook his head before pushing his door open. "You drive me crazy in a different kind of way than this girl."

"Rude." I climbed out of the car, relieved he didn't have feelings for me, for Hailey's sake. It would be too heartbreaking to have another guy she liked be into me instead. "I'm tempted to not even help you with your girl problem, but go ahead and tell me about her." I hoped he was talking about Hailey. She might be less heartbroken if it was someone other than me, but she'd still be heartbroken.

"I don't know how to prove to her I'm ready for a long-term commitment. She thinks I'm a big flirt."

"Hmm." I considered his problem as we walked toward the bakery. Actually, my problem. I had to figure out who he meant. He didn't know very many local girls, so if she was a local, it could be Hailey. But he'd also traveled home. Maybe his trip hadn't been just about seeing his mom. "That's a tough one. Did she tell you that's what she thinks of you?"

He shook his head. "Not in so many words. She's sort of kept her distance since I got back. Like when we went surfing. I was out of my mind when I saw her there, but after everything I did for her, she barely thanked me. She couldn't get away from me fast enough."

There was the clue I'd been looking for. It had to be Hailey. Who else could it be? Jami and I were the only other girls there, but he hadn't rescued us. "I don't think she was anxious to get away from you. I think all the excitement probably got to her, and it didn't have anything to do with you."

"I guess that could be it." He opened the bakery door for me, and we walked in. The smell of yeast and cinnamon filled the air, and my stomach growled even though I'd already eaten a slice of pineapple cake at the last place. "But what do I do now? I've got to prove to her I'm solid; I'm not going anywhere. She's hasn't had enough of that in her life."

"You have to do something big," I said, getting more excited the more he spoke. "Some grand gesture to show her your feelings. Something she's never seen you do for anyone else." I may have completely miscalculated Elton being perfect for Hailey, but I was right about Blake.

"You're right! And I think I know what it is." A smile crept across his face. "It's going to be so perfect!"

"What?"

"It's a secret. You'll find out soon."

The girl at the counter waved and asked how she could help us. There wasn't time to press Blake for details before he reached across the counter to shake the baker's hand and introduce us.

I'd have to wait a week to find out what he was planning for Hailey, but in the meantime I could get her prepared. Surprises were great, as long as the surprisee had some idea it was coming. Hailey would need a little time to practice her happy-surprised face so the pictures I'd be telling the photographer to take would turn out perfect.

My excitement over telling Hailey to be prepared for a surprise waned somewhat when I walked into the shop to find the huge mess on my worktable I'd asked her to clean up still there while she sat on the couch sending Snaps while Xander slept.

"Did it get busy while I was gone?" I asked as I picked up the trash can and brushed cut stems, leaves, and ribbons into it.

"Not really," she said before striking a pose. The click of the camera grated on my ears. I picked up the two pairs of clippers and dropped them into the plastic bin where they belonged, preferring the sound of metal hitting plastic to the shutter-flashing sound coming from Hailey's phone.

"Oh, sorry." She stood and tucked her phone into her back pocket. "I was about to clean that up. I just needed a quick break after Xander fell asleep."

"Yeah, I get it . . ." I didn't really, but I didn't know how else to respond. I wanted to treat her more like a friend than a project, but she was also my employee. I wouldn't be doing her any favors if I didn't expect her to act like the responsible worker I needed her to be.

I took a deep breath and said what had to be said. "When I ask you to do something, I really need you to follow through. We've got a lot of orders to get out, and things will only get busier the closer we get to Valentine's Day. You've got to stay on top of things so we don't get behind."

"I'm really sorry." She shrank into her shoulders. "I promise I'll do better."

"I know you will." I hoped so anyway. The longer she worked for me, the less likely it seemed she would.

When she grabbed a broom without being asked and started sweeping, I decided to let go of my irritation with her.

"Hey, I've got some good news for you." I smiled wide.

"What is it?" She stopped pushing the broom and returned my grin.

I put a vase away and grabbed a rag to wipe down the table, letting her excitement build until she tapped the broom on the floor demanding I tell her.

"Someone has a surprise planned for you," I sang.

"Who? What kind of surprise? When?" She threw questions at me faster than Miley Cyrus and Liam Hemsworth went through engagements.

I ran the cloth over the table. "I can't tell you who or what, but I'll give you a hint about when." I wanted her to be prepared, but I didn't want to ruin the surprise altogether. "Soon."

She peppered me with more questions for the rest of the week until I wished I'd never said anything to her, especially because her anticipation turned into one more distraction at work for her. That's the last thing I needed when I had a party and a wedding to finish planning on top of all the orders I was getting.

Still, her excitement added a layer of eagerness for me. As much as I didn't like the fact that Taylor rarely had time to spend with me that wasn't devoted to planning her wedding, I was looking forward to her pre-wedding reception.

When the actual day arrived, there was no way I could have known the party would be the disaster it became. The venue was perfect—not too fancy but not too casual either. Taylor loved the luau theme but still wanted good food and dancing. And nobody barefoot. That was important to her. Hawaiian shirts were fine, but bare feet were not.

We'd rented a room that overlooked the ocean and had an outdoor patio with fire pits. The fires kept us warm enough to enjoy the sunset—a perfect combination of reds and yellows that matched Taylor's wedding colors—but the night was cool enough to keep people inside where the music and dancing were happening. Perfect.

I'd even convinced Daddy to go. He never would have agreed if Taylor weren't my oldest friend, but since she was he forced himself to go, as long as I promised not to make him stay long. Since I had to be there early, Parker brought him, which also made things easier for Daddy.

Once they arrived and I had all the party details under control, I went through the poke bowl buffet line then scanned the room to find where they were sitting. I spotted them at a table across the room but not far from the dance floor. For some reason, seeing Parker help Daddy into his seat reminded me of the last wedding we'd been at together: my sister's. I remembered how he'd held me tight and danced with me when all I'd wanted to do was cry.

As happy as I was for Taylor, I was going to need a dance with Parker, just like I'd needed one at Caroline's wedding. His seat next to the dance floor plus the fact that the DJ wasn't going light on the slow songs made for a perfect setup. I'd be sitting right by Parker when the next slow song came on.

I made my way across the room and set my bowl in the spot next to Parker. "Is this seat taken?" I assumed it wasn't and was nearly in it before he answered.

"I'm supposed to save it for Hailey," he said with a sheepish look and a glance behind me. I followed his eyes over my shoulder to see Hailey standing there.

"Thanks, Parker!"

I'm sure she didn't mean to be rude as she nudged me out of the way to get to the seat—*her* seat. It felt a little rude though. Maybe even a lot rude. Especially when she scooted my bowl out of the way without a word.

Daddy sat on the other side of Parker, which meant I couldn't. I opted for the next best option and took the seat to Daddy's other side.

Before I'd even pulled out the chair, Hailey had monopolized the conversation, telling Parker all about her latest math quiz. This one hadn't gone as well as her big test, and she was convinced it was the teacher's fault.

"I don't understand what he's saying," she said. "How can I when he barely speaks English?"

I cringed, but Parker nodded politely. It was then I saw Blake wandering around with his food, and I realized I had the perfect place for him to sit. I stood and waved him over to our table.

"There's a seat next to Hailey," I told him when he was close enough to hear me over the music.

He looked down at Hailey then back at me. "How about the one next to you? Is that taken?"

I frowned—hopefully not noticeably. My plan had been for him to distract Hailey so I could talk to Parker, but I couldn't tell him no without it being awkward.

"Sure." I plopped back down and pushed my food away. I needed cake, not fish.

To make matters worse, Blake waved the Bateses and Jami over when he saw them looking for a seat. There had been no way not to invite them after Taylor had announced her engagement while Nancy and Martha were at our house. I'd tried to find a way, but Blake had pointed out that since Jami was friends with all of us, she should be invited, which meant her aunt and grandma had to be invited too.

Nancy took a seat right next to Blake and immediately leaned over him to talk to me.

"Everything is beautiful. Just beautiful." She stopped talking long enough to take a breath and press her hands to her heart. "I've never had a poke bowl. Is that how you say it? Poke. Like you would with a stick?" She made jabbing motions with her chopsticks.

"Pok-ay," I said, but she kept talking, uninterested in the answer to her question.

"I usually don't eat fish, but I'm trying it today—"

"Here." Blake interrupted her and stood. "Trade me seats so you won't have to talk around me." He picked up his bowl then slid Nancy's into its place. She had no excuse not to move then, so after thanking him four hundred and thirty-four times, she sat down next to me, he sat next to Jami, and my night went from bad to worse.

By that point I figured nothing else could go wrong. I was wrong. So wrong. Because as Nancy sat down, she caught a glimpse of two more people looking for a place to sit. She waved them over before I could stop her. She didn't know Elton and Erica; it was just my bad luck they happened to be the last two people who didn't have somewhere to sit. I hadn't wanted to invite them either, but Weston did all of Elton's marketing, so I didn't really have a choice.

"Oh no," I moaned. I didn't mean for anyone else to hear it, but Parker's smug grin and laughing eyes told me one other person had at least seen me mouth it.

The couple sat down across from me and said their hellos to everyone. Somehow Erica's didn't make it to me. I was okay with that.

"Isn't this an interesting choice of food?" she asked, stabbing at the food with her chopsticks. "I hope the crab is real. I suspect it's crab with a *K*."

"It's not." I forced a polite smile. "It's real." Poke bowls were Taylor's favorite, and it had been my suggestion to serve them since they were a Hawaiian dish. It hadn't been cheap, but since I'd helped plan the food, I made sure to cover what she couldn't without her knowing. But somehow Erica seemed to know and wanted to criticize me for it. Or I was being paranoid.

Except then she had something to say about the flowers. "What an interesting way to decorate the table," she said, picking at the mini pineapple sticking out of the arrangement of blooming artichokes, roses, and carnations, which rested on an areca palm frond.

"Thank you." I was proud of the clever way I'd mixed together a variety of plants from Hawaii. Judging by the way she'd wrinkled her nose when she said "interesting," we had differing opinions about my design.

"I'm sure Taylor loved it," she shot back.

"She did," I said, smiling through gritted teeth.

"I love them!" Hailey exclaimed. "I want to do the same thing for my wedding." She paused and glanced at Parker. "If I ever get married, that is."

I was about to answer Hailey when someone tapped my shoulder. I looked over to see Blake leaning toward me behind Nancy's chair.

"I'm going to do it!" he loud-whispered.

"Do what?"

"My big gesture. For Jami."

The music and Nancy's chattering kept the words from reaching me before Blake stood. Then they sucker punched me twice. First as I realized the big gesture I'd encouraged him to do was happening on Taylor's big day. The second one landed as I realized his gesture was for Jami, not Hailey.

And by that time Blake was already halfway to the mic.

Chapter 26

THE SONG PLAYING CAME TO an end. Blake whispered to the DJ then picked up the mic. I held my breath, wanting to crawl under the table but opting instead to close my eyes.

"We're here tonight to celebrate Weston and Taylor," Blake began, and I opened one eye. So far it wasn't bad. "Weston and I haven't been close, but as I've gotten to know him over the past few months, he's become the big brother I always wanted."

Okay, that was sweet.

"Lucky for me, he is actually my big brother."

The crowd laughed, I opened my other eye, and Blake paused until the room went quiet again, which was sooner than he seemed to expect.

"Watching my brother with Taylor has really taught me a lot about what a relationship can be." He paused again, and for a second I thought he was going to tear up. Everything he'd said had been about Weston and Taylor, so I started to breathe again. Not quite normally—he did still have the mic in his hand—but I thought it might be okay.

And then he opened his mouth again. "That's why I'm up here right now—to thank them." A couple of people clapped, but nobody else had a chance to join them. "And to tell the woman I love I'm ready to commit."

And there it was. I whipped my head from Blake to Jami, whose face, even in the dim light, burned redder than a sunset during wildfire season.

"She's too shy to come up here, but I want everyone to know I've loved her from the first moment I saw her sitting in our university's library." Blake zeroed in on her, and she lifted her head to return his gaze. "Jami, I love you."

I tore my eyes away from Jami to Blake, wondering how he could know that when they'd only met a few months ago and why he needed to announce it at Taylor and Weston's celebration.

"I know this is fast. So fast most people probably don't know we've been dating. And everything you know about me may make you doubt me." Blake walked toward our table, clutching the mic and staring at Jami. I stared at the cord. It wasn't long enough to stretch all the way across the dance floor to Jami, her shaking hands clasped in her lap. "But I promise I'm not the player you saw at school."

The cord went taut, but Blake took one more step, and the mic nearly flew out of his hands. He stopped, looked around for help, and Weston stepped forward to take the mic from him.

"I promise I will never take your love and your friendship for granted," Blake said loudly, projecting his voice as he continued his walk and his speech mic-less.

There were a few *aww*s in the crowd. One from Erica, for sure. I scanned the room to see who would dare think it was okay for Blake to steal the spotlight from Taylor. My eyes landed on her at the same time she looked my way. We exchanged wide-eyed looks, but then she smiled, shrugged, and took Weston's hand as he returned to her side.

"You were right to think I'm not the kind of guy who could settle down." Blake stuck his hand in his jeans pocket, and I knew then what his big plan was. I glanced at Jami to see if she knew too. The tear glistening in the corner of her eye told me yes.

Blake pulled a black box out of his pocket when he reached our table, and then he went down on one knee and lowered his voice. "But that's not who I am." He opened the box to show her the ring. Nancy gasped. It was the least I'd ever heard her talk in my entire life.

"I want to spend the rest of our lives together. I love you." Blake's eyes pleaded with Jami as seconds ticked by without a response. As irritated as I was with him, I really hoped she'd say yes; otherwise things were going to be really awkward for the rest of the night. And he'd be heartbroken.

That's when I remembered Hailey. She was going to be heartbroken. After the weeks of tears and self-doubt when Elton rejected her, I didn't even want to think how she'd react to Blake ditching her for Jami. *Jami,* who I hadn't been able to convince her wasn't boring or quiet. Hailey was going to be a hot mess.

Except, when I braved a peek at her, she didn't look heartbroken at all. Anything but, actually. In fact, she was the first one to clap after Jami nodded and pressed her lips to Blake's.

Then everyone clapped, and the music started again. Blake led Jami to the dance floor and wrapped her in his arms. Weston and Taylor joined them, followed by a few other couples. I glanced at Parker as Elvis sang.

I caught his eye. He smiled. I smiled. The world stopped. I was finally going to get my dance.

And then Hailey tapped his shoulder and leaned close to his ear, whispering something. He nodded. They stood and walked to the dance floor. Elton and Erica followed. Daddy, as the gentleman he always was, asked Nancy to dance, leaving silent Martha and me at the table.

After however many years of being speechless, Martha decided that was the moment to break her silence. She reached over, patted my hand, and with a smile wide enough to reveal her missing molar, said, "Don't worry, dear, there are plenty of fish in the sea. You'll find someone who's right for you."

I should have been thrilled to hear her voice again—I was sure everyone else was going to be—but the only thing I could think was how much I wanted her to mind her own business. Of course, she didn't. Once she'd opened her mouth and noise came out, the floodgates were open. While everyone else swayed back and forth in the arms of someone she loved—or at least liked—I listened to Martha reminisce about falling in love with her husband at first sight.

"Really?" I feigned interest while keeping my eyes on Parker and Hailey. I should have been relieved it wasn't Jami in his arms. But he and Hailey were both laughing. A lot. "Love at first sight? Not everyone can claim that," I said to Martha, but what I really wanted to know was what Hailey and Parker thought was so funny.

"Oh no. I hated his guts the first time I met him," Martha answered, catching my attention again. "First Sight was the club where we worked. He tended bar and I . . . well, I was a dancer."

And now she had my full attention. "A dancer?" There was only one kind of "dancer" working at a place called First Sight.

"Sometimes people can surprise you, can't they?" A smile crept across her face with the stealth of a cat after the butter left on the kitchen counter. "You think you know them—who they are, how they think, what they like—but you really don't."

I chewed the inside of my lip and took my time before I nodded in agreement. I'd thought I knew what Elton wanted, but I'd been wrong. I'd thought I knew what Blake wanted, and again, I'd been way off target. And as much as I'd thought I knew Hailey and what she wanted, I'd struck out twice. Three times, if I counted my efforts to get her to succeed in college.

But one thing had become clear to me as I watched her and Parker dance: he was the one she'd be heartbroken to lose, not Blake. The question was, would she lose him, or did he feel the same about her?

"By the time you get to be my age . . ." Martha interrupted my thoughts, which I should have been grateful for because they were going to a dark place. "You learn to hold your judgments until you know all the facts."

I tore my gaze from the dance floor back to Martha. Was she lecturing me about being judgmental? Because it felt like she was being a little judgy.

I opened my mouth to ask her what she meant, but the music ended, and Blake took the mic again as everyone else headed back to their seats.

"I don't want to dominate the party, but I've got one more thing to say." Blake held the mic in one hand and kept his other arm wrapped around Jami's waist. I wondered if anyone else was getting as annoyed with him as I was for making the night about him instead of who it was really supposed to be about. My question was answered as my eyes wandered to Parker. Even from twenty feet away, his pinched expression and folded arms told me he felt the same.

"I have to thank my brother and his fiancée for showing me what love is all about," Blake continued with a tender glance at Jami. "Watching them made me less afraid of commitment and absolutely sure I could spend forever with one person, as long as that person was Jami."

A collective *aww* went through the crowd, and even I lost some of my annoyance. Maybe even most of it. But definitely not all of it.

"So, let's raise our glasses." Blake ran back to our table and grabbed his glass of water and Jami's too and then ran back to the floor where he'd left her standing, looking frightened but happy.

A long pause followed as waiters frantically hustled around the small room passing out the glasses of champagne that weren't supposed to go out for another fifteen minutes.

"And *now* let's raise our glasses." Everyone followed Blake's lead. Guests who were sitting stood, and a hundred champagne flutes were held mid-air. "To Weston and Taylor. Thank you for showing us all what true love is. May you have all the happiness you deserve and more."

Clinking sounds filled the air, reminding me of the wind chime Mom had made from sea glass she'd collected during a hundred or more walks on the beach. She'd given it to Daddy for his birthday days before she died. It hung on the porch above the chair Daddy sat in every night, playing music for him as he watched the sunset. Until that moment the thought had never occurred to me that maybe the sunset wasn't the only thing that brought him to the same spot every night.

As if he'd read my mind, Daddy came up behind me and kissed my cheek. "You okay?" he whispered in my ear over the clapping of the crowd.

"Fine, Daddy. Thanks." I leaned into his chest to assure him.

Except I wasn't fine. I'd always thought Daddy couldn't be lonely with me around. Now I knew what he had to feel every day, because I felt it myself watching Parker and Hailey. The burning in my chest I got every time I saw him with someone else wasn't because I might lose his friendship. It was because I didn't want to lose any part of him. I wanted all of him for myself.

Watching them smiling and raising their glasses, I couldn't be sure Parker was in love with Hailey, but I knew without a doubt she was in love with him. It was written all over her face, more obvious than a big, blinking *You Are Here* sign.

I wondered if my feelings for Parker were as obvious as hers. I doubted it, but then again, maybe that's why I hadn't seen much of him lately. Maybe he could see how I felt even before I could and didn't want to hurt me because he didn't feel the same. Or, worse, he was in love with Hailey.

The only way to know for sure would be to tell him how I felt, but I didn't know if I was ready for that kind of honesty. It could only turn out two ways: our friendship would be over if he didn't feel the same, or my friendship with Hailey would be over if he did. Neither was a great option, but if I was being honest, I'd take the second over the first.

Except I really didn't want to hurt Hailey. She'd had enough hurt in her life and didn't need me adding to it. So I smiled at her and let her beaming face lighten my own mood as we all sat back down at the table, minus Blake and Jami, who had disappeared.

"Wasn't that sweet?" Erica asked as she took a bite of the cake a waiter set in front of her. Cake Blake and I had picked out the same day I'd encouraged him to let the girl he loved know how he felt. The girl I'd thought was Hailey. Hailey, who sat shoulder to shoulder with Parker and had just taken a bite of his cake.

"Sweet, yes, but not very polite to steal the spotlight from Taylor and Weston." I took a bite of cake and swallowed my regret along with the pineapple sponge cake covered in whipped frosting. The cake didn't taste nearly as good as it had the week before.

The corners of Erica's lips curled up. "I used to be jealous of people in relationships too. I couldn't figure out why everyone but me seemed to be able to fall in love." Her voice was syrupy sweet, but her eyes didn't match the concern she tried to fabricate from nothing. "Then I decided to om-power myself and get rid of everything blocking my path to happiness."

"Is that right?" I pushed my cake away and dropped my crumpled napkin onto the table. Under the table Daddy patted my shaking knee.

"We could help you clear some of that negative energy that's getting in the way of your relationships," Elton said to me then looked at Erica for backup. "That's what Om-powerment is all about."

"Excuse me?" *I* had negative energy?

"I had a boy I was in love with once." Nancy, of course, had to get in on the analysis of my love life. "I was sure he felt the same about me. He never spoke to me or sent me flowers, but I saw it in his eyes."

I looked around the table, hoping someone would stop Nancy before what she was saying got worse, which it would. It was Nancy, after all. I was still too speechless from Erica's "om-powered" advice to say anything myself.

"At least, I thought I saw it in his eyes." No one was stopping Nancy. "Now I realize it was just my imagination. When he got engaged to another girl who worked with us, I thought I'd never get over it." Her eyes drifted around the room while she spoke, only landing on me occasionally, making it obvious who the story was for.

"I wish I had gotten over him sooner. I could have married someone else, but I guess it's too late now." Nancy sighed then smiled at her cake. "I hope you won't make the same mistake I did, Liza." With all the sorrow of someone who's flushed a recently acquired and expired pet goldfish, Nancy dug into her cake.

"Which mistake? There's a lot of them to avoid," I muttered but not under my breath enough to keep Nancy from hearing.

I've never actually seen a kicked puppy, but I imagine its face would look a lot like Nancy's did with her drooping, sad eyes and quivering chin. She stared at the tablecloth and slid her fork back and forth, clinking it against her knife. "I've made a lot of mistakes, that's for sure. I wouldn't wish the life I've had on anybody. I don't know what I could have done differently, but I should have done something . . ."

The silence at the table and Nancy's inability to whisper made every word she muttered to herself loud enough for us all to hear. I scanned every face at the table for a hidden smile or a laugh, any kind of sympathy or understanding. We all thought Nancy was ridiculous . . . right?

Apparently not. No one would look at me. All their sympathetic looks were directed toward Nancy.

"I'm sorr—" I started to apologize, but Parker stood up and held his hand across the table.

"Nancy, would you like to dance?" he asked.

"Oh, yes. I'd love to." Nancy bounded out of her chair faster than I'd ever seen her move. I caught Parker's eye to thank him, but he pressed his lips tight and shook his head in a way that made my chest tighten with embarrassment. I broke away from his cold gaze and stared at my lap. I swallowed hard and brushed away some imaginary cake crumbs.

"I think it's time for me to get home." Daddy set his carefully folded napkin on the table. "Would you drive me home, sweetheart, or do you need to stay?"

I looked around the room until my eyes landed on Parker and Nancy. He had her laughing at something, which made me feel better, but he wasn't going to be dancing with me. Taylor and Weston were busy with their guests, and Blake and Jami still hadn't reappeared.

"I'll stay and clean up," Hailey offered. "You can go."

Since I wasn't needed—or wanted—I left.

Chapter 27

I WAITED A FEW HOURS before texting Parker. I knew he was mad, but I didn't really know why. I'd been rude, but I hadn't meant to be. It just slipped out.

How is Nancy? I texted.

Hurt, he replied within seconds.

I'm sorry.

I'm not the one you should be apologizing to.

That was true, but I'd tried to apologize to Nancy, and he'd asked her to dance before I could.

I'm going to. Why are you so mad?

My phone buzzed, and Parker's picture popped up.

"Hi," I answered carefully.

"I'm not mad. I'm disappointed." He sounded mad. "I know you're a compassionate person, but sometimes you are frustratingly clueless."

"Clueless?" And was *frustratingly* even a word?

"Yes, clueless." His voice rose. "The worst thing that's ever happened to you, you don't remember, so you live this charmed life, oblivious to other people's problems."

"What problems am I oblivious to?" I walked across my room and peered through the blinds into the backyard and Parker's apartment. All I could see was a light shining through his bathroom window. "I've been helping Hailey with her problems. I made friends with Jami because you thought she needed one. I threw a wedding party for Taylor so she wouldn't have to deal with it—"

"You can't solve everyone's problems, Eliza!" This time he came close to yelling. I'd never seen—or heard—him lose his cool before. "Sometimes people need empathy and kindness." He sighed, and the despair in it floated across the ether into my ear and under my skin, touching every nerve of my body.

"I've known Nancy most of my life," he said softly. "From the time she was a reluctant debutante who got her own BMW for her sixteenth birthday. I knew her when she was in college and attempted suicide after something happened that no one talked about but everyone knew. She hasn't been the same since then, which should be enough for anyone's empathy. I wish that were the last bad thing that happened to her. It's not. In her lifetime she's gone from having everything to nothing. And you make fun of her for living in the past."

"Okay. I get it." I did, too. I knew she used to have money, but no one had ever told me the other stuff about her. I slumped into the easy chair by my window and stared at the lone light shining from his apartment. "I'm sorry."

"The worst of it is you don't show her any gratitude for taking care of you for so many years."

"That's not fair," I responded. I had vague memories of her babysitting Caroline and me until I went to kindergarten, but they weren't happy memories. They weren't sad either, just there. "It's not like she did it out of charity. She got paid to take care of me."

"She did a lot more than she got paid to do," Parker answered with a firmness that swept away my wavering surety. "Your dad was a mess. When he could pull himself together enough to go to work, he stayed there. Nancy practically lived at your house."

"Nancy?" A rusty memory of someone pushing me in a swing at the park floated into my head. I knew I loved whoever was doing the pushing, but I'd always assumed it was my dad. It must have been Nancy.

"I didn't know, Parker." If he was telling me all this to make me feel even worse, he'd done it and more. "I'm sorry."

"I know you are." All the anger had gone out of his voice. "Just . . . be more aware of people's feelings."

He hung up without saying goodbye, and the sting of his words kept me up most of the night. I couldn't decide who I was most upset with: him or me.

It turned out, by the next morning, it was Hailey. She came into work late, and I couldn't help but wonder how she got home the night before and if Parker had been her ride. I told myself my annoyance was with her tardiness, not with who her imagined ride was. She'd been late before. A lot, actually. But after six months, I decided it was time to set some boundaries.

I answered her cheerful hello with, "I thought you were going to be here a while ago."

"I'm sorry." She set Xander in his playpen but picked him back up when he complained. "Xander's been fussy all morning. I think he's teething."

My resolve softened as I looked at the baby's tear-stained face. "Here," I said, holding out my arms. "Let me see what I can do." She passed him off to me, but he only wailed harder.

"Thanks for trying," she said taking him back. Dark circles under her eyes stood out even with her heavy makeup. "And thanks for being cool about me showing up late."

"Just try not to let it happen again." I sat down at my computer and turned it on. I'd gone easy on her, but I hoped my message had come through.

"Can you believe Blake and Jami?" she asked over Xander's cries.

"No!" I turned away from the computer, ready to forgive her for being late because I'd been dying to talk to someone about what had happened. Taylor had been my first choice, but she was too overwhelmed to talk to me with the wedding only a week away. "I didn't see that coming at all."

"You didn't?" Xander's cries almost drowned out her words. She bounced him up and down, but it didn't help. "I thought something was up with them. Every time he looked at her was like . . ."

She said something mildly inappropriate that got lost in Xander's sobs.

"You really didn't know?" Her voice rose as she rummaged through her diaper bag until she found a pacifier and popped it into Xander's mouth. "I thought for sure you would. You two were so tight."

"Blake and me?" I shook my head. "We're just friends." I made a split-second decision then to find out what was happening with her and Parker. But I couldn't come right out and ask. "To be honest, I thought you were kind of into him."

"Me?" Hailey handed her pacified baby his favorite stuffed dinosaur and set him back in the playpen. "No way. He is so not my type."

"Really?" I turned back to my computer. If she told me there was something between her and Parker, I didn't want her to see my face. "I thought that's who you meant when you were talking about someone who rescued you."

"What?" A chair scraped across the concrete floor, and she sat down behind me. "No. I was talking about Parker. Blake never rescued me."

"What about at the beach? He swam into the riptide to help you." I scrolled through my email, trying to take my mind off the pounding in my chest.

"Oh, that!" She laughed. Hard. Like couldn't-catch-her-breath hard.

"What's so funny?" I eyed her over my shoulder. I didn't find anything amusing about her almost drowning.

"Wanna know a secret?" She didn't wait for an answer. "I was hoping Parker would be the one to rescue me." She laughed again. "I got myself out of it when I saw Blake coming. I knew I'd end up rescuing him."

I turned all the way around. "You faked the whole thing?" I didn't know whether to smack some sense into her or shake it into her. What kind of mother gets herself caught in a riptide so she can be rescued? "What if you hadn't been able to get out? What would have happened to Xander?"

She rolled her eyes. "I've been in a million rips. Me and my friends used to get caught in them all the time just for kicks. The only people who drown in them are the dumb clucks who fight them."

I turned around to hide how mad I was at her and to take a breath. "It seems like a stupid chance to take," I said and clicked on an urgent email.

"You're right. I'm sorry." She rested her elbows on her knees and plopped her chin into her hands. "I do stupid things when I'm in love. You saw me with Elton, and I wasn't into him half as much as I'm into Parker."

I closed my eyes before reading the message. Hailey needed my support, not my lectures. Being a friend meant listening even when I really, really didn't want to. And so, I turned around again to face whatever she had to say.

"It's okay. We all do stupid things." I rubbed her back, and she tilted her head to smile at me. "But how did Parker rescue you?"

She sat up now, anxious to tell me. "Math. He helped me pass my math class."

"Oh." I was expecting something much bigger than that. Something more rescue-y. "Yeah, that makes sense." *Sort of.* "Soooo, is there anything besides that I should know about? Is he into you too?"

"I think so," she answered. "Why else would he help me? You said yourself you thought he liked me."

"That's when I thought you were talking about Blake, but Parker helps a lot of people. He'd save the whole world all by himself if he could. I wouldn't read too much into it." I turned back to the computer to get away from the hurt on her face. The hurt I'd put there.

"So are you saying you don't think he likes me?" she asked. Out of the corner of my eye I saw her cross her arms and legs.

"I don't know if he does or not; I'm just saying not to read too much into his tutoring you." My words were as much for me as they were for Hailey. "Has he said anything to you?"

"Not in so many words, but I could tell when we danced how he feels." She uncrossed her legs and swooped her hair over her shoulder to finger-comb it. "I had my head on his shoulder, and I could totally feel his heart beating. Every time we're together it's like we can't get close enough to each other. We haven't kissed or anything like that, but I can tell he wants to. I just keep telling myself to take it slow. I've already got a kid, and I don't want to be the kind of girl who just hooks up with guys anymore."

I only caught about half of what she said, and not because I didn't want to hear it. I'd opened the urgent email, and it had my full attention. "Hailey—" I interrupted. "Do you know what this order is?" I pointed to the message I'd just read. "It says they want to make sure we have hydrangeas for their order today, but I haven't seen any order."

Hailey gasped. "Oh no!" She jumped out of her seat, grabbed the mouse from me, and navigated to the program that recorded our online orders. "Oh no!" This time she added a curse word too. "I don't know what happened! I thought for sure I put the order in here."

She opened the file where the order should have been. It wasn't there, and no amount of scrolling would make it appear. I took the mouse back from her and navigated back to our ordering program to see if I could find the original order.

"There it is." Hailey pointed to an order, and I opened it. "I don't know how it got marked as filled."

I read through the order, feeling sicker to my stomach with each passing second. "This is for a funeral, Hailey, and the order is huge." I checked the time. I had four hours to not only put together three big arrangements and get them to the funeral home but to get some hydrangeas, which weren't technically in bloom for another few months. "There's no way I can get this done."

"I'm so sorry." Hailey stood behind me, so I couldn't see her face, but her voice told me she was on the verge of crying. I was too, for that matter. "I really screwed up, didn't I?"

"Yeah, you really did." Maybe if I hadn't already been annoyed with her for falling in love with Parker I would have soft-pedaled what she'd done. Or maybe not. She'd messed up big time. "I have to order hydrangeas a day in advance this time of year. I have no idea where I'm going to find them local."

"What can I do to help?" she asked, but Xander had started to cry again. She got him out of his prison and held him so close I didn't know who was comforting whom.

"We need to call every florist within a fifty-mile radius and see if they have what we need." I stood up from my spot at the computer and pointed for her to sit down. "Then we need to ask them to make the arrangement for us and pay whatever it costs, even if we lose money. We won't have time to pick up the flowers and arrange them."

"I'll start on the two arrangements we have the flowers for," I added before handing her my phone. We had to keep the store line open in case any other customers tried to call. I guess I'd sufficiently scared Hailey, because she didn't say another word to me. I was okay with that. It would be easier to let her go at the end of the day.

Chapter 28

By some miracle we got the order done and to the funeral home on time, but after paying the other florist and driving all the way to Carlsbad to pick up the arrangements, I didn't make any money. If I counted the cost of gas, I lost money. Plus I still had a stack of other orders to fill when I got back to the shop, which were already late. Those I could do alone, but I wouldn't be closing by five o'clock. First, though, I had a harder job to do.

When I walked into the shop Hailey was cleaning up the backroom. I should have been happy about it, but it's something I never did until the end of the day when all my orders were done. I'd have to get everything back out that she'd just put away.

"I know you have to fire me, so I'm going to quit so you don't have to," she said before I'd even put my purse away. I appreciated her making things easier for me, but I also saw hope in her eyes. She didn't think I'd really do it, but I knew I had to. If this had been her first mistake, I could let it slide. But even after months of training, she still couldn't arrange flowers without damaging so many it cost me more to have her do them than I could make selling them. And, obviously, she still didn't know how to work with our ordering system. I may not have been in the flower business to make loads of money, but I also wasn't in it to lose money.

"I'm sorry, Hailey." I didn't know what else to say. Her whole body deflated like one of those giant jump houses kids have at birthday parties. They're the happiest things in the world when they're filled with kids bouncing and laughing, but as soon as they're all crumpled up on the ground, they're a depressing reminder that everything good has to come to an end.

"It's really okay." She wiped her thumb under her eye. "You've been the best boss I've ever had—"

"I'm the only boss you've ever had." I walked to her and wrapped her in my arms. "We're still friends, right? You may not be cut out for the flower business, but you're definitely cut out to be a bestie. I don't know what I'd do without you and Xander."

"Obvs." She pulled away and rubbed the bottom of her nose, keeping her eyes pointed at the ground. "I'm gonna need some time to get over feeling so dumb. I tried so hard to do this job right, and I messed a million things up."

"You messed a few things up, not a million." I walked to the front counter and pulled out a box of tissues from under it. "The thing is, you don't have a passion for flowers, and that's okay. I'm good at this because I love it." I handed her a tissue, and she blew her nose.

"I wanted to love it because you do, but I still can't figure out what the big deal is about flowers." She reached for another tissue, and I noticed her nails. They were hard to miss with their electric-blue polish. But on the ring finger of each hand the nails had an intricate beach scene painted on them.

I grabbed her hand for a closer look. "Hailey, these are your best yet."

The sun on both nails wasn't just orange. It had shades of red in it. And the umbrella on the beach had something written on it. I held her hand closer to see what it said. "How did you write *Tommy Bahama* so small?"

The pride in her eyes moved to her smile, and her tears were gone. "I was going to write *Corona*, but *Tommy Bahama* was more of a challenge, so I tried that."

"Well, you nailed it, girl. No pun intended." I let go of her hand and looked at her. For the first time I saw who she was and not what I thought she should be. "You love doing this, don't you?"

"Nails?" She shrugged and walked to the playpen to pick up Xander even though he was perfectly happy. "I mean, yeah, I like it. I love helping people feel pretty. Everyone can have smokin' nails. But it's not like a real job I could do for the rest of my life."

"Why not?"

"I don't know." She shrugged again. "That's just what you told me. You said I'd need my own salon to make any money."

"You need to forget what I told you. It was probably the stupidest thing I've ever said."

"Really?"

"Really. You should do what you have a passion for. Quit wasting your time here and in college classes you hate. Go do what you love. Life is too short not to."

She didn't answer right away, but a light turned on. For the first time she had this air of confidence around her. Super weird, because she'd just been fired.

"I think I should finish college," she said finally. "I want to keep taking business classes. But maybe I could do nail school too. Then I could open my own shop, like you said." She moved Xander to her hip and picked up her diaper bag.

"I think that's a great idea." I wanted to hug her, but I touched her arm instead. "I'll send the brides who hire me to you for their nails. You're going to be the hottest thing in town."

"You really think so?"

"As long as you quit taking my advice, I know so."

I helped her pack up her things and walked her to the back door. I pushed it open, and someone yelled, "Whoa!" from the other side, sending my pulse racing.

Parker stepped from behind the open door, and my heart slowed to a flutter. An annoying flutter that had nothing to do with the shock of seeing him. If he and Hailey had something going on, my heart had no business acting like a kid on Christmas morning.

"Hi!" Hailey squeezed past me through the doorway and stood on tiptoe to kiss his cheek. "What are you doing here?"

"Trying not to get crushed." He pulled Hailey out of my way.

"Sorry, I didn't know you were out here," I said and brushed by him to get to Hailey's car. I was carrying the playpen, and it was heavy. Everything felt heavy at the moment.

"Let me take that." He reached for the playpen's nylon handle, his hand touching mine.

"I'm fine." I jerked away, nearly knocking myself over with the force.

His forehead creased with a question he didn't ask, but I guessed it had something to do with why I was being so rude.

"Hailey's car is right there," I said more gently and jutted my chin toward the rusted Honda Civic with mismatched doors. She shouldn't have been driving a hazard like that, especially not with a baby in it. But I reminded myself it was the best she could do.

"What's with all the stuff?" he asked as he opened Hailey's trunk for me.

I dropped the playpen into the trunk, and Parker took the diaper bag off Hailey's shoulder and set it next to the playpen.

"She'll need that up front," I said.

"I'm going to find a new job," Hailey answered the question I'd avoided.

"Why?" Parker's concern brought the same burning to my cheeks I'd felt the night before when we talked on the phone. How could I defend letting Hailey go after he'd basically told me to be nicer?

I looked to Hailey to answer. She stared back at me.

"We decided she should pursue what she loves," I answered finally.

"That, and I totally screwed up an order." Hailey grabbed the fist Xander was beating against her chest and kissed it as though he were the one who needed comforting.

"You got fired?" Parker asked.

Hailey nodded at the same time I shook my head. Parker's eyes bored into me. I could feel them trying to see through my skull into my brain, looking for the sensitivity chip that must have come dislodged.

"I'm sure it wasn't bad enough to be fired." He stepped closer to Hailey, blocking my view of her.

"I didn't fire her. I let her go," I said.

"What's the difference?" he asked in a voice more gentle than I expected.

"We both decided she should use her creative talents doing nails." I peeked around him at Hailey, who still held Xander's fist close to her mouth as she rocked him on her hip. "That's what she loves."

Parker moved closer to me but looked back at Hailey. "Really?"

She nodded, but her red-rimmed eyes made her nodding less convincing and my decision less certain. I thought I'd done the right thing, but maybe I'd let my jealousy over Parker's feelings for her influence me. Maybe I'd made a bigger deal of her mistakes than I should have.

Except, I reminded myself, my Yelp reviews had gone from excellent to good since she'd started, and a lot of the negative comments were about Hailey's customer service.

"Are you okay?" Parker directed the question to Hailey but then looked back at me. He stood close enough to gently put his hand on my elbow, and Hailey's eyes followed Parker's touch then went back to his face. He would have noticed the tears that sprang to her eyes had he been looking at her instead of me, but he didn't.

"You know what?" Hailey's voice trembled. "I'm fine." She turned her back to Parker and me and swung the passenger car door open. "I've been on my own my entire life, and I don't need charity from anyone. Especially not from some snob who's had a perfect life or a guy who thinks he's too good for me." She jerked the front seat forward and shoved Xander into the car seat in the back.

"Hailey!" I didn't know what to say beyond that. Not that she could have heard anything over Xander's wails or the hollow clang of the door being slammed shut. She hurried past us, bumping me out of her way.

"Wait, Hailey—" I grabbed her arm, but she twisted away from me.

"No, seriously. I don't need you or Parker." She yanked her car door open. "Just leave me alone," she added before slamming the door shut and starting the engine.

"Let her go." Parker moved me out of the way as she backed up the car.

"She was fine ten minutes ago."

She drove down the alley, and tears welled up in my own eyes. Every relationship in my life was officially a mess. Caroline and Taylor didn't have time for me, Parker thought I was oblivious, and Hailey hated me. The only person I could count on was my dad.

"What got her so mad?" Parker asked and led me into the store.

"I have no idea. She seemed excited about making a new start until you showed up." My eyes were drawn to the spot where Xander's playpen had been for the past eight months. I felt as empty as it looked. Then it hit me why she freaked out.

"Did you come here to see her or me?" I asked him.

"You." He bit his lip. "I've got something to tell you."

He loves me. The thought flickered through my head, but then I remembered our conversation from the night before. He couldn't love me when I treated people the way I'd treated Nancy. And now he had Hailey to add to that list. She'd be at the top of his People-Eliza-Is-Mean-To list if he felt the same way about her that she did about him.

I took a deep breath to gear up for what he had to tell me. "Is it about Hailey?"

"No." He shook his head slowly. "Why would it be about Hailey?"

He looked genuinely confused. I opened my mouth to tell him how she felt but then changed my mind and shook my head instead. "I don't know."

"I thought Hailey might be here but figured I could text her later," he said. "You're the one I have to apologize to before I go."

He'd come to apologize? That was a surprise. But then the rest of his sentence hit me. "Go where?"

"I found a place in L.A., which is where I need to be to grow my nonprofit." He rubbed the back of his neck. He always had a knot there. I kept telling him yoga would help, but he never listened. "I've taken advantage of your dad's charity for too long."

"You're moving?" I didn't care about the apology anymore. He'd been right about everything he'd said, so there wasn't a reason for him to apologize.

He nodded.

"When?" I almost would have preferred the news that he had feelings for Hailey. At least then I'd still get to see him. L.A. wasn't far, but it may as well have been a million miles away as often as I got there between taking care of Daddy and my shop.

"This weekend." He stuck his hands in his pockets and stared at the floor. "There's not really a reason to wait."

"You're not going to Taylor's wedding?"

He shook his head, a slow, almost imperceptible movement. "She's more your friend than mine, and I don't have the money to spend on tickets to Hawaii."

"I can get you tickets!" He'd been gone for years and I'd been fine without him, but now I didn't know how that had even been possible. And I didn't know how I'd face all the emotions I knew Taylor's wedding would bring up without him by my side.

"Eliza, you can't keep throwing money at every problem that needs to be solved." Parker looked as surprised by what he said as I felt. He took a step toward me, but I turned around and began pulling ribbon from the shelf. His words stung as much as the tears I fought back.

"I'm sorry. That was too harsh," he said softly.

"It's fine. I'm used to you telling me what I'm doing wrong." I kept my back to him and unwound ribbon to make a bow, but I could no more make a bow right then than I could solve a calculus problem.

"Listen, Eliza . . ." He touched my arm then stepped in front of me and tried to make me meet his gaze, but I kept my eyes on the floor. "I'm sorry. I'm sorry I say things that make you feel like what you're doing or who you are is wrong. I think you're pretty close to perfect."

My eyes darted up. "You do?" There was a softness in his eyes I hadn't seen in months, and it gave me the overwhelming urge to tell him I loved him. So many things in my life were changing and uncertain, but that's the thing I knew without a doubt. I loved him.

Even with that certainty I didn't know for sure that he felt the same. If he didn't, everything about us would change. We would never again have the easy friendship we enjoyed. We might not even be friends. I couldn't risk that, so I didn't. I didn't say anything about how I felt.

"Of course I do." He moved the hand he had on my arm to my fingertips. "I'm sorry I said all those things last night. I know you were upset about Blake, and I should have been nicer about it."

"I was upset, but that wasn't an excuse to treat Nancy the way I did." I took a chance and moved my fingers so they were firmly in his palm. "You said everything I needed to hear." *Everything I needed to be a better person.*

"But it's not my job to . . ." He squeezed my hand, triggering a jolt of hope that ran the length of my arm to my heart. "It's not my job to lecture you. You're not a kid anymore. I didn't mean to treat you like you were my little sister or something."

"True. I'm not your sister." I moved closer to him, and our eyes locked.

"No, you're not." Parker leaned toward me, and heat rippled through me. He must have felt it too, but his reaction was the exact opposite of what I wanted. "But you are practically family." He let go of my hand and stepped back. "I should treat you better, especially when you've been going through a hard time."

There was my answer. He still thought of me like a sister, not like a grown woman he could fall in love with. I didn't know if he was in love with Hailey or not, but I knew for sure he wasn't in love with me.

"Thanks for coming to say goodbye," I said, my voice barely above a whisper. Normally I would have hugged him, but I couldn't do it then. Instead I stepped around him to walk to the cooler. "I've got a couple arrangements to get done."

"Okay." He followed me to the cooler where I opened the door but didn't step in, hoping for some kind of encouragement before he left. "I'm sorry about missing the wedding."

"You should probably tell Taylor, not me."

"I will."

"Okay." I turned my head toward the inside of the cooler. "I should get back to work. Good luck in L.A."

"Thanks."

That's all he said before he walked out the door, leaving me to wonder if I'd just made the biggest mistake of my life for letting him.

Chapter 29

Flower arranging is the best problem-solving technique I know of. If I can put aside a problem long enough to make a big bouquet, it's probably not a problem worth solving anyway. If it is something big enough to focus on, I usually have a solution by the time I put the last flower in its place.

But my Parker problem? That was two-fold: one, I was in love with him, and two, he was moving to Los Angeles. It took two big arrangements to figure out what to do, because it obviously wasn't something that could be put aside. Unfortunately the solution I came up with didn't really do anything to solve my Parker problem, but it did send me in the right direction.

Instead of replaying my conversation with Parker over and over a million times so I could figure out what I should have said to make him stay, I made an apology arrangement for Nancy. Lilies and roses. Basic, but I knew she loved them. I even happened to have a stuffed Scottie dog I added to it. As soon as my last customers picked up their orders, I closed up shop and drove to Nancy's.

I heard laughing before I knocked on their door, and I was sure it came from their third-floor apartment. But seconds after I knocked everything went silent inside. I could have sworn I'd heard footsteps coming to the door, so I knocked again. And then I knocked a third time.

Martha finally answered, but she only opened the door wide enough to peek her head out and say, "Hello, Eliza."

I'd worked at Daddy's office with Martha one summer. I was seventeen, and she was . . . well, she was just old and cranky. Every time I'd made a mistake—which was often—she'd say my full name in the same tight voice she'd just used, emphasizing the "za" with the disappointment of someone who'd discovered they'd been served a steak with only a butter knife to cut it.

"Hello, Mrs. Bates." I hadn't called her that in years. I was an adult, after all. But she'd reduced me to that same seventeen-year-old girl who couldn't understand why it was so important to file paperwork in cabinets when computers had been invented to save people from such a boring job.

"What can I do for you?" She still hadn't opened the door all the way.

"I was wondering if I might come in and talk to Nancy for a minute. I brought her these." I held up the flowers as proof I'd come in peace.

"She's a little busy right now." Martha glanced over her shoulder and let the door open a couple more inches. "We've got a wedding to plan for, you know."

"I know, and I'm so excited for you both!" I smiled wide. I'd found something to say that might convince her to let me in. "And for Jami too. Blake is a great guy."

The door opened a fraction of an inch more. "You didn't seem very excited at the party. You seemed mad. Or disappointed." She cocked her head to the side. "Maybe even jealous."

Martha literally had not said more than five words to me in the past five years, and suddenly she had a lot to say that I didn't want to hear. Did people really think I had been rejected by Blake? I thought back to my conversation with Parker. He'd said something about my being upset with Blake. Did he think it was because I had feelings for Blake and not because Blake had hijacked Taylor's whole wedding party and made it his own? Because that would explain a lot about why things got so weird between us. It also might mean . . .

"Liza?" Martha's voice brought me back to the present and the task at hand.

"Sorry. I got distracted." I had to call Parker. The art of flower arranging had worked, and I'd found the solution to my problem when I wasn't even looking for it. Except now I had a bigger problem: apologizing quickly enough I'd have time to call Parker but sincerely enough for Nancy to believe me.

"I understand if Nancy doesn't want to see me." I held the flowers toward Martha, who didn't get the hint she should take them. "I really am sorry I was so rude. It didn't have anything to do with her, I was just . . ." Just what? How could I explain the person I was mad at that night was Erica for implying I wanted to be in Jami's place, when really, I wanted to be in Hailey's place? Hailey was the one who'd sat next to Parker and who he held in his arms. And—

"I suppose I could ask her if she'd like to see you." Martha opened the door wide, but I'd been knocked in the head by an epiphany, and I had to leave.

"Give her some more time." I shoved the flowers into Martha's chest. If Nancy did forgive me—which was likely, considering her kind nature—I'd be stuck there for hours talking to her. "I'll come back in a few days and see if she's ready to talk then," I blurted then bolted for the metal stairs, taking them as slowly as my racing heart would let me until I got to the second floor, out of Martha's sight. Then I ran down them because I had to see Parker.

I'd finally put everything together. Parker hadn't been acting weird because he had feelings for Hailey. He'd been acting weird because he had feelings for me. But he thought I had feelings for Blake. An easy mistake to make considering how much time Blake and I had spent together. Erica's stupid comments at Taylor's reception hadn't helped either, but then, neither had my stupid comment about being upset with Blake.

I had to let him know who I really wanted to surf and laugh and dance and . . . other stuff with. Not Blake. It had never been Blake. It had always been Parker. From the time I was a little girl who followed him around begging for piggy-back rides to the awkward tween who had a crush on the very grown-up college boy to now, when we were both grown-ups and he could love me as something other than an annoying faux sister. He could love me as me, faults and all.

And I suspected he did.

At least, I really, really hoped he did. Otherwise I was about to make the biggest fool of myself possible. But I had to do it.

I pulled into my driveway twenty minutes later. Traffic, red lights, and a charger-less phone with a dead battery had all conspired against me. What should have been a ten-minute drive took double that, and I had no way to call Parker.

I shouldn't have been surprised when I went around back and found his apartment dark. I knocked on the door anyway. No one answered. Then I rang the doorbell and peeked in every window I could. They all reconfirmed what I already knew—he wasn't there.

I walked the short distance back to my house and went inside. I still had options. Or option, anyway. I'd have to call him. For some reason the thought of telling him face to face how I felt was less scary than doing it over the phone. Maybe because face to face I could gauge his body language and abort the whole mission if it looked like it was headed off course. I couldn't do that over the phone.

"Eliza, is that you?" Daddy called from upstairs like he always did when I came in. As though it would be anybody else.

"Hi, Daddy!" I climbed the stairs quickly. I needed to call Parker before I lost my nerve, but I couldn't run to my room like I wanted to without hugging my dad first.

"I put dinner in the oven a few minutes ago," he said as I kissed his cheek. "It will be ready in fifteen minutes." He motioned for me to sit next to him. "Tell me about your day."

Fifteen minutes? I couldn't wait that long plus the time it would take for us to eat. I had about fifteen seconds before my adrenaline rush wore off and my brain took back over in time to talk me out of calling Parker.

"I will in a minute. I have to do something first—" I started to say.

"Parker left for L.A. Did you know he's moving there?" Daddy glanced from me to the couch, looking as confused about why I still wasn't sitting by him as he was about why Parker would ever want to live anywhere besides right behind us.

But if I sat down, my legs wouldn't want to get back up to carry me somewhere for the private conversation I needed to have. "He told me, but I thought he wasn't moving until this weekend."

"He'll be back in a couple days to get his stuff," he answered. "I don't understand this sudden decision. He came over half an hour ago, thanked me for everything, and said he'd be back Friday to pack up."

"I'll be right back, Daddy." I ran to my room, with Daddy calling after me wondering what was going on. I ignored him. If Parker had left thirty minutes before, I'd beg him to come back so we could talk, and I'd explain to Daddy later.

I dialed Parker's number, my heartbeat increasing each time I pushed a digit. He didn't answer, so I hung up and dialed again. And again. And three more times without an answer. He had to be driving and he had Bluetooth, so there was no way he wasn't hearing his phone.

Which could only mean one thing: he didn't want to talk to me.

But I wasn't ready to give up. I thought about it, but the stakes were too high. I'd spent half a lifetime afraid of falling in love. Now that I was in it, I was going to fight for it.

Please pick up. I texted him just in case he was stopped in traffic and would glance at his phone then waited thirty seconds to call again.

It rang and rang with no answer.

I'd imagined a romantic scene where I'd knock on his door, he'd open it, I'd tell him I loved him, and he wouldn't say anything—just take me in his arms, lifting me off the ground, and finally, *finally*, his lips would be on mine.

None of that was happening now.

The ringing changed to a beep, and his voice came on asking me to leave a message. I almost pressed end, but I knew if I hung up again, I'd never be able to say what I wanted to say. And I had to say it, even if it meant spilling my emotions all over like a first-time skater on an ice rink carrying one of those giant mugs full of Coke. Or Mountain Dew. Or whatever it was people who carried sixty-four-ounce mugs of soda drank.

"Don't move to L.A., Parker," I blurted. "I know it would make your life about a thousand times easier, but don't do it. I should have told you that when you said goodbye today. I should have told you a lot of things. I don't know why I didn't." I blathered, saying anything that made it from my brain to my mouth out of the million reasons he should stay that were darting through my head. I paused long enough to grab one of them. The best one of them.

"Here's the thing. I love you." My brain slowed down, and so did my heart. I'd said it. I'd said it, and nothing had exploded or imploded or . . . ploded in any way. I could say more. I could say everything. He might not want to hear it, but I had to do it.

"And I think you may love me too," I went on. "At least, I hope you do. Because I really can't imagine my life without you. I think I've known that for a long time, but it wasn't until I had to think about that possibility that I realized I didn't want to think about it. Ever.

"Please come home. Please." I didn't know what else to say. I'd said everything I had to, and even if it turned out he didn't love me back, I felt lighter. I didn't know how I'd bear it if he didn't love me, but at least I could stop pretending I didn't love him.

"Okay. I think that's all. Except, please call me." I pressed the phone to my ear like I might be able to hear into the future and skip right to the part where he was supposed to tell me he loved me too.

I couldn't hear anything. *Obvs,* as Hailey would say. All I could do was wait.

Wait. And hope.

Chapter 30

It took all of five minutes of waiting and Parker not calling before disappointment washed over me with all the fury of a rogue wave. But those minutes seemed like a lifetime. The thought of waiting another lifetime or, even worse, a bunch of lifetimes before I heard his voice again was too horrible to think about. Thoughts of *What if I've ruined everything?* and *What if he never wants to see me again?* circled around my head, forming an angry whirlpool attempting to suck every good wish I had into a dark abyss.

I left my room and found Daddy on the couch right where I needed him to be so I could snuggle into him like I had as a child when I had bad dreams. I laid my head against his shoulder and curled my legs against his side.

"What's got you so scared?" he asked, wrapping his arm around my shoulder.

"I don't know," I said into his chest. "Being alone, I guess."

"You're not alone." He patted my arm, but there was little comfort in it. I could hear the worry in his own voice. "I'm right here."

"I know, Daddy." I wrapped my arm around his waist and squeezed, determined to keep him there forever. But forever was a long time. An impossibly long time. Someday I wouldn't have him to comfort or protect me anymore.

I clung tighter and inched closer to him, squeezing my eyes shut to force that most terrible idea of all out of my head. Everything was changing too fast. Caroline was having a baby and living farther away from me than she had our entire lives. We'd gone from talking a couple times a day to barely once a week. Taylor was getting married in five days, and I talked to her only slightly more than I talked to my sister. Parker was leaving. Hailey hated my guts. Jami and Blake . . . well, I didn't really want to see them anyway. (I could be annoyed with Blake without actually being jealous of Jami.)

Even Nancy and Martha were mad at me.

I literally had no one but my dad.

I let out a deep sigh, and a tear escaped with it, sliding across my nose and down the tip of it until it dropped onto Daddy's shirt. I stared at the tiny water spot, imagining how big it would grow if any of the other tears beating on my chest made it out. It wasn't a pretty picture.

I uncurled my legs and sat up, wiping my cheek.

"It's just you and me, kid." Daddy had said that to me a million times since Caroline had moved out. He didn't know how true it was.

I rested my neck against the arm he had spread across the couch and stretched my legs out on the coffee table. "Yep," I said, crossed my arms, and stared at the ceiling. Tomorrow I would reach out to Hailey and try to repair a breach I had no idea how to repair. I'd finish the last details of Taylor's wedding plans, and I'd wait and hope for Parker to call. Until then, I'd watch old movies with my dad.

Which is exactly what I did. But first thing in the morning, I texted Hailey and asked if we could talk. I probably should have done it sooner, but I justified my wait by telling myself she needed time to cool down. In reality, I didn't know what to say to her. I didn't think she really had a right to be mad at me because Parker wasn't interested in her. Unless she thought he and I were interested in each other. I'd give her credit for figuring out how I felt about Parker, but if I wasn't even sure how he felt about me, how could she be?

Putting that question aside, there were a million other things I'd done that she did have a right to be mad about. Trying to control her life, pushing her to do something she didn't really care about instead of pursuing something she loved, treating her like a project. That last one was the biggest and worst. That one she should be mad about.

I gave her an hour, but when she didn't respond, I tried calling. I shouldn't have been surprised when she didn't answer, but I was. I also should have left a message. Instead I gave her the benefit of the doubt and assumed she might be in class or some other important place. So I gave her two hours before I tried again.

Two hours of torture. The shop was slow, and I hadn't taken any orders for bridal flowers because I'd blocked out five days for Taylor's wedding. Before everything with Hailey, I'd debated whether to leave her in charge so the shop wouldn't lose money while I was gone, but I'd decided no. Bullet dodged there. But after months of having Hailey and Xander around when it was slow, the silence was unbearable. So was waiting for Parker to return my call while I counted down the hours I'd given myself before trying Hailey again.

When my self-imposed timeline finally came to an end, I dialed Hailey's number. Still no answer, but this time I left a message.

"Hey," I stammered. I'd meant for it to come out casual and totally normal, but my nervousness and guilt escaped. "I'm really sorry." *But for what?* "I don't know what upset you yesterday, but I've done a lot of things before then that you should be upset about. Maybe that's been building and it all came out at once." I was blabbering and had no idea what path to take to get to the point I needed to make. "Anyway, call me, please."

I hung up then decided to send a Snap. She was more likely to open that anyway. I took a picture of the spot where Xander's playpen used to be and captioned it *Miss you guys.*

Then the waiting game began again. I'm really not good at games. Especially the waiting ones. Every time I looked at the time, sure at least an hour had passed, it turned out to only be fifteen minutes. Hailey didn't open my Snap, Parker didn't return my call, Taylor answered my *How's it goin'?* text with a thumbs-up emoji that told me she was too busy to talk, and no customers came in. I couldn't even call Caroline because I knew she was at work.

The whole world was trying to avoid me.

I finally decided to close up shop and go surfing. Even if the waves were mush, they couldn't disappoint me anymore than my friends had. They especially couldn't disappoint me anymore than I'd disappointed myself.

Turned out, they weren't disappointing at all, and by the time I'd caught a few good sets, my spirits were lifted. That is until I got out of the water and checked my phone. Caroline had texted that she needed to talk. I was in such a better mood I didn't anticipate what she had to tell me would be bad news.

"I can't come down to stay with Daddy while you're in Hawaii," she wailed.

"What? Why?" I wailed and dropped the towel I'd been using to dry my hair.

"I've had some spotting," she said, and suddenly I understood why she was crying. "The doctor thinks everything will be okay. The heartbeat is still strong. But he's put me on bed rest for at least a week."

I would have cried for myself if she'd been canceling on me for any other reason, but this one was too big. "Of course you can't come. I wish I could come to you."

"But we'd still have the same problem, wouldn't we? What to do with Daddy?" She took a long, ragged breath. The thing that made her such a great sister is that, of course she wasn't just upset about the baby; she was upset about not being able to take care of our dad so I could go to Taylor's wedding.

"It's okay." Being four hundred miles away from her had never felt so far. "You worry about keeping our baby safe."

She took another jagged breath that ended in a whimper.

"I don't mean worry. I mean everything will be okay." I grabbed my board and my towel and headed for the stairs, cradling the phone with my shoulder. "You just take care of you and the baby. I'll figure out something to do with Daddy."

"I'm so sorry."

"Don't be sorry. Go lie down. This is the perfect excuse to binge on Netflix."

We said goodbye, and I made my way up the street. I couldn't help but check out back when I got home. I wished Parker were there to help me talk Daddy into going to Hawaii with me. If anyone could do it, it would be him. Even then the chances would be slim.

I peeled off my wetsuit and hung it across the fence before going inside and calling for Daddy.

"Out here, Eliza," he called back. Of course he was sitting on the deck; the sun was setting. Where else would he be?

"I'll be out in a sec," I said and went to my room to put sweatpants and a hoodie over my damp bikini. I'd shower later, but right then I had to try and convince my dad to get on a plane and fly over the ocean. I could barely get him in a car anymore, so I had a next-to-impossible task ahead of me. I took my time sliding into my warm clothes, hoping for some inspiration about how to fix all of Daddy's little quirks that kept him from living life.

Caroline and I never pushed him to get help for his quirks because they weren't a huge inconvenience. Neither of us minded taking care of him, and neither of us felt much of a desire to go far. That is until Caroline and Preston fell in love, and Daddy's care fell entirely on me. Even then I didn't mind. I loved living with him. But in a matter of hours it had become a huge problem. I couldn't miss Taylor's wedding.

With warm clothes on, I took a deep breath and prepared myself for battle. That David kid had beat a giant with only a slingshot, so maybe I had a chance too. That is, if you believed in those Bible stories. I wasn't a church-going girl, and I'd only gone to Vacation Bible School because Taylor had, but at that moment I chose to be a believer.

I carried a blanket to the patio in case Daddy needed an extra one and sat down next to him. He had the fire going, but it was still chilly. I held the blanket open to spread over both of us, but he shook his head so I wrapped it all the way around myself.

"Did you talk to Caroline?" I asked.

He stared at the fire and nodded. The flames outlined the worry etched on his face.

"She and the baby will be okay." I snaked my hand out of the blanket and put it over his clenched fist. "The heartbeat is still strong. It doesn't sound like this is too serious; she just has to be careful."

"I should be there with her." He unclenched his fist then clenched it again, clutching his pant leg with it. "Your mom would want me to be. But the thought of getting in the car or, even worse, an airplane . . ." He closed his eyes and shook his head while his chest vibrated unevenly with each shaky breath he took. "I can't do it." He opened his eyes and looked at me. "What's wrong with me?"

"Nothing." I had never seen him cry. He'd never been a super manly man who wouldn't let himself—he just didn't cry. So it scared me to see tears about to fall from his watery eyes. "Nothing is wrong with you. You don't like to travel. Lots of people don't—"

"I hardly leave this house," he interrupted. "I can't even make myself do it to go take care of my daughter. And Caroline says you're going to miss Taylor's wedding. All because I'm a doddering old man. What kind of father am I?"

"A perfect one, in every way." I let go of his hand and threw my arms around him. "I don't even know what 'doddering' means, but I'm sure you're not that." Unless doddering meant afraid to fly. Even if I'd had the courage to ask him then, I knew he wasn't getting on any planes.

But another idea had come to me. I let go of him and rested my head on his shoulder. "Listen, Daddy. What if I had someone come stay here with you so you wouldn't be alone, and I went and visited Caroline before I flew to Taylor's wedding? Would you feel better knowing I was with her?"

He pulled a tissue from his jacket pocket and wiped his nose while he thought about it. "I would, but I don't need anyone to stay with me. I'm not that old. I can take care of myself for a few days while you're gone."

"Of course you don't *need* anybody, but I would worry too much about you if you didn't have some company." I took his hand in mine and held it tight. "I couldn't leave for an entire week without knowing there was someone here to get your breakfast or bring you an extra blanket when you sit out here at night. Especially since Parker won't be around."

The muscles in his neck tightened as he worked his jaw back and forth chewing on the problem. "Who would you get?"

That was a good question. "Nancy?"

"She couldn't leave Martha, and they've got that wedding to plan for."

"They could both come."

"A week with Nancy would drive me from marginally crazy to full-blown asylum patient."

I giggled. At least he could laugh at his mental . . . at his quirks. "Okay, so no Nancy." That didn't leave a lot of other possibilities. Maybe Elton and Erica, but I shot that idea down before my brain could do anything more than toy with it. The last thing I wanted was Erica going through my things looking for more ways to judge me.

That left one person. One person who happened to not be speaking to me at the moment.

"What about my friend Hailey?" It felt good to call her my friend. At least, I hoped I could still call her that. "The one with the baby?"

"I know who Hailey is." His shoulders relaxed. "Would she bring the baby?"

"She'd have to." I hadn't thought about that potential deal-breaker.

An eternity passed before he answered, and with each eon I became more convinced I was out of luck.

Until he said, "I could use some practice with babies before I have a grandchild of my own."

I bolted up. "Really?"

"I like her. She doesn't talk too much. And I like the baby." Daddy's voice didn't exactly rise with excitement, but I could hear it in there. "She might like a vacation at the beach."

"She'd love it!" I was so excited I actually clapped until I remembered the only hurdle standing in the way of my plan: Hailey hated me at the moment.

But that could be overcome because I needed her. I *needed* her. She was my friend, and I needed her help.

Chapter 31

Parker hadn't returned my calls or my texts the following morning. As much as I wanted to send him one more text to make sure he'd listened to my call, that would have been too humiliating. Plus, I had more pressing matters to deal with. Hailey still wasn't answering my texts either, and she was my last hope for making it to Caroline's bedside and Taylor's wedding.

I sent one last plea, begging her to please, Please, PLEASE call me. I waited an entire hour before I decided I'd have to go into full-on stalker mode, track her down, and talk to her face to face. She'd moved out of transitional and into Section 8 housing recently, but I'd never been to her place. I knew she didn't have class on Tuesday afternoons though, so I closed the shop, punched her address into Google maps, and crossed my fingers that she'd be home.

Google led me to a brown-brick twelve-story apartment building that looked like it had been built in the seventies. It was nicer than I'd expected. Hailey lived on the tenth floor, so I found the elevator, stepped in, and hit the button. As the door was about to shut, someone called to hold it. I stuck my arm between the closing sheets of metal and squeezed my eyes shut, hoping this wouldn't be the day an elevator door actually chopped off someone's arm. The doors clanked and opened without maiming me, so I opened my eyes to find Hailey standing in front of me looking as angry as she had the last time I'd seen her.

"What are you doing here?" she asked, clutching Xander in one arm and a bag of groceries in the other. The doors shut, and the elevator groaned with the burden of carrying us up ten flights.

"I came to see you." I reached to stroke Xander's black hair, but she pulled him back.

"Why?" Her canvas bagged slipped and she shifted it higher on her shoulder.

"Let me take that." I reached for the bag, but she moved away from me again.

"I told you I don't need your help. I'm not a charity case." Her eyes narrowed, shooting daggers faster than the knife-thrower I'd seen at a street fair once. Except she wasn't trying to miss me.

"I know you don't, but I need you." I reached for the bag again. She hadn't stopped metaphorically knifing me in the heart, but she didn't back away. "Let me take that bag, and let's talk."

I slung the bag over my shoulder and stared above the door at the numbers lighting up as we reached the next floor. Three more to go.

"I don't want to talk." She said the words, but without confidence, as she stared up at the numbers with me.

"I know. I don't blame you, but I'd appreciate it if you did."

The door dinged as the elevator reached the tenth floor. "My apartment's a mess," she said as I followed her down the dimly lit hallway that was dark enough to be depressing but not dark enough to hide the stains and tears in the industrial-grade carpet.

"That's okay."

She reached a brown door with one of its numbers hanging upside down and stuck her key into the lock. She slowly pushed open the door then stepped aside so I could walk in. "This is it. I told you it was a dump."

I glanced around the room looking for something to compliment. A futon with a dirty white cushion flanked one wall. An old TV with a VCR/DVD player sat atop cinder blocks opposite the futon, with a crateful of video tapes next to it. I walked to the crate and picked up an old Barbie movie. "I used to love this one when I was a little girl. I had it on DVD."

"Yeah, I bought the whole crate for a couple bucks at a garage sale." She set Xander down on the floor and handed him his favorite toy. I tried not to look at the worn brown carpet I suspected had once been beige.

She took the bag off my shoulder and walked to the kitchen. She didn't have far to go. The whole living room and kitchen combined couldn't have been more than four hundred square feet. Then I realized there was a small crib under the window.

"Xander sleeps out here?" I asked and walked to his crib. Dust covered the metal blinds over the window. I took the cords that hung too close to Xander's crib—and his reach when he was in it—and tucked them between blind slats.

"We both do. It's a studio apartment." She took cans of formula and blocks of cheese out of her bag.

I looked around again. There were two other doors in the room. One was probably a bathroom and the other a closet. Their entire living space was smaller than my bedroom suite.

"You didn't get any apples?" I asked when she'd finished emptying her bag. She loved apples.

"Apples are way out of my food stamp budget," she said in a tone so laced with sarcasm and accusation I didn't dare point out a couple apples cost less than a bag of chips—even if they didn't last as long. Maybe that's why she skipped them. Chips had a longer shelf life.

"So what did you want to talk about?" She walked out of the kitchen and crossed her arms. "You obviously don't need my help at the shop since I sucked at that—"

"You didn't suck."

"Whatever." She rolled her eyes. "I didn't like working there anyway."

That hurt. "Well, I liked having you work there."

She huffed, but her shoulders slumped too as she let go of some anger. "You're just saying that because you need something from me."

"No, I really mean it. I miss having you and Xander there. Even though it's only been one day, it's not the same."

At the sound of his name, Xander whimpered. "Can I pick him up?"

Hailey gave me a terse nod. "So you need me to come back?"

I could have said yes, but it would have been for selfish reasons. I liked having Hailey around, and I could work around her clumsiness, but I'd still be treating her like a charity case. She'd never be successful there, and she'd never pursue what she was good at if she stayed. In any case, I'd already hired a contract florist to take care of the shop while I was gone, so I took Xander in my arms, stood up, and shook my head.

Her face fell, then hardened, and she grabbed Xander from me. "Why are you here? Isn't it enough that you fired me then humiliated me with Parker after I told you how I felt about him?"

"What do you mean I humiliated you?"

"I don't tell anyone what I'm feeling, but I spilled my guts to you. I tell you all about how into him I am, and you don't say anything about him being totally into you."

"What are you talking about? Parker doesn't see me as anything more than a friend, as far as I know." Saying the words aloud brought home the reality I'd been trying to ignore. Parker hadn't returned my call. "I thought maybe he did—I really, really hoped he did—but you're not the only one who's spilled her guts to someone and been hurt. At least you only told *me* how you felt."

"You want me to feel sorry for you?" She held tightly to Xander, even though he squirmed to get down. "This is the first time you haven't gotten what you wanted."

"I know." I thought I'd be able to talk Hailey into forgiving me, but I was losing hope. Hope I'd be able to see my sister, hope I'd be able to go to Taylor's wedding, and, most of all, hope Hailey and I could be real friends. "But the reason I wanted him wasn't to hurt you. I really do love him. I have for a longer time than I ever realized."

She set Xander down, and I reached into my pocket for my keys and said, "I should go." I hoped she'd tell me not to, but she didn't. "I really am sorry, Hailey. I know I treated you more like someone who needed my help instead of as a friend. I thought that was being a friend to you, but it wasn't. You need to know I do like you. I think you're amazing, and I'd love to keep you at the shop so we could hang out every day and I could see Xander. But you can do so much more than that, and I've kept you from doing what you want and being who you want for too long."

Hailey kept her eyes on the floor, and I waited for her to say something. The only one who did anything was Xander, who wobbly crawled to me and hit my painted red toenail. He sat up and planted himself at my feet. I was about to step over him when he grabbed my toe. I couldn't exactly walk away with a baby dangling from my foot, so I stayed until he let go.

"Now I'll go." I sounded more lighthearted than I felt. Stepping over him instead of scooping him up and covering him with kisses nearly broke my heart. I made it to the door before I couldn't take another step without telling him goodbye. "Can I give him one kiss?" I turned around and asked.

Hailey raised her eyebrows then nodded. I walked back to Xander and did exactly what I'd wanted to do since I'd walked in. I had to breathe in that baby smell and touch that soft hair one more time.

Hailey took a step closer, and I thought she might take him from me. "You never told me what you needed," she said.

"Caroline's on bed rest," I answered and held Xander closer, hoping her words meant I'd be able to keep holding him. "I need someone to stay with Daddy for about a week while I go see her and then go to Taylor's wedding."

She flinched when I said Taylor's wedding. Of course, she'd been invited, but she didn't have the money to go. I would have paid for her, but I'd decided that would have insulted her. She'd see it as welfare, and she hated taking welfare for the necessities, let alone for luxuries.

But after the flinch, there was a look of pride. "You want me to stay with him?"

I nodded. "Daddy wants you to stay too."

"Really?"

I nodded again. "You and Xander."

"Really?" she repeated.

"We don't have anyone else we both feel comfortable helping us out." The smile on her face encouraged me to go on. "You can set up Xander's playpen in my room. Daddy doesn't need to be taken care of—he just doesn't like to be alone. You can hang out at the beach or do whatever you want. I'll even pay you."

Her face clouded. "So you need me to work for you?"

I shook my head and backtracked. "No. I need your help as a friend. If you don't want me to pay you, I won't. I'll feel terrible about it, but I'll do it if it makes you feel better."

"It will make me feel better. I already owe you for the 'scholarship.'" She made air quotes, and I felt my cheeks flush.

"You know about that?"

She frowned and nodded then let a smile creep up her lips. "I went to the administration to ask if my scholarship could go to someone else if I withdrew. They had no idea what I was talking about. I put it all together and figured out you're the one who gave it to me. I get why you did, but when I was mad at you, it made me feel like more of a welfare mom."

"You're not a welfare mom."

"I am, but I won't always be." She shifted her weight and stood taller. "Taking care of your dad will help me pay you back."

"If that's what you want, that's what we'll do." I wanted to cry with relief. Something had finally gone right. "Can I hug you now?"

She smiled wider and threw her arms around Xander and me.

When we broke apart, I handed Xander back to her. I had some packing to do and flights to arrange. Between flowers for Nancy and begging for forgiveness from Hailey, I'd repaired two relationships I'd made a mess of. If I focused on those wins, I could almost forget my biggest loss. The more time that passed without a call from Parker, the more convinced I was that I'd ruined the most important relationship in my life.

Chapter 32

Hailey arrived bright and early the next morning with enough luggage to make me wonder if she thought I'd asked her to move in. At that point, though, as long as I got to see my sister and go to my best friend's wedding, I didn't care if Hailey did move in permanently.

I hugged Daddy goodbye and climbed into my Uber. I tried not to think about the fact that I was going to be farther away from him than I'd ever been. I was twenty-four years old and flying an hour away from home by myself for the first time. I should have been scared. A part of me was. But I buried that feeling with the push of a Play button that brought Taylor Swift on the flight with me.

I used Miss Swift to distract me from worrying. It worked until I was buckled into my seat and the airplane taxied down the runway. Then all the thoughts I'd been trying to avoid for weeks—make that months . . . okay, years—made it to the forefront of my mind before I could pull up another playlist to drown them out. I let myself see, for the first time, how like Nancy Bates's life mine was. I may not have had the same love for cats or Scottie dogs, but I had the same kind of codependent relationship with my dad that she did with her mom. Both of us used our needy parents as excuses not to move forward in our own lives.

When that realization hit me, followed closely by the recognition that the farther I got from home the more free I felt, followed by the reminder that Parker still hadn't called me, I came apart. Tears sprang to my eyes and rolled down my face before I could stop them. Once they started it was full-on Hurricane Eliza, with heaving sobs, saliva, and snot spilling out of mouth and nose. The lady sitting next to me handed me a package of tissue then scooted as far from me as possible.

The emotional storm didn't stop in baggage claim or on my Uber ride to Caroline's. It didn't stop after I'd made it safely to her house. It followed me through her front door and into her room, where I curled up in bed with her before even saying hello.

"You made it," she said and held me in her arms.

All I could do was nod. I was still sobbing too hard to talk.

"When you're ready, tell me what's wrong," she said and gently stroked my hair. "I'm sure all this isn't about me and the baby, but just in case, the bleeding has stopped. The doctor thinks everything is going to be okay but wants me to stay in bed for at least another week."

"Oh, that's so good to hear," I said and then cried harder out of relief.

She pulled me tighter, and I rested my head on her shoulder until I'd calmed down enough to talk. "I miss Daddy already, but it feels so good to be away. I didn't know I'd feel like this."

"Oh, Sweetie." Tears sprang to her eyes. "I should have known. I thought you were perfectly happy taking care of him. I should have known it would be too hard to do by yourself."

I reached across her belly to grab the box of tissues sitting on her side table. I dried my eyes, but by the time I'd blown my nose, my eyes were wet again. "I am happy. I love him. I love living at home. I'm happy." I wiped my eyes and nose again. "I guess I didn't realize taking care of him would be so hard. I didn't know I'd have to give up so much."

"You found a way to get here and go to Taylor's wedding." She took a tissue for herself and dabbed under her eyes. "It won't always be this hard. Once I have the baby, I can help again."

"I know you will, but you'll also have your own life." I didn't know how much to reveal about what I was feeling. How could I tell her how trapped I felt, how hard it would be to have my own life if I couldn't leave Daddy for more than a week, and not make her feel guilty for leaving me alone with him?

"You've got your shop and your friends, and you've never been interested in getting married." She went into big sister mode, determined to solve my problems and make me happy again. "I promise, as soon as we can, Preston and I will come stay with Daddy so you can have a break. We'll come as often as you need us to. And Parker is always right there to help too."

I guessed she didn't know about Parker moving to L.A., and I wasn't sure I should be the one to tell her. I definitely couldn't tell her about my feelings for him. She was my sister, but she was also his sister-in-law.

So I told her what she wanted to hear. "You're right, and I'll be fine." I took a deep breath and shut my eyes. It had been a long, heart-wrenching thirty-six hours. I needed a nap. "I guess I'm just emotional with everything that's happened over the last few days."

I curled up closer to her. She turned on the TV to some old movie, and I was asleep before the opening credits finished.

Caroline and I spent the next day watching all the cheesy Valentine's Day movies we could find. They shouldn't have cheered me up since my chances with Parker seemed dead in the water, but somehow they did. Or maybe it was being with my sister that did it.

All too soon, it was time to get on my flight to Hawaii. I hadn't flown since I was five years old and Daddy took Caroline and me to Yellowstone National Park. We'd flown to a little airport in Idaho to get there, and the ride was so rough Daddy had rented a car and we drove home rather than get back on an airplane. That was the last time he'd flown anywhere. Which meant it was the last time I'd flown anywhere. There'd been a spring break trip to Mexico I was supposed to go on in college, but Daddy had talked me out of it the week before.

Getting on the plane to Hawaii after a day with Caroline was the most exciting thing I'd done in a long time. But then, anyone who didn't get excited about flying to Hawaii would have to be crazy.

And anyone who didn't get a little scared flying over the ocean for five hours would have to be a little crazy too. We hit enough turbulence that by the time we landed, I was even more excited about getting off the plane than I'd been getting on it. Part of the excitement may have been that I'd finally get to see Taylor and have a few hours with her before she was officially more Weston's than mine.

She met me in baggage claim and had me in a hug nanoseconds after we saw each other.

"I'm so happy you made it! I can't believe it actually happened! I didn't think you'd be able to leave your dad," she gushed while rocking me left and right.

"It's just the two of us today," she added after she let me go. "I told Weston he was on his own because I only want to spend time with you."

"That's exactly what I need." I put my phone away, determined not to check it again to see if Parker had called.

Even though she'd chosen a remote location so she could have a casual wedding, Taylor still wanted flowers. We could have ordered them in advance, but it would have been so expensive. Arranging all the flowers was my wedding gift to her. Unfortunately it also meant that as much as I wanted to sit in a cabana by the beach and take a nap, I needed to scope out the local flower markets I'd found online.

I'd already planned out Taylor's wedding bouquet and the *haku* she wanted instead of a traditional veil, but seeing all the different flowers surrounding the airport had me rethinking what I wanted to do for her. As we walked to the car I stopped at every planter to inspect each new flower. I thought California had a lot of the same flowers as Hawaii, but I'd been wrong. I found at least five different flowers I'd never seen before.

"I hate to say it, but this is not the time to stop and smell the flowers," Taylor said. "Unless you're planning to sneak back here tonight to steal them."

"That's not a bad idea." I stopped again, but she grabbed me by the arm and pulled me away before I could bend down to get a better look at a huge orange blossom I suspected was in the gardenia family.

Taylor dragged me to the car, and we went on our way. With barely twenty-four hours to get everything done before the ceremony, she'd made the right move. But once we were on the road, I spilled everything about Parker. I had to tell someone. It'd been torture waiting as long as I had to unload.

So I told her the whole story, from the moment I'd figured out I couldn't live without him to the second where I'd hit End after pouring out my heart.

"And? What did he say when he called back?" she asked, clutching my hand as she pulled into our first market.

"He hasn't." I pulled my hand from hers and opened the car door.

"He hasn't?"

I shook my head. I knew this is where we'd end up, her wanting a happy ending for me and me not being able to give it to her. You'd think she would have known how things would turn out when I'd started the whole story with, "I think I did something really stupid."

"Are you sure?" she asked.

"I've checked my phone about a million times since Tuesday. I think I'd know if he'd called."

"That's weird," she said. "It seems like he'd at least text to tell you he wasn't interested." She followed me out of the car and put her arm around me. "I know you wanted to hear from him right away, but give him time. He never rushes into anything. My guess is he's thinking things through, so don't give up hope."

I nodded and walked toward the first stall in the market. They had the same orange flower I'd seen at the hotel, and I wanted to focus on it so much more than I wanted to focus on the humiliation gnawing at my gut like an angry beaver.

Thoughts swirled in my head like an overloaded washing machine. Taylor's words had the hope I'd lost trying to squeeze its way back into my heart, but I wasn't sure I wanted it to. I wanted to believe the only reason Parker hadn't called was because he was "thinking things through," but there was still a chance he just hadn't called. And depending on which way I approached it, the odds of either one of those reasons being true were pretty high.

"Have you checked your email? Maybe he sent you a message days ago declaring his undying love for you and *you* haven't answered *him*." Taylor's eyebrows rose to an accusatory angle.

"Why would he email me instead of calling?" I asked, knowing she was just trying to make me feel better, but a part of me wondered if she might be right. Because of course I hadn't checked my email. Who checks email anymore? I mean, other than work email. I didn't even know which address he would have sent any message to. Probably my old high school one, which I couldn't remember the address to, let alone the password.

"I don't know, but you can't give up on him." She lifted her chin and stared me down. "This has to happen. It's meant to. Especially now that Blake ruined all my plans to have you as a sister-in-law."

"Yeah, I wish it were meant to be. More and more I'm thinking nothing is going to happen." I grabbed a bucket and stuck a couple bunches of the orange flower in it.

"Oh, please." Taylor rolled her eyes and shook her head. "Something has been happening since the minute Parker came back to town. You two are the only ones dumb enough not to have seen it."

"You think he likes me?"

"Oh, I think he more than likes you. And I know you more than like him." She pursed her lips and nodded. "You luuuuurve him."

"Stoooop," I pleaded. Of course I loved Parker, but hearing Taylor repeat what I'd already revealed left me feeling raw and vulnerable. Especially when he still hadn't called.

"You luuuuuurve him, and you want to maaaaaarrry him," she sang, swaying back and forth to her teasing rhythm, which I did not appreciate.

"Shut up." I looked down the open-air aisles at all the stalls full of flowers. I wanted to deny her accusation, but I would have been lying, and Taylor would have known it.

What I did do was refocus my attention on the thing that was actually happening: Taylor's wedding. She needed flowers by tomorrow. A lot of them. And I needed to make the bouquets, haku, and table arrangements out of those flowers. That's what *needed* to happen.

But the only thing I *wanted* to do was check every email account I'd ever had—and there were a lot of them—to see if maybe, possibly . . . *hopefully* what Taylor said was true.

"Check your email," she ordered.

"I only have my work email on my phone."

"Check. It," Taylor demanded. Bossy Taylor was not to be disobeyed.

I did as I was told. Even though I geared myself up for the worst, it still hurt when there wasn't anything from Parker in my inbox. I sucked in my lips and closed my eyes to let the disappointment settle back into my gut. Then I showed the empty inbox to Taylor. "See?"

"Fine. Now try the others."

I shook my head. I'd have to work up the nerve to be disappointed again. "Tomorrow is your big day. Let's get your flowers."

She stared me down again, and for a minute I thought she would try and argue me out of it. But the fact was tomorrow was her big day, and if we didn't get working on the flowers, she wouldn't have any. My Parker problems would have to wait.

Chapter 33

Choosing the flowers took less time than I thought it would, mostly because Taylor rushed us through the stalls okaying everything I held up so we could get home to the email she was certain waited for me if I could figure out which account Parker had sent it to. I was less certain and would have been happy taking my time finding the perfect flowers, but she was the boss.

Three hours and six full buckets after getting to the market, we had everything we needed and barely enough space in the car to get it all back to the hotel. It was a cramped but delicious-smelling ride.

The parking lot was nowhere near our room, of course, so we each carried three buckets in so we wouldn't have to waste time trekking back to the car. I hung a bucket in the crook of my elbow, did the same with another bucket on my other arm, and then picked up the last bucket with the tallest flowers.

"I hope we can find our way to the room. We might as well be blindfolded," I said to Taylor.

"We only have to make it to the bellhop, and then he can put them on his luggage-hauler thingy, and we'll be golden," Taylor answered.

Unfortunately there was a line of cars at the door and no bellboy/person (if we want to be PC) available to haul our flowers for us. So we kept walking, slowly. Very slowly. I peeked between the flowers whenever possible to make sure we were headed in the right direction and prayed people wouldn't want to be trampled by a walking garden, no matter how beautiful, and would get out of our way.

I shuffled through the lobby, walking extra carefully to keep from spilling any water on the marble floors and making my journey even more treacherous. I made the mistake of taking some deep yoga breaths to stay centered and balanced, literally, but only succeeded in breathing in a nose full of pollen. I was in the process of de-pollinating my nostrils with some serious snorting in order to avoid some even more serious sneezing when I heard my name.

"Eliza?" It was Parker's voice saying my name, but I couldn't be sure if it was actually him or my imagination.

"Is that you behind there?"

I heard him again, but I still couldn't see him.

"She's the other one." I heard Taylor say in front of me. So either we were both hearing voices, or . . .

"Parker?" I asked through the flowers. "Is that you?"

Suddenly hands wrapped around the bucket in my arms, it was taken away, and there was Parker in front of my face instead of an armful of plumeria.

"What are you doing here?" A lump caught in my throat. I still didn't know if he was real or if I was in a kind of dream. The really good kind.

He set the bucket down without answering me and then took the other two hanging from my arms and set them down. I glanced at Taylor, who had Weston by her side along with the flowers he must have taken from her arms. I caught the smile creeping up her lips just before Parker wrapped me in his arms.

If I'd had time to think about it, his embrace would have been surprise enough, but then he leaned in, and I knew he hadn't flown across an ocean for a hug. His lips met mine before my brain had time to process how my world had changed in a matter of seconds.

My body, on the other hand, didn't have to process anything. Kissing Parker for the first time felt like something I'd done a thousand times before. It was the most natural thing in the world, like every part of us, except our brains, had always known this is where we'd be. Standing in a hotel lobby in Hawaii, surrounded by flowers, locked in each other's arms and lips.

His kisses were sweet and tender, with a touch of mint. Even if he'd had airplane breath, I still would have kissed him, but the mint? It helped. He broke away before I was ready and put his hands on either side of my face. Our eyes met, and then our lips did once more.

"I got your message," he said.

"So you came all the way here to answer it?" I'm not going to lie: a tear fell. Maybe out of relief, maybe out of joy from the kisses—they were that good—but whatever the reason, my eyes were wet.

"Well, no. I emailed you—" He let his hands drop to his side.

"My work email?"

"No, not your work email, your *lizabellesurfs* one. Why would I pour out my heart to your work address?" Parker stepped back and asked, as though he hadn't spent most of his life as Mr. Practical. Who knew he had a romantic side?

"I told you!" Taylor blared through the lobby loudly enough for people to turn and look at us. Not that we didn't have an audience already. People kissing in the middle of a lobby will draw a crowd, apparently.

Parker tipped his head toward Taylor in agreement. "It was more of a love letter, not a flower order. I wanted to be sure you heard all the things I've wanted to say. When you didn't answer, I went home, but you'd already left for San Francisco. I didn't have any other choice than to get on an airplane to tell you in person how I feel."

I put my hands on either side of his face. "Then I'm glad I'm not so old school to check my email every day." I raised up on tiptoe and kissed him. "Now, tell me what you came to say."

"I thought I already had." He kissed me again, but not so tenderly.

"Hmm." I broke away, closed my eyes, and smiled while I regained my bearings. When the room stopped spinning, I looked at him again. "I still want to hear it in words."

His mouth twitched in the familiar way it always did when he was about to tease me. I waited for it, but then his eyes softened. "I love you." He shrugged. "I can't remember a time when I didn't. Like a sister when you were little, then as a friend, and now . . ." He sighed and laced his fingers in mine. "Now I love you for the kind, intelligent, beautiful woman you are. I love you for helping me see my faults and making me want to be better."

"I do that?" I asked. "I thought you just did that for me."

"No." He closed his eyes and shook his head. "I lecture and criticize you. You?" He tucked a rogue curl that had fallen in my eye behind my ear. "You inspire me. I've never been happier than when I heard you say you love me. I think I listened to that message a thousand times to make sure I wasn't imagining it."

I unwound my fingers from his and ran my hand through his hair. "You can hear me say it in person a thousand times every day." And I kissed him again.

As much as I would have liked to stand there kissing him all day, obviously we couldn't. After all, the real reason we were kissing in Hawaii at all was because of Taylor and her wedding. And there was work to be done for it.

Aside from the kissing and the *I love you*s and the general feeling of bliss, another benefit of having Parker there was that I could put him to work. He and Weston carried the flowers up to the suite Taylor and I were sharing. Within a matter of minutes the room looked more like a flower shop than my little shop at home.

We separated the flowers into the buckets by what they would be used for. I had to do the haku and the bridal bouquet on my own, but I showed everyone else how to do the centerpieces for the few tables and the other decorations. I couldn't think of a better place to be in that moment than with my best friend, her fiancé, and my boyfriend—could I call him that yet? I decided yes. Yes, I could. And I could kiss him whenever I wanted, so I did.

"We're never going to get these done if you keep kissing him," Taylor finally said after she'd had enough of our PDA.

"Fine. You're right." I looked at the clock to see just how right. The answer? Way too right for comfort. "I'll move over here to keep from getting distracted." I picked up my flowers and the half-finished haku and carried them to the other side of the room.

"You know I can move over there too," Parker said in a husky voice that wasn't entirely teasing.

"Not until you're done clipping those fern thingies," I answered sternly. "Then I have a reward for you." I gave him a slow, sultry wink.

"Oh, barf," Taylor exclaimed and dropped the floral tape I'd motioned for into my lap. "Were Weston and I as bad as you two?"

"Worse," I said almost before she'd finished her sentence.

"So much worse," Parker added.

We all joked and teased back and forth for hours while we finished the flowers. It wasn't exactly the afternoon I'd envisioned with Taylor or that she'd envisioned for herself the day before her wedding, but it was perfect. Parker was perfect. Everything was perfect.

Except for one little thought that kept begging to be scratched like an itch in the middle of my back that couldn't be reached without some serious contortions. I ignored it with only a little discomfort until the end of the day, after Parker and I had finished the flowers, gone to dinner with Taylor and Weston, and then snuck off by ourselves for some time alone.

We held hands and walked the flower-lined path of the hotel grounds, watching the sun set over the ocean.

"Your dad's already seen this sunset," Parker said, and I knew then my question couldn't wait anymore.

"You're right. And I forgot to call him." Worry washed over me, followed quickly by a landslide of guilt.

"It's been kind of a big day. He'll understand."

I stopped walking, and Parker stopped too. My heart beat hard with the question I didn't want to ask. The question that could make my best day turn to my worst. I looked into his smiling face, not wanting to change the happiness there—the happiness I knew had to be shining in my face too. But I had to do it.

"We have to talk about Los Angeles," I said slowly. Carefully.

He licked his lips then rubbed them together. "What do you want to know?"

"Are you still moving there? I know it's not that far, but it's far enough." I held my breath and waited for the answer.

"That depends," he answered, and his smile slipped behind the shadow crossing his face.

"On what?"

"You."

"What about me?"

He shrugged and shook his head. "I don't want to leave you. Not now."

"I don't want you to go, but you can't put that on me." I let go of his hand. Everything I'd hoped for and almost had was vanishing as quickly as the setting sun. "We can try long-distance . . ."

"You wouldn't want to live there?" he asked then quickly added, "Someday?"

I shook my head. "You know I can't leave Daddy."

"I know." He stared at the ground and chewed his lip then lifted his head and met my eyes. "And I can't leave you. So I guess that settles it." He took my hand and tried to walk again, but I stayed planted.

"What do you mean? What's settled?"

"I'm not moving," he said as matter-of-factly as if he'd decided not to order dessert.

"What about the commute? I thought you hated it." I still refused to move, even if he did think his life decision was no more important than a piece of cheesecake. Not that cheesecake isn't important. I'm pro-cheesecake.

He stopped and took my hand again. "The only reason I wanted to move is because I thought you had a thing for Blake. Even with him out of the picture, I couldn't watch you fall for another guy."

"Me and Blake? We were only friends. And why didn't you think I'd fall for you?"

He looked down at me and raised an eyebrow. "One, you spent a lot of time together. I thought I was going to go crazy, and I didn't want to go through that again. Two, I didn't think you thought of me as anything other than an annoying faux brother."

"So you were going to move?"

"It was that or get my heart broken every time you fell for a new guy."

"Or you could have just told me how you felt instead of being a wuss!"

A slow smile spread across his face. "In retrospect, that would have been the better choice."

"Ya think?"

He put my hand to his lips and kissed the knuckle of my middle finger. "The important thing is I'm not going anywhere now."

"Good." I pulled my hand away from his mouth and let my lips take its place.

Chapter 34

The next three days were a whirlwind of activity. Taylor and Weston exchanged vows on the beach surrounded by a few close friends and family, including Blake and Jami, who flew in that morning. We danced the rest of the night, and then I had two days to do whatever I wanted. And what I wanted was to cram as many minutes with Parker as possible in that forty-eight hours. I got no argument from him about that.

We'd never been on an official date before, so he planned one that lasted the entire two days we had together. It included romantic dinners, breakfasts, picnics, snorkeling, tubing down a waterfall, and surfing—obviously. For those two thousand eight hundred and eighty minutes, I didn't worry about Daddy, the shop, or anything else—except when I texted Hailey to make sure Daddy wasn't just saying everything was fine so I wouldn't feel bad about leaving him.

She promised me everything was actually fine, but even reading her texts reminded me I'd have to tell her about Parker and me when I got home. I'd have to tell Daddy too, but his reaction would be a much better one than the one I expected to get from Hailey. Hers would be more along the devastated rather than delighted side of things. It had to be done, though, and as soon as I got on the plane, I dreaded every second that brought me closer to the time I'd have to tell her.

"She's going to hate me," I said to Parker for the millionth time as we circled LAX.

"She's not going to hate you." He kissed the top of my head. "She might be hurt, but she'll get over it. She'll realize what she had for me was a crush, nothing more."

"I don't know. I hope you're right." I closed my eyes and took a deep breath, waiting for the jolt I knew would come as soon as we touched down.

"Do you want me to talk to her?" He wrapped his arm around me, taking away a fraction of my fear of landing.

"No, it has to be me." The bump came as the wheels hit the ground, followed by a second bump as the wheels hit the ground again. I clenched my eyes tighter, waiting for the stop I knew had to come, but I still worried it wouldn't.

"I've got a feeling your talk with Hailey will go a lot more smoothly than this landing," he said as the plane finally stopped at our gate.

"I hope you're right."

Parker being Parker, of course he was right. But this time I didn't mind. In fact, he was so right things couldn't have gone more smoothly if we had teleported home.

When we pulled in front of my house, I noticed a car I hadn't seen before, but I didn't see Hailey's car anywhere.

"I'll drop my bags and come over," Parker said.

"No, let me talk to Hailey first." As much as I wanted him right by my side, it would be easier on Hailey if he wasn't.

"Okay, if you're sure."

I picked up my suitcases and nodded. "One hundred percent sure. But I wish I weren't."

Parker went around back to the apartment Daddy had already said he could keep, and I went inside my house, balancing a suitcase on my thigh while I pushed the door open.

"Daddy, I'm home," I called and dropped my luggage. I'd haul it to my room later, after I'd faced the more difficult task ahead of me.

"We're up here!" Hailey called. Xander imitated his mom and babbled his own hello. Any other day that sound would have been enough to cure whatever was ailing me, but not on the day I had to break the worst news ever—for Hailey—to her.

I walked slowly down the hall, pretending I was still on island time. When I got to the kitchen, I was greeted by not only my dad but also by Hailey's friend Ashton.

He and Daddy both stood up as I entered the room, but I passed by him with only a confused glance and went straight to the arms Daddy had stretched out for me.

"Did you have a good trip? Are you tired? Did you eat anything that made you sick?" Daddy peppered me with questions, but I had some of my own. Namely, what was Ashton Martin doing in my house, and why was Hailey standing really close to him? Like, we're-a-couple close?

"I'm fine, Daddy. Just tired." I put my arm around his waist, and we walked to the couch and sat down. "The food was delicious. The wedding was amazing. It was the best."

I looked at Hailey, who had taken a seat on the couch opposite us, right next to Ashton. "I can't thank you enough for being here with my dad so I didn't have to worry about him."

Daddy patted my knee. "You worry too much about me."

"I wonder where I get that from." I leaned my head on his shoulder and wanted to fall asleep right then, but there was still the question of Ashton to be answered.

"Hi, Ashton," I said.

"Hi. Good to see you again."

Xander pulled himself up on Ashton's knees, and Ashton picked him up to blow a raspberry on his naked belly.

"Ashton's staying for dinner," Daddy said casually, as though he always invited strangers to eat with us.

"Oh, hey!" Ashton jumped up. "Do you have bags? Can I bring them in for you?"

"Yeah, that would be great. Thanks." It would also give me a minute to ask what was going on without being flat-out rude. Obviously no one was going to offer up an explanation on their own. "They're by the front door. I'll take the baby."

I held out my arms for Xander, and Ashton handed him to me before going down the hallway. As soon as he was out of sight, I looked at Hailey. "What's going on? Why is he here?"

"Are you mad? Your dad invited him—"

"I'm not mad," I interjected.

"Hailey's car broke down on the freeway a couple days ago," Daddy said. "Ashton towed her to his shop and brought her back over here. He's loaned her a car and was so helpful I had to invite him over. What would she have done without him?"

She blushed then looked toward the door as the sounds of my luggage rolling on the hardwood got louder. She jumped up and ran to him as soon as she saw him. "I'll show you where to put them."

The two went down the hall, rolling one of the suitcases together while he carried the other.

"He's a nice young man," Daddy said. "I think she likes him."

"You do?"

"That's what she says."

"She told you that?"

"Yes." He gave me a stern look. "Apparently she's the only one who will tell me anything, because she told me about you and Parker too."

"She what?"

"She showed me the pictures on that pictogram thing."

"Instagram? What pictures?" It wasn't a surprise there were pics of us on social media, just a surprise Daddy had seen them. I took out my phone and pulled up Taylor's Insta account with Daddy looking over my shoulder.

"There's one of you and Parker kissing." He pointed to the picture. "Of course, I'm not surprised or disappointed. I only wish you'd told me."

"I'm sorry. I wanted to wait until we got home and I could tell you in person." And so I could tell Hailey first, but apparently I didn't even need to do that. "And Hailey was okay with it? She wasn't upset?"

"Why would she be upset?" Before he could say any more, Hailey walked back into the room.

"Where's Ashton?" I asked.

"Bathroom," she answered with a shy grin. Her lipstick was smeared.

I had two minutes, probably less, to get all the info I wanted from her. "You're really okay with Parker and me?"

"Of course." She waved my comment away like a pesky fly. "That was a stupid crush. Obvs you guys are perfect for each other."

"Kinda like you and Ashton?" I asked.

"Maybe not that perfect," she answered just before Ashton appeared in the hallway. "Where is Parker anyway? Didn't he come home with you?"

"He's out back. I'll tell him to come over." I stood up and pulled my phone out of my pocket. "What's for dinner anyway?"

"Hailey cooked. She's an excellent cook," Daddy answered.

"She's excellent at a lot of things." I texted Parker to come over. I'd have to tell him he was right about Hailey too, but I'd never been happier in my entire life about being wrong.

That night after we'd watched the sunset with Daddy and Ashton had taken Hailey and Xander back to her apartment, Parker and I sat alone on the patio. We were wrapped in a blanket in front of the fire, looking at the wedding pictures Taylor had posted on Insta.

"Who took this one?" I asked pointing to the culprit that had outed Parker and me before we could tell anyone ourselves. There we were on the beach, our lips locked, with the sun glowing pink over the ocean behind us.

"I don't know, but you should thank them," he said, nuzzling his chin on the top of my head.

"Seriously." I scrolled through the pictures of Taylor walking down the sandy aisle, flower petals scattered around her. Then the ones of her and

Weston exchanging vows, rings, and kisses. The moments after their I-dos, when we all took out bubble wands and filled the air around them with huge, floating orbs. Cutting the cake, throwing the bouquet, walking off into the sunset together. We relived the entire wedding.

"You still don't want any of this for yourself?" Parker asked. His breath warmed the top of my head. Being in his arms warmed everything else.

"What? A wedding?"

"Not just that. Marriage. The whole thing."

I thought about it. The idea had never appealed to me until I'd seen him walk into my shop six months ago. Every minute I'd spent with him since then had lessened my resolve to never get married. "I could possibly be persuaded."

He shifted in his seat to face me then put his put his fingers under my chin and tipped my head up. "I can be very persuasive."

"Prove it," I said, already breathless with the anticipation of his kiss and everything I knew would follow.

About the Author

Brittany Larsen loves a lot of things, but yoga, Jane Austen, and the beach are all at the top of her list. At the very, *very* top are her husband and three daughters, who share her yoga, Jane, and beach love, in varying degrees. The placement of her white dog and black cat on that list depends on what "surprises" and/or animal carcasses they've left for her to find. She lives in Orange County, California, and is the author of *Pride and Politics* and *Sense and Second Chances*.